CORPORATOCRACY

RULES

CORPORATOCRACY

RULES

A Diana Hunter Thriller

Joan Francis

Lobathian Publishers

CORPORATOCRACY RULES

A Diana Hunter Thriller

For information

LobathianPubs@aol.com

ISBN: 978-0-9821370-2-4

Printed in the United States of America

I wish to thank my

Palmdale Partners in Crime

for their assistance and encouragement in

producing this book.

ONE

By 9:30 a.m. I was headed for Maude McCallvoy's compound which sits on top of a mountain on the west side of Los Angeles. I carefully wound my way up a steep, narrow street, past modest little houses that were wedged into every semi-level spot that could be created out of the narrow canyon. From the middle-class homes along the road, one would never guess that one of the richest women in America lived at the top. It seemed quite medieval, actually, with the vassals in the bungalows below and the castle crowning the hill.

The request for this meeting had come through Richard Barton, my friend, hair dresser and disguise master. I told him there was no amount of money that would make me take an assignment from Maude to spy on her son, Robby. He just laughed at me and said, "Oh, yes you will, and it won't be for Maude's money, it will be for your own curiosity. You'll be compelled to find out if the Old Black Widow is trying to have Robby rubbed out or something."

He knows me far too well, but he missed the mark on this one. The real curiosity that drove me to meet with Maude was: why me? Maude and I did not move in the same circles and had met only because we both used Richard's beauty shop and spa, Rick's Coiffures Americain. When we were scheduled at the same time, our political discussions were usually explosive. I learned from Richard that the stylists called us the Gingham Dog and Calico Cat, and he took great glee in pointing out that those two ate each other up. Half the shop wanted him to schedule us together so they could watch the fireworks and make bets on the outcome. The other half threatened to walk out *en masse* if he ever put us in side-by-side chairs again.

Our debates had made me curious and I had researched a bit about the old gal and learned it was no wonder we disagreed. Her grandfather had been a wildcatter who struck it rich in Texas and Oklahoma. With his new wealth in oil, he returned to Philadelphia and claimed a bride from the old-money class, in fact the daughter of one of the founding families. The McCallvoys have been making money with money ever since.

Every year Maude was the largest single contributor to the Republican

Party. Her political viewpoint could be summed up by the old comic strip character, General Bullmoose, in *Lil Abner*. "What's good for General Bullmoose is good for the USA." Her hero was Ronny Reagan and his trickle-down economics. Her friends were those who wield the power within corporations, banks, and government offices. In short, Maude was a member in good standing of that shadow-power behind the curtain; those I had come to call our ruling Corporatocracy. What possible reason could she have to hire a private eye like me when she commanded an army of corporate security people.

She had married a handsome loser from one of the "right" families, but when he consistently lost or spent great gobs of her inheritance, she tried to divorce him. The ensuing court battle for control of her fortune was vicious and was carried in all the tabloids. Then, at the height of the scandal, her husband died under mysterious circumstances. A coroner's inquest absolved Maude of any wrong-doing, but the tabloids didn't: they dubbed her the "Black Widow Heiress." For some perverse reason I have never dared inquire about she has prolonged the memory of this appellation by constantly wearing a black widow brooch with a giant ruby shaped like a widow's hourglass marking.

She reclaimed her maiden name, scooped up her only child, Robert, and moved from Dallas to this fenced and guarded enclave in California. From here the widow minds her web of corporate power that spans the globe. About the only thing she has never been able to control is Robby.

Rounding the last curve, I pulled up to a massive electronic iron gate, said my name into the little speaker box, and the gate slid open. As I drove forward, the waiting security guard eyed my baby blue '57 T-Bird and noted my plate: PRE10D. Then I saw his appraisal drop as he surveyed the damaged paint, torn upholstery, and non-original features such as my push-button combination door locks. With obvious disapproval of its condition, he told me to park the Bird on the other side of the guardhouse.

I pulled up under the shade of a beautiful old live oak that actually grew right on the fence line. The builder had thoughtfully jogged the wall inward so the old tree could continue to grow there, its massive limbs hanging majestically over the wall into Maude's yard. I wondered if Maude was responsible for this ecological brownie point. If so, it was a side of her I had not seen before.

The grounds seemed to cover the entire mountain top, and from the gate I could see nothing but dense shrubbery. The guard loaded me into a golf cart and I watched expectantly for my first glimpse of the mansion. We drove along a path that ran around the perimeter of the property, but I never got even a peek at Maude's mansion. Instead of being taken to the house, I was escorted to a small garden in the rear of the place. Boxwood hedges, trimmed to plastic perfection, were arranged in unimaginative symmetry. Within the rectangles of boxwood were the almost bare sticks of severely pruned roses. This sterile formal garden was out of character with the natural sprawl of native chaparral covering most of the mountain top. It also gave the place a cold and emotionless feeling. To add to the chill of the garden, the morning had brought the first cool overcast of fall. As I stepped out of the golf cart, I wished I had brought my jacket.

Maude was seated on a hard wrought iron bench and rose stiffly to greet me. "Diana, thank you for coming to see me. I appreciate you arranging your schedule."

I mumbled what I thought was an appropriate response and waited uncomfortably for her to continue.

Maude is five foot ten and, though lean, has a large bone structure with broad shoulders. She has thick wavy, gray hair, slate gray eyes, high cheekbones, and a square face. A beauty in her youth, perhaps, but with her size and determined square jaw, newspapers and magazines of the day more often referred to her as "a handsome woman." Even in her sixties she is still attractive.

She offered me a bench across from her and began pouring coffee from a pot that sat on the glass-topped iron table.

"I hope coffee and these excellent scones will make up somewhat for my lack of hospitality. I apologize for the location of our meeting, but I did not wish to have anyone of the household overhear us. I hope you understand."

I wondered what was wrong with her office but said lamely, "No problem."

She handed me the cup of coffee, and waited expectantly. As I had learned at Ricks, talking with Maude was like playing three-dimensional chess. Both of us are especially gifted in the art of reading other people, discerning the subtle unspoken clues that tell you what people are really thinking and doing. Today, however, she was going to have to say everything out loud so there was no doubt about what she was asking me to do.

When I failed to respond appropriately she said, "I need to know that you understand. I want none of my household or anyone else to know of our conversation. Is that very clear?"

Maude is one of the most powerful individuals I have ever met. She doesn't have to be overtly forceful, but simply radiates a quiet power. More than once I have seen her on a news show and noted that she could quell powerful adversaries with a single, subtle look. As she waited for an answer, that look was focused on me.

It took more nerve than I really felt to keep from looking away from Maude's penetrating gray eyes, but I learned at a young age that the only way to deal with a powerful personality was to stand your ground. I suspected my willingness to go toe to toe with her was half of the reason Maude enjoyed our little debates. I doubted that there were many people in her life who didn't crumble into submissiveness under her gaze.

"I understand what you are saying, Maude, but I think I need to explain how I work. What I discuss with my clients is always held in complete confidence within my organization. However, my associates must be told as much as they need to know to assist me in any project. Is that clear and acceptable?"

"Richard Barton and who else?"

"That too must be confidential."

Her expression gave away nothing as we held each other in an unflinching game of eyeball chicken. When she did speak, her change of subject was disarming.

"We have had many famous debates at Rick's. You and I have spoken of almost everything and you certainly have never held back any opinion or judgement concerning my affairs. There is one subject, however, that has single-handedly garnered more news and television coverage than anything, yet we have never discussed it. Why is it that you have never mentioned Robby?"

My anger flared. I had avoided Robby out of consideration, courtesy, and taste. Maude's question seemed to consider me no better than the gossips who thrived on such personal scandal. Some of that anger was in my voice as I answered, "He falls into the category of other people."

"What do you mean?"

"My dad used to say that intelligent people talk about ideas, average people talk about things, and inferior people talk about other people. I gave you credit for being intelligent, Maude. We talked about ideas. Your personal soap opera with Robby is your own business."

She took a deep breath and her stern facial features softened into a hint of a smile. Looking away from me, she picked up her coffee cup and said softly, "Thank you, Diana." Then, pulling a newspaper clipping from her pocket, she abruptly changed to an all-business tone. "Here, what do you think of this?"

In huge print it read:

THE FAT CATS ARE PICKING UP BILLIONS OF DOLLARS WORTH OF
PROPERTY FROM SUBPRIME FORECLOSURES AND THE TAXPAYERS
PICK UP THE BILL. DON'T BE LEFT OUT IN THE COLD!

GET FORECLOSURE PROPERTY FOR

NEXT TO NOTHING

Come to a FREE LECTURE and learn how easy it is to grab your share of land out
of the thousands of foreclosures.

Get free legal aid from

Legal Aid for Los Angeles Land

LA LA LAND

The article went on from there with a biography of Dorica June Grizel, the head of LA LA Land, and with testimonials from people claiming to have picked up three bedroom homes for fifty bucks. I read as much as I could stomach and then put it down and looked at Maude. "What's the scam?"

"That's what I want you to find out."

"To what purpose? This doesn't look like something Robby would be into."

"No, it doesn't."

Some strange note in her voice vibrated a warning on an instinctive level but I couldn't interpret a meaning. I made no response and just waited for an explanation. She quit looking directly at me and made a close study of her scone.

"Robby was working at a downtown mission which tries to help homeless families. He had been there for about two years and no one had yet 'made him' as he says. You probably know from newspaper accounts how he always lives and works under some false identity. Then about three months ago he disappeared from the mission, and as usual I had to send out the hounds to try to find him. One morning last week he showed up at the office asking to 'borrow' a secretary, make calls to my title company, and speak to one of my attorneys. He just dropped in as if there hadn't been years of . . . We even managed to have lunch together after he finished his business. It was the most we had seen of each other in years. He was interested in this Dorica June Grizel. He didn't volunteer too much and I didn't ask. Over the years we both have learned that if we wish to have a peaceful time together we have to keep the conversation away from his various endeavors."

She stopped speaking again and I prodded. "Do you think he's working for this LA LA Land?"

"Yes. But he evidently now fancies himself some sort of detective. He and Ralph Jenson, my attorney, were at it behind closed doors for over an hour. Jenson later told me that Robby had a lot of questions regarding what kind of evidence it would take to get the District Attorney to file against someone for real estate fraud. Jenson's a civil contracts attorney and said he told Robby he couldn't help him in a criminal law matter."

She sipped her coffee and nibbled on her scone. She was stalling and seemed uncertain how to proceed. Most unlike her. She was also hiding something. Very much in character.

"So what is it you need, Maude?"

"I need someone on the inside to see what Robby is involved in."

"You want me to do that? Why don't you use the people you normally use to track Robby?"

She looked at me icily and returned to her role of corporate director. "My dear Diana, please do not presume to advise me. I have an entire corporate security force at my command and I have also chosen many an outside investigator when needed. If I have chosen you for this job, I have my reasons. Don't think I have failed to check you out thoroughly. In the process, I may have leaned a bit heavily on Richard. I must say I admire his close-lipped loyalty."

"Okay, but before I take your case, I still have to know, why me?"

Her eyes glazed over and she looked away. Whatever her answer was going to be, it was either a lie or an evasion. "From what I have learned, your methods of operation are appropriate to my needs," she said in a dismissive manner.

I waited in silence for more. Something wasn't right here.

"Look, Diana, Robby and I have played this little game for so many years he knows all the people I normally use. Besides, I know that you are very good at researching a paper trail. That's a lot of what Robby is doing. Just researching property deeds that he seems to think reveal wrongdoing by this LA LA Land bunch. I need you to find out what Robby has learned."

I was trying to decide if this sounded straight but was given no time to think. One thing Maude knows is how and when to close a deal.

"Despite my difficulties with Robby, I, as a mother, still want to be sure he is safe. There aren't too many people I would trust with this assignment. I will pay you well for your services." She reached into her pocket and handed me a piece of paper.

"I want complete secrecy. No one on my staff at work is to know about this and, of course, no press. On that paper you will find the phone number of a secure line where you can contact me with your reports. All verbal, nothing in writing."

She then handed me a small key with a tag attached. "You will find a $20,000 retainer in cash in this safety deposit box, which I took the liberty of opening in your name."

And I had been thinking of asking her for a $5,000 retainer. The little voices in my mind, which I think of as my internal board of directors, were in a complete uproar. The cautious one was screaming warnings that bordered on paranoia and was pointing out that Maude was concealing something from me. I would like to believe that Richard was right and that it was my curiosity that won out, but I have to admit that someone on my committee was saying, "Take the money and run."

TWO

Merle, our building elevator operator, glared at me and asked, "Floor?" as if she hadn't taken me to the eighth floor every day for the last year.

I rent an apartment in a building on the corner of Eighth and Ocean Way in a seedy little patch of the county known as Bluff Beach. The rent is just $350 a month and the place is only eight blocks from the beach, but of course it's a dump and not up to code in anything. Worst of all, I am forced to take my life in my hands by getting in the elevator with Merle.

Bluff Beach was sort of overlooked when L.A. and Long Beach annexed property for their cities. There was, of course, good reason no one wanted it. In the 1920s it had only speakeasies; in the thirties, gambling houses; in the forties and fifties, bars, prostitutes, and tattoo parlors. By the sixties it had become so foul and dangerous, that even liberty sailors avoided it.

Hippies discovered it in the early seventies and moved in. As they morphed gradually into yuppies, they began to change the landscape of the town. In the late eighties a few smart souls incorporated it into a small city, declared it a redevelopment district and began to build like crazy. Now the downtown has the rough bustle of a boom town. The good news is you can still rent cheap if you're willing to forego the manicured suburbs. The bad news is you get a derelict building, an antique elevator, and Merle.

There are no push buttons in this elevator. Merle has to manually control the rise and fall of this antique and usually has to shift back and forth a time or two before she's able to stop close enough to floor level to let people get on or off.

She stood there, resolutely waiting for my answer. There was no cure for it. I had to tell her the floor every time. "Eight, Merle, same as it's been every day for the last year. Eighth floor."

Merle is about five foot four, thin, and has badly dyed red hair, which is also very thin. Her small features are highlighted with lipstick and eyebrow pencil the same shade of red as her hair. She tops the hair with a white pillbox hat that matches white cotton gloves. She wears a yellow jacket trimmed with white lapels over every dress in her three-dress wardrobe. This combination of hat, gloves, and jacket seemed to be her own idea of a proper uniform rather than anything specified by the management. I doubted the "management," whoever they were, ever entered the building, much less Merle's elevator. She had run the elevator in this building for twenty-three years, and though I suspected she had too many ups and downs in her life, I would never have the nerve to pry.

She focused on her elevator controls and mumbled something inaudible as she began to maneuver the small box up to the eighth floor. She jarred the thing to a stop approximately at the eighth floor. I stepped to the door ledge and down five inches to the hall floor. "Thanks, Merle," I said cheerily.

"Your phone's not fixed."

At first I thought she was mumbling to herself again. Then her words penetrated and I realized she was speaking to me. "What?" I asked.

"Your phone's not fixed. The key didn't work and the alarm made such a racket the phone man just left again."

I felt the hair prickle on my neck. "Merle, are you saying there was a man at my door today and he set off the alarm?" She looked at me as if the question had offended her and shut the elevator door. My attempt to stop her was futile.

Thanks to my friend and mentor, Sam Dehany, my apartment door lock is biometric. I simply press my thumb to the bell button and the system reads my print and automatically unlocks the three locks. Anyone trying to pick the lock would set off an alarm and alert the little guard on duty in my apartment. If I had understood what Merle was saying, that was exactly what happened today.

I unlocked the door, flipped on the lights, and peered in cautiously. As I stepped inside, Yeabot rolled over to the door and greeted me with, "Hello, Mother. You have two phone messages."

I couldn't help smiling. Yeabot, my robot always lightened my mood. Yeabot's little white plastic body is about three and a half feet high and he looks like a cross between R2D2 and the Pillsbury Dough Boy. My friend Sam invented him while on government payroll and when he wanted to retire from the intelligence community he wanted his unfinished robot design to retire with him. Since that would not be acceptable to the federal government, Sam hired Hunter Investigations to help convince his bosses he had gone crazy and had nothing but unworkable nonsense in his robot plans. Though I had occasionally pulled a scam or two before, I was in over my head from the moment I said hello to Sam. However, despite the fact that this scam had to fool both real life foreign spies and the U.S. Government, we did get Sam and his robot out of the service. I have since wondered whether it was my "creative" solution or Sam's expertise in black ops that won the day.

Sam retired with nothing but a modest pension, and he will never be able to benefit from the robotics designs started on government time. He paid me for my help by making this robot for me and programmed it to be a combination of computerized secretary, database genius, waiter, and security guard. I love the little guy. In addition to Yeabot's practical assistance, he delights my sense of fantasy with his ability to talk to me. I named him for the Navajo talking God, Yeibichai but Sam could never remember that so he called him Yeabot and the name stuck.

"Yeabot, was there a security breach today?"

"No, Mother."

"Good! Just Merle's crazy nonsense." I certainly would take Yeabot's word over Merle's. Then I thought about how precisely you must speak to a robot. "Yeabot, was there an attempted security breach today?"

"Yes, Mother. Would you like a printout?"

"Yes, please, Yeabot."

He rolled across the room, tapped into my printer, and printed out an incident report. Reading it, I learned that at 9:45 a.m., fifteen minutes after I left my apartment, someone had attempted to open the door with an unauthorized key. The alarm sounded and Yeabot was alerted and reported the incident to Sam. At 9:50 Yeabot turned off the alarm and waited on guard until Sam drove over from San Pedro. No further attempt was made. End of report.

Merle thought he was a "phone man." Burglar or spy, I wondered. I also wondered if it was coincidence that it occurred at a time Maude knew I would be away from my apartment. Was she trying to make sure she knew what I was doing? I made a mental note to ask Sam to check for bugs and taps. It was nice to know my security system worked, but very unnerving to know someone had put it to the test.

Putting that worry aside, and settling down to business, I played my messages, returned a couple of calls, and prepared a report for the mail. Then I turned to Maude's case.

I had questioned her extensively, forcing her to recall every name, number, and song Robby had told her regarding LA LA Land. She refused to let me speak with her attorney, repeating her instruction that none of her staff was to know about my investigation. What I got from her didn't amount to much, but I suspected that a complete background on Dorica June Grizel would be likely to create more leads than I could track down in six months anyway.

I dialed Jenny's number and was relieved to get her machine. On the last case she worked with me things had gotten a bit too chilling and she had a few moments when she wondered if she would get back home to see her husband and two kids. When it was over she told me I must have a death wish and that I had dragged her into things without being honest about the danger. I wasn't sure she would be too eager to jump into a new case. That terrified me more than any hazard from my investigations. Other than my father, Jenny was the longest relationship in my life. But now her life had settled into the normal, the husband and two kids thing. That made us light years apart even though we lived within twenty miles of each other. I left her a carefully worded message.

"Hey, Jenny. I have a new case. It's just straight investigation, and Maude McCallvoy is the client. Needless to say the retainer is substantial. Please start the background research on an outfit called Legal Aid for Los Angeles Land and its principal, Dorica June Grizel. There is a lawyer partner too. Don't know his name yet. Spare no cost. We want everything we can get. Please meet me at Rick's tonight with any information. Thanks."

I hung up and then dialed Richard. He answered the phone himself.

"Hi, Richard."

"Hello, Diana. You must have talked to Maude. Her menacing calls have stopped."

"Yes, and Jenny and I need a special tonight. You free?"

"Stop at the Maison de Paris and bring something wonderful for dinner and you're on."

"Okay. By the way, what's the idea of blabbing all you know to Maude?"

There was a very long pause, then Richard stammered, "But, but, I didn't. Honest to God, Diana, she did everything but hypnotize me. I never told her any details of other cases. What did she say?"

"Richard, I'm teasing. What she said was she 'had to admire your tight-lipped loyalty.' From her tone of grudging admiration, I can guess what kind of pressure she put on you."

"Did she really say that? I'll try to remember that the next time she orders me to the rack."

"Thanks, Richard, we'll see you tonight."

THREE

"We cannot eat until you put that stinking bag of rags outside."

"Okay, okay."

I was reusing my Bag Lady Betty outfit from a previous case and it still had a strong residue of a stinky cream that Sam had concocted as a means of keeping folks from checking me out too closely. I put it outside in the trunk of my car and returned to the salon.

Richard's Beverly Hills salon was of Moorish style architecture and had once been a Moroccan restaurant. He had chosen this building for a specific reason. Richard was, without a doubt, the world's greatest fan of the movie *Casablanca*. He had refurbished the building into an elegant, luxurious beauty salon and spa with decor resembling *Ricks Cafe Americain* in *Casablanca*. You entered through giant wooden doors carved to match those in the movie. The waiting room was dimly lit by Moroccan lamps that were hand made of sheep skin stretched around wrought iron frames. Diffuse light shown through fine black lines that artists had punctured in the skin with a needle. A ceiling fan with broad rattan blades rotated slowly overhead. Clients were seated in fan-shaped rattan chairs arranged around tile-inlaid tables and were offered cool drinks while they waited to be called for their treatments. Occasionally Richard hired impersonators to appear at Rick's as Bogart and Bergman or Sidney Greenstreet and Peter Lorre. Naturally he named place *Ricks Coiffures Americain*.

We sat in four of the big whicker chairs and dug into our gourmet take-out. Jenny was very quiet and didn't join in the small talk. Finally I asked, "Well, Jenny, did you come up with anything interesting on Dorica?"

She pulled out a yellow notepad and recited mechanically, "I checked public filings for fictitious business, voters, marriage, real property, and unsecured property tax rolls. The only items of much interest were her DBAs. The names she used on her Doing Business As forms made little sense until I noted the acronyms:

Greater Real Estate Education Development filed in 1984, acronym GREED, and the California Association for Securing Homes filed in 1982 is CASH, and Personal Income Group for Greater Investment filed in 1986 is, of course, PIGGI."

Richard looked up and asked, "Greed? Piggy? What kind of a weirdo are you into here?"

"Yeah, don't you love it," I said. "What else would you expect from the founder of LA LA Land. Five dollars says she's a con and one who relishes taking people for the sheer fun of it. Was there anything in between the eighties and her current gig?"

Jenny looked up at me with an expression I couldn't read. "Only if you count two years in the Federal pen; and yes, it was for fraud."

"Good work! Anything else?"

Jenny looked back down at her notes as she shook her head. "Not much. There's not a single piece of property in Dorica's name or her various business names, and the address she used for her voters registration was a private postal drop."

"How 'bout litigation?"

"Jackpot. I ran litigation in L.A. Superior Court. The printer began to clatter and only stopped after three full pages. Dorica was party to twenty-seven lawsuits in various superior court locations throughout the county. I tried muni court and came up with fourteen more. She must have bought BMWs for half the attorneys in the county."

"I tried consumer public filings and found she had forty-two judgements or liens filed against her or her corporations between 1982 and 1986. They amounted to millions of dollars and were from all over the state. Here's the strange thing, though. There was not a single foreclosure. Also, there's not a thing on record after 1986."

"So. What do we have?" I started ticking things off on my fingers as I sorted them out. "We don't know where she lives. We know she runs some kind of real estate scam and yet owns no property. She must own something. The question is, how does she hide it? We know she had lots of litigation, judgements, and debt up until 1986 and now seems to be clean. We don't know how she cleaned up her act. You sure she had nothing since then?"

"Nothing. She did her two years and disappeared, may have been out of the country. But I do know how she cleaned up all the debt. She filed bankruptcy in a tiny court, almost to the Oregon border, on 12-2-1986. I would never have found it without the database. I do love the electronic age."

"Very good, Jenny. Now we need to find out who owns the property the school is in?"

"Got it. LA LA Land property is owned by the Founder's Trust Inc., which in turn is owned by something called Simboyd N. A. Address for Simboyd was Box 7892, Honolulu, Hawaii. The reverse directory gives the occupant of that address as Very Private Postal. Another mail drop."

"Are these companies fronts for Dorica?"

"Unknown. Secretary of State has never heard of Simboyd N. A. Founder's Trust Inc. was incorporated in 2005 in Delaware and was authorized to do business in California. The president is in Mexico City and the agent for service is Europa-Continental Corporate Management."

"Mexico, Hawaii, letter drops; why do I get a feeling these folks may be trying to hide something? Can I use your phone, Richard?"

"Of course."

I called the operator in Hawaii and got a number for Very Private Postal and dialed it.

"Very Private Postal. May I help you?"

"You better," I growled. "Who is this?"

"This is the manager, Mr. Peterson. Who is this?"

"This is box 7892. You got somebody new working there or something? Our last shipment ended up with some other person's address on it. I needn't tell you how serious a problem that could be, do I?"

"No, ma'am. How di . . ."

"We are both lucky that the local carrier knew where that package was supposed to go, aren't we?"

"Well, yes, I . . ."

"Now listen very carefully, Peterson. First we are going to check your instructions. Read me the address you have for our packages."

"But, I . . ."

"No buts, just check it."

A short silence followed, then pages rustled. I held my breath. Then the slightly indignant voice from the other end of the line said, "One Avenue of the Stars, Suite 2700, Los Angeles, CA 90067."

"Good," I growled. "Now make sure everyone uses it. Any more goof ups and we find a new service." I hung up quickly before he could form any questions of his own.

"What?" asked Jenny.

"That Hawaiian mail drop gets Simboyd's mail and ships it right back here to L.A. Unfortunately not to LA LA Land as I expected. Some high rent number in Century City. Oh, well. That gives us another lead. Looks like any real answers we get are going to have to come from LA LA Land."

I looked in the mirror and realized what Richard was doing to my hair. "No, Richard, it can't look pretty. It has to look dirty and matted and dull, like I slept on it for weeks."

Richard closed his eyes, took a deep breath, and let it out in a dramatic sigh. "Ah, yes. Tonight we are turning a silk purse into a sow's ear."

"Diana," said Jenny, "it's already 11:00 p.m. There is no way you will get a bed in the shelter tonight, and downtown L.A. is no place for a camp out. Women on the street really do get mugged, beaten, raped, and killed. Why don't you wait until morning before you hit the street? Then you can have all day to wander around in your stinky outfit and get a room at LA LA Land."

"No, it's okay. I have a safe plan all worked out." That, of course, was a brazen lie and Richard and Jenny looked at me as if they knew it was a lie. The truth is, if I don't act impulsively, I might not act at all.

"Right," said Jenny. "Well, I've done your research, but that's it. I'm not going to play street person for you. I think it's nuts and I . . ."

"No, no, Jenny, I'm not going to ask you to come in through her homeless hostel." I interrupted her and talked fast. I couldn't let her say the words. It would be too hard to get her to take them back. I couldn't let her say she wasn't going to play anymore. "You, ah . . . you just come in as a San Fernando Valley housewife looking for a career. I understand that tuition is free for the homeless until they sell some property. Then she takes tuition out of their proceeds. Your tuition will run about a thousand bucks. Here is a checkbook on a case expense account I set up for the purpose." I quickly handed her the checkbook and waited to see how she would react.

"Oh, and when exactly were you going to tell me about this?"

"Exactly, right now, this evening. That's why I asked you to meet me here, to discuss the case and set up plans. If you have any other ideas on how to do this, give."

Mechanically she took the checkbook and opened it. "Margerie Halsteader," she read aloud, and then repeated it several times. "Margerie Halsteader, Margerie Halsteader."

I was relieved to see she was trying to get a fix on what kind of character she was to be with that name. "That way Margerie will be in a position to learn how the paying public is treated, and Betty can see how the homeless fare. Then we can compare notes."

"No breaking and entering? No safe cracking? No surprise plans you get me into without telling me what we are doing?"

I smiled. "No. Just take her real estate course, keep your eyes and ears open, and see what you can learn." I then threw Jenny a line from an old Danny Kaye movie that had inspired our pretending since the tender age of six. "Get it?"

Studying the checkbook, she answered automatically. "Got it."

"Good," I said, finishing the bit. She was still with me.

FOUR

I had parked my car at the El Pueblo Athletic Club and stashed my purse with the night clerk at the desk. I considered just taking a room until morning but I was already in my Bag Lady Betty outfit, and the truth was I was curious about life on the street.

Wandering around Bunker Hill admiring the art work, fountains, architecture, and gardens was fun and allowed my mind to wander too. I was thinking that Jenny was right. I had created a strange and dangerous employment for myself. The game had been necessary to rescue Richard, but why didn't I stop after that? I could live on my regular case work. Was I an adrenaline junky, or just addicted to the money?

As I left the hill and went into the dingier and more threatening parts of town, I walked steadily and lingered nowhere. "Safer as a moving target," I mumbled. As soon as I voiced that thought, it occurred to me that it could be an analogy for the way I lived my life and dealt with relationships. With that thought I decided to curtail all introspection.

I patted my coat pocket, feeling for the reassuring lump of my stun gun. It didn't provide the same level of security as my Walther 32, but the stun gun was legal. Once again I cursed Los Angeles police and sheriffs' policies for refusing to issue P.I.'s permits to carry concealed weapons.

When I am downtown, I begin breathing very shallowly, because at street level the air tends to smell like the back end of a bus. It's like, if I don't breathe too deeply I won't get that crud in my lungs.

Tonight the diesel and gas fumes were somewhat less concentrated. Unfortunately that only cleared my nasal receptors for the smells of human filth. Urine and feces and trash of all kinds have naturally increased with the increased numbers of homeless. I wondered why the city couldn't put out a few portable outhouses, and then wondered if the vagrants would use them.

In the next block I heard music. Across the street I saw a woman and two men sitting on the steps of a doorway sharing both a bottle of wine and a ghetto blaster. I considered hanging around and listening for a while as they sang and moved to the music. Almost instantly I abandoned the notion as a really stupid idea. For one thing, at this spot the odor of urine was strong enough to chase me away all by itself. More importantly, I got looks from the trio that let me know that an audience was not welcome.

Down on Spring Street I saw many sleeping vagrants, dark bundles huddled in smelly alcoves. Those who were awake were mostly men, sitting or standing in small groups. Petty drug sales were made openly on every block.

I can't see people living on the street without wondering how they got here. What combination of fate and choice leads to this? What is it like to live this way? Could I prevent it from ever happening to me? I think so. I think I am independent and resourceful enough to take care of myself. Are drugs, booze, and mental illness or laziness at the bottom of all such cases? How does it happen? What do they think? Unless I could talk to these people and learn their real story, I would never be able to know.

Near Third and Spring, I walked past three young men dressed in baggy pants with the waistline hanging down past their butt crack. One was seated on a circular planter with his knees spread wide and his hands on his crotch. The body language was explicit: sexually aggressive and threatening. With nothing but his position he was saying, "Fuck you and the society you rode in on." With his facial expression he added, "I'm big enough and bad enough to do it." The other two stood on each side of him like his alert and watchful soldiers. The three eyed me so hostilely that I was wishing I had stayed at the club or up on Bunker Hill.

As I walked past them, the leader stood up. I heard their shuffling steps as they sauntered slowly down the sidewalk after me. I couldn't run fast enough to get away and I sure couldn't fight them off. Jenny's warning about rape, assault, and murder suddenly seemed like wisdom.

I looked up and realized I was now in front of the Ronald Reagan State Office Building. How appropriate that this is the scariest place in town. Half the reason there are so many homeless street crazies is because of Reagan. He began the trend by shutting down most of the state mental hospitals and dumping the patients out on the street.

That thought gave me the germ of an idea. No one likes to engage one of the street loonies. Looking at my reflection in the glass door, I began to talk to it. My friends slowed their pace but were still walking toward me. My mumbled, incoherent words became a rant interspersed with an occasional angry yell. I could see them hesitate just a few paces away.

Throwing my hands up, I gave the reflection one last burst of wrath and then turned abruptly and walked toward the three men. My tirade returned to a mumble as I talked earnestly to the air and made no eye contact with the gang. The leader stood, arms folded, legs spread wide, blocking the sidewalk. It was all or nothing. Just as I reached him I threw up my arms again and raised my voice to a yell repeatedly warning one and all that the Jabberwocky was coming. I saw his eyes open wider and his hands come off his chest, positioned for defense. I waved my arms frantically landing several glancing blows on his chest. He looked first astonished then angered as my flailing arms effectively pushed him aside. His two pals closed ranks and I was encircled by the three of them. I dropped my voice to a whisper, still talking to no one in particular and making no eye contact. From a whisper I gradually raised the volume again. I stopped talking suddenly and listened. Then I screamed as shrilly as possible. The leader put one finger in his ear and rubbed vigorously. The other two watched him for direction.

I turned my back on the leader, went back to a mumble, and started to walk between the other two. Their shoulders locked together like magnets and they spread their legs to a braced stance as I came up hard against their chests. I could feel a large automatic in a shoulder holster on one. So much for the effectiveness of gun control.

I heard the leader say, "Hey, man, you watch, that Jaba Jaba gonin' get you." All three men laughed. The wall of chests parted and I was permitted to pass. As I hurried on down the sidewalk, I could hear them speaking quietly as they repositioned themselves on the steps. My relief was mingled with a slight adrenaline shakiness.

I had already had enough night life and moved out as fast as my little legs would carry me toward safer ground. A block up the street a thin young man appeared from a darkened doorway and began pacing me. Though it was cold, he wore nothing but a pair of green cotton shorts and a T-shirt. His incoherent discourse could have been a duet for my last act. I reached inside my coat pocket, wrapped my hand around my stun gun, and tried to walk a little faster. As I turned back up Fourth, Green Shorts stopped as if he had reached an unseen frontier he could not cross.

Supposedly, the doors to the state hospitals had been shut so patients could be freed into the loving care of relatives. Reality was it freed the state of the expense of caring for them and imprisoned them on dark, dangerous streets.

I was still looking back over my shoulder at Green Shorts when I stumbled over something on the sidewalk. I fell forward, my head barely missing a brick retaining wall. As I fell I let out a small yell and heard an answering cry of alarm from the alcove to my right. I scrambled part way up and found myself looking into two huge frightened eyes, which were sunken and outlined in dark circles. She looked to be in her mid-thirties. Her hair was light colored and hung unkempt, straw-like.

"I'm sorry," I said. "I, I just tripped." The blanket she had wrapped around her moved and two more pairs of dark frightened eyes peered out at me. Two children, maybe two and four, huddled on the street with their mother, wrapped in a thin hospital blanket. "Oh my God," I said.

The mother poked the heads of the children down under the blanket. Then as fast as a striking snake, she pulled out a two-foot-long piece of pipe and aimed it at my head. I was on my feet and backing out of her alcove in two fast heartbeats.

We stared at each other for several seconds as I tried to think what I could say or do that would help. She didn't look like she would be open to introductions and I couldn't think what to say to her. I reached into my coat pocket, took all of the money I had brought with me, and I tossed it, money clip and all, at the woman. At first she jumped back, then she looked at the money. When she looked at me, there was no expression, not even curiosity.

"It's money," I said. "Maybe you and the kids can get a room or some food." She just continued to stare at me. I backed away slowly. When I was about six steps back she reached down and picked up the money and pulled it under the blanket.

What I had seen in that alcove was more than I was prepared to deal with. Children, little more than babies, huddled on the street. Third World countries, maybe, but the United States? I tried to close my mind to the memory of those three sets of frightened eyes, and headed back to Broadway as fast as I could without breaking into a run.

On normal day trips I find Broadway to be a fascinating street. It's like taking a trip through exotic cultures, with Chinatown on one end and Latino retail on the other. The Latino district has that atmosphere of a foreign bazaar which tourists enjoy on Olvera Street or in Tijuana, yet this street is for real shopping, not tourists.

Shop owners open up the whole front of the store and display their wares as far out toward the sidewalk as they can get away with. They stand there, hawking their goods like carnival barkers, while Mexican radio stations blare pop music from the doorways. Here you can find every type of clothing from shorts to wedding dresses, as well as luggage, electronic gadgets, jewelry, and household goods. Little sidewalk stands like the ones in Mexico vend fresh fruit right alongside taco and burrito stands, hamburger shops, bakeries, and even fried chicken franchises. It's a fun marketplace, in the daytime. Tonight, it was just another lonely street with iron security grates on all the shops.

Despite the retail activity at street level, most of the upper floors of the buildings are empty. LA LA Land took advantage of all this under utilized space and located in a lovely old 1920s building adorned with an elaborate frieze. The bottom floor of the building began life as a vaudeville theater and then converted to a movie theater. It still has the classic old marquee out front. At one time that marquee carried the names of the latest films and the greatest stars, but by the fifties, folks were heading for the suburbs and going to movies at the drive-in, and the stately old theater was relegated to second-run films and B movies. Then it became a porno movie house, and finally was closed altogether. Today the marquee tells the world that this is LA LA Land.

Walking around to the back of the building, I climbed up the dimly lit stairway. I didn't really expect the sleepy guard on the other side of the iron gate to let me in, but I was establishing my credentials as a hungry vagrant. He responded kindly but firmly.

"Listen here, honey, we open at 5:00 a.m. Come back then for a nice breakfast and a bath. Now get outta here. You most definitely need that bath." Additional cream from Sam's stinky concoction was not needed. The residue left on my clothes was quite sufficient.

I wandered back up to Bunker Hill killing time, and went back to LA LA Land about 4:35. There was already quite a line outside the little back door to the hostel. I got in place quickly. After my brief experience on the street, I was looking forward to LA LA Land as a place of warmth and safety, which of course only proves that my thinking was as naive and stupid as the rest of Dorica's suckers.

FIVE

A greater variety of people stood in this line than my preconception of the homeless had led me to expect. Of course, some were obviously under the influence of drugs or alcohol and others were talking to people or things that weren't there. But also in this line were families: mother, father, and small children, looking normal and cared for.

My attention was taken by an old man and woman who puffed up the sidewalk toward us like a tiny train maneuvering their small cargo in a single grocery cart between them. Like the little engine that could, the woman was in front, one hand tenaciously coupled to the front of the basket, pulling it as she marched up the street in heavy-soled men's boots. Her wrinkled face was set in lines of bitterness and determination and framed by a crisp all-weather khaki-colored hat. Like her boots and hat, her khaki pants and faded plaid jacket were selected for their practicality and durability. Dressed in similar attire, the old man trudged behind in a shuffle-footed gait, following like a forlorn and engineless caboose. His hands clinging to the handle of the cart, his head and shoulders bent, he looked more like he was holding himself up than pushing the cart. How could such frail old people live on the street? What had life done to them? How could this be in America?

With a growing sense of guilt, I searched the crowd for the dark-eyed mother and her two toddlers. Why hadn't I told her about LA LA Land? Why hadn't I asked her to come here with me? What was the matter with me that I stood tongue-tied? I had seen a young mother with very young children, sleeping on the street, cold, afraid, and probably hungry. The only response I could muster was to throw money at her and run away.

I sat down on the pavement as several others were doing and waited for the door to open. As I watched, I was shocked by the sudden realization that I had more in common with these people than I would ever have imagined. I too had found my lifestyle suddenly changed. I had been a spoiled Beverly Hills wife married to an aerospace CEO. Then came the Congressional investigations into bribery and kickbacks. In the wink of an eye Martin disappeared with his secretary and a couple billion dollars of his employer's cash. I may not have ended up on the street, but I came very close; and I certainly lived an unorthodox existence now. "There but for the grace of God go I," I whispered.

An elderly black gentleman limped stiff-legged up the sidewalk and took the place in line behind me. He was dressed in a worn but neat maroon polyester suit, with vest and hat, and carried himself with dignity. From one arm hung what I first took to be a cane. However, he opened the little device and revealed that it was a folded, tripod stool. He took pains to place it exactly as he wanted and then seated himself upon it. From his suit coat pocket he pulled a small transistor radio, plugged the ear phones into his ears, and turned it on. From his other pocket, he pulled a newspaper. As he opened the paper, he looked over the top of it, directly at me, letting me know that I had been caught staring. I couldn't help smiling at his resourcefulness. "You're really prepared," I said.

He didn't make a smile with his mouth but his eyes seemed to soften as he apparently decided I was harmless. "Gotta be," he replied.

Encouraged by this response, I dared to push my acquaintance further. "It's quite a long line already. You think they will have enough breakfast for everybody who shows up?"

He considered me over the top of his paper. "Nope," he answered and went back to the paper.

I could take a hint. Making no further attempts at conversation, I went back to my people watching. My attention was focused on a young father who was talking quietly and earnestly to a sullen boy of about eight, when the old gentleman behind me asked, "This your first time to LA LA Land?"

I weighed my answer. Should I admit it, and if so what would he ask next? He read my hesitation instantly.

"The first timers that's in the first fifty in line always gets in," he said. "But ya gotta be 'prepared' to be one of them what gets a bed and stays a full week."

"Really," I said. "What do you have to do to get a bed?" He ignored me and read his paper. I leaned a bit closer. "You know, it's kinda scary out here and I sure would like to know how to stay in there. I don't have much, but I've got about seventy-five cents in change."

He continued to read but his right hand lowered, palm upward. I took off my rubber boot and shook out the change I had stashed there and placed it in the old man's hand. He deftly slipped it into the watch pocket of his vest.

"When you go in they'll ask you if you ever been here before. Say no. Then, if you're too nuts or too drunk they just give you a cup of coffee and a donut and send you on. If you seem okay they put you in line for a shower, and if you need 'em, they give you clean clothes. Since you stink, you better take the new ones."

I had difficulty keeping a straight face. I thought my Bag Lady Betty perfume fit in quite well down here. Maybe I was just getting used to it.

"Then they might let you stay around if you talk to 'em a bit. That's when you need to really be prepared," he added knowingly.

With that he ducked behind the paper again and no amount of persuasion could induce him to tell me what he meant by that last hint.

At thirty seconds before the hour, my friend folded his paper, turned off the radio, and put them in his pockets. As he stood, he folded his little stool and placed its rounded handle over his arm. The door to LA LA Land opened and the line began to shuffle in. He eyed me as we walked. "You real hungry?" he asked.

"I could eat," I replied.

He was silent again and then said, "You like pancakes?"

Now it was my turn to study him. I thought I got his measure. He wanted my pancakes. "Not too many at one time," I answered.

He broke into his first real smile. "Good!" he said. "After your shower you find me in the dinin' hall. Maybe we can talk some more."

I couldn't help smiling at this old fox. "What's your name?" I asked.

He eyed me a moment. "You may call me Walter. What do I call you?"

The way he phrased the question made it sound as if it was a forgone conclusion that the name would be an alias. I wasn't sure if that was because everyone here used them or because this guy was on to me already.

"Betty," I replied.

He smiled and nodded to me and we followed the line in.

SIX

There were few formalities to get in the door. As Walter had told me, the drunks and crazies were given a donut and coffee and ushered away. I passed inspection and was directed to the showers. When I came out, I found that they had taken my clothes and replaced them with a clean, good-fitting polyester pantsuit and a white blouse that was missing the bottom button.

Gratefully I dressed in the clean-smelling clothes. I thought of all the old clothing I had given away and hoped it had gone to someone who felt as good about getting it as I did. What an eye opener, and I had only been on the street part of one night. Maybe I was on the wrong tack with Dorica. Perhaps she really was providing a benefit to the inner city.

From the cafeteria line, I spotted Walter. He had been watching for me and waved me to his table, where he sat with three other adults and five small children. He had saved me a place. As I sat down, I noticed that he had already emptied his plate of pancakes and was working on the eggs and toast. He introduced me to the other adults and I traded hellos with Mary Anne, Jim and Aurelia. Mary Anne said that her husband, Ben, was in the office but I would meet him later.

"This," said Walter as he introduced me to the children, "is my friend who don't like pancakes. See, I tol' you I would find someone besides me who didn't like pancakes."

Two children were already working on a plate of cakes. Two other young children greeted me with unabashedly hungry grins, while the older boy looked at his lap to avoid looking too openly eager.

"It's a crazy thing," explained Walter, as he forked the pancakes from my plate to the children's. "They give adults three pancakes and children just one. That's against nature. Have you ever seen a child walk? No, and you won't. They skip, they jump, run, trot, jog, dance, climb, and balance on the curb. They do all sorts of things, but they never just walk. If adults worked as hard as kids, they might need them three cakes, but they don't, so they just gets fat."

I smiled as the kids poured syrup and dug into the pancakes. Walter looked sideways at me with a hint of a grin. "I'll bet you thought I was goin' to eat all them cakes myself, didn't you? Uh huh."

Not only had I misjudged Walter but he had read me perfectly, right down to the sub-text. I made a mental note never to play poker with this gent.

"Well, you better get with eating your eggs or these kiddies will eat them up too."

I gladly tended to my eating.

Mary Anne said, "Thanks for the pancakes, Betty. I hope John didn't twist your arm too hard."

I was confused for a second and then realized my "Walter" was their "John." "No, and you're welcome. Did you meet John this morning?"

"No, we met him about five weeks ago when we first came to LA LA Land."

"Oh, you've been here for that long?"

"Yeah, with John's help, we found out how to get a work fellowship."

"What's a work fellowship?"

"It allows you to stay here six weeks and work off your care by helping in the kitchen, the laundry or outside fixing up houses that are being bought and sold. That way you can go to the classes free."

"What classes?"

"On Dorica's real estate system for buying property. We got so excited when we found one but . . . well . . . it didn't work out for us. Now our internship is up and I don't know what we are going to do."

My next question came out sharply incredulous. "How could you possibly hope to buy a property if you're, well, down enough to be here?"

"It's all part of Dorica's method. If you find a good property that is under market value, she can get you a hundred percent loan. Just the rent from that property we found could have put us back on our feet."

In the current market this sounded ludicrous but it was obvious that Mary Anne believed it even after her pipe dream had vanished.

Aurelia looked concerned. "Is Ben still determined to talk to Mrs. Grizel about it?"

Mary Anne nodded. "Since someone else bought the property we worked he's going to ask her if we can extend our work fellowship."

"What are you going to do if she refuses?"

"If she says no, . . . well, Ben says he's going to tell her he knows the deal was crooked and that he's going to the authorities."

Walter's expression darkened and he looked back down at his coffee cup.

"What makes him think it's crooked?" I asked.

"Mac told us four weeks ago. He said this would happen. That we would work up a property but before we had a chance to buy it, it would be sold to someone else."

"Who's Mac?"

"He works here. What do you think, John? Will she extend our stay?"

Walter/John let no emotion show on his face but his pause and long look into Mary Anne's face said it all. "If that's what Ben's up to now, honey, you're not goin' to stay even overnight."

Mary Anne's face went pale and she fought back tears. "We have no place else to go!"

I felt the panic in her voice and saw again those three pairs of eyes in the dark.

"Mary Anne, do you have any family or anything that could help for a while?"

She shook her head.

"How about another shelter?"

"We've tried. Maybe in time but not now."

"If you had a place to stay could you find jobs? What did you do before?"

"I don't know. If we had a place to live I could wait tables and Ben could work as a security guard . . . different shifts so one of us could be with the kids. Ben had a good job when he first got out of the Navy. That's what brought us to California. We bought a house and the whole nine yards. But then his company moved their manufacturing plant offshore and Ben was laid off. His unemployment ran out and the other jobs he found didn't pay enough, and then the balloon payment came due on the mortgage . . . well there was no way. We managed to live in an apartment for a while, then a motel. Last month we ended up . . . We have applications in for programs to help both of us get retrained into some career where we could make a living. That sort of thing takes so long." She looked at her children and the pain on her face about did me in.

We emptied our second cups of coffee and the kids started running around the hall. LA LA Land clerks were going around the tables, talking with everyone, taking names, and making notations on a clipboard. Walter leaned over to me and spoke quietly. "Now's that time for us to talk more, just like I promised. When they gets to you, talk smart enough to show you can read and write, but don't act so smart like you might figure out too much by yourself. Understand?"

I nodded.

"And this here's important, when they asks for your Social Security number, tell them you don't have it on you but you can get it. Got that?"

I nodded again. I started to ask Walter how he knew all this when loud voices from the entrance of the cafeteria drew everyone's attention.

Mary Anne looked up and moaned, "Oh Ben!"

I followed her gaze and saw Ben. He was a tall man with light brown hair and a short beard. He was terribly thin and his hair was a bit disheveled, but he still carried himself with the that straight posture instilled by his military background. His facial expression, however, was frantic.

He was arguing with a greasy-looking fellow with neck-length black curls, sideburns, mustache, a pocked face, and the eyes of a used car salesman. The slimy looking fellow was punctuating his sentences with a shoving action as he pushed Ben toward the main stairway. The entire room could hear him telling Ben to get his belongings together and get out by noon.

Mary Anne's eyes rimmed with tears. As she rose and started gathering her children, those tears cascaded down her reddened cheeks. If Ben and Mary Anne could not stay here, they and their three small children would be on the street tonight. I thought about my last night and knew I couldn't let that happen.

I turned to Walter, but he had disappeared.

As I started to follow Mary Anne I was stopped by a young, eager fellow with a volunteer badge on his shirt and a clipboard in hand. Keeping one eye on Mary Anne, I gave information to the volunteer. Following Walter's instructions, I found myself invited to stay and attend the meeting tonight when Dorica herself would bring the sermon to the great unwashed masses in the old theater downstairs. On second thought, we were now washed masses. No overnight or internship was offered, however.

Before I had finished my little interview, Ben, Mary Anne and their kids headed for the sleeping rooms. By the time I caught up with them they had already gathered their few belongings and were walking toward the front entrance off Broadway.

When I stopped them and said, "I need to talk with you," I saw resistance in both their faces. "Please, just a minute. It's important." With a doubtful look to one another they acquiesced reluctantly.

We walked down the front stairs and into the foyer of the theater. As soon as we were clear of others I blurted out, "I have a place for you guys to stay." Needless to say the looks I got were incredulous, and I couldn't help a small laugh. "I know," I said, "sounds screwy. But I don't want you guys on the street and I can help. I'm a . . . not exactly what I appear to be and I know of an apartment in Bluff Beach that's vacant. It's dumpy, but it's furnished and clean and you can stay there and get back on your feet." They looked at me like I was one of the crazies. "Really, please believe me."

Ben studied me with great distrust. "If you're not exactly what you appear to be, just exactly what are you?" he asked.

I considered what I could tell them that would gain their trust. "I really don't have time to go into that, but I'll tell you what. You know the El Pueblo Athletic Club?" Mary Anne nodded. Ben just glared. "It's member only and rather exclusive and only a few blocks from here. If you walk there and they know your name and let you in will you believe I'm on the up and up?"

SEVEN

Ben wasn't buying it, but Mary Anne put her foot down. The looks on the three kids' faces were the clincher. His suspicions were far from gone, but with no other real option, he reluctantly agreed to go to the El Pueblo to check my story. If they really got in, they agreed to wait for my friend to give them a ride to the promised apartment.

I saw them off at the Broadway entrance to the theater and then headed for the public phone in the lobby to call Jenny. I didn't have any money on me, but dialed her using my calling card number.

"Hello."

"Hi, Jenny. I need a favor."

"Diana? Of course you do. Where are you? Are you all right? What happened last night in L.A.?"

"Yes, I'm okay but don't have time for a lot of explanations. I'm temporarily at Dorica's homeless hostel and have to get back upstairs and see what I can do to get to stay here awhile, so please, just listen."

"Okay, shoot."

"I met a couple here who worked up a property for Dorica and are witnesses to the whole scam."

"Sounds like the lead you need."

"Yeah, except there's a problem. They're homeless and they and their three kids all got kicked out of here this morning. I, ah, I sent them over to the El Pueblo Athletic Club and I need you to drive into town and scoop them up."

"Oh, I'm going to 'scoop them up,' am I? And what do I do with them?"

"They had no place to stay, Jenny, and I don't want to lose track of them. We need to talk with them. Please rent that apartment next to mine, the one with the furniture, and give them a little walking around money."

"Oh, I see. We're adopting them! What do I use for cash?"

"Use the checking account I gave you from Maude's retainer. Taking care of our sources has to be a legitimate investigative expense."

"OK. Listen, I got tons of stuff on that Dorica person. You want it now?"

"No, no time. I'll be back to you as soon as I can. Thanks, Jen."

I hung up before she had time to draw a breath and ask another question. She would do fine on her own. Making a quick call to the El Pueblo, I told the desk that the Cannons were my guests and asked that the staff make them comfortable until someone came to pick them up.

The El Pueblo is one of the posher old clubs in L.A. It has an Olympic size pool on one floor, his and hers gym and workout floors, an indoor track, racquetball courts, and one floor for lounging, drinking, reading, working, or playing pool. There are five different restaurants varying from snack bar to haute cuisine. There are also three floors of hotel suites. My membership was the only status symbol I was able to hang onto after my ex husband, Martin flew south. It delighted the proletariat rebel in me to send my new homeless friends there.

The pay phone was just off the side entrance to the grand old theater auditorium, and as I walked past I pulled aside the curtain and peeked in. The theater still held much of the elegance of a past era and I stepped in to take a better look. This side door brought me into the auditorium about two thirds of the way down the aisle. As I was admiring the ornate old ceiling, the creaking of the wooden floor and the soft rustle of the burgundy-colored curtain turned my attention to the front of the theater. I looked over to the exit at the right side of the stage and saw the curtain still moving. Someone else had been in the theater and had ducked out in a hurry. Could that someone have been listening to my phone call or was it just another hostel guest looking around the old theater?

I ran over and looked through the curtain. No one was in sight but there were three possible exits. There was a passage that led to the backstage area; off to the right was a street door with a lighted exit sign, and in between was a winding staircase that I guessed went up to the hostel floor. A faint sound of footsteps came from the staircase.

Rather than chase him up the same stairs, I ran to the other exit on the left and took the stairs two and three at a time. I opened the door at the top and came out into a busy hallway on the third floor.

EIGHT

As I slipped out into the upstairs hall, a gray-haired gentleman was quietly easing the door closed on the right exit. He was fairly tall and lean but seemed stooped and burdened by whatever life had brought him.

This bent, discouraged looking figure must be the person who had been in the theater downstairs. What bothered me was that I had seen him before. Ben and Mary Anne and I had almost run into him as we turned a corner in the hall. Now I wondered. Had he really just been walking innocently down the hall toward us or had he been listening to our conversation? He disarmed my suspicions somewhat when he shuffled down the hall and appeared to be totally unaware of me.

Gray Hair and I both joined the rest of the guests of this strange hotel as they formed a rather ill-defined line in front of a large office. Conversation buzzed noisily as we all waited to see who would be lucky enough to get a bed pass.

Suddenly, from the office there was a scream so piercing and so filled with terror and pain, I fully expected to see someone being murdered. The crowd became absolutely still.

Through the glass partition I saw a wooden reception counter with several guests lined up in front of a swinging gate. None of the guests in line seemed to be source of the scream.

I pushed through the crowd and let myself into the office. As I searched the six desks beyond the counter a woman at the first desk leaped up from her typewriter, pulling frantically at her blouse and screaming, "Get it off! Get it off of me!"

The unpleasant fellow with the pocked face and sideburns who tossed the Cannons out was sitting at a desk in a glass cubical at the back of the office. The name plate on his door read Gunter Hengst. He rose from his chair, and at the same moment a woman emerged from a private office on the left. The woman was tall and slender with piles of thick, black hair beautifully coifed in an elegant, puffed

Victorian hairstyle. This must be Dorica June Grizel.

Everyone was in motion. Most of the crowd was backing away from the screamer and Dorica was on the phone calling for help.

Without thinking, I pushed past the crowd, let myself in the swinging gate and headed for the terrified woman. Gunter was ahead of me. She let out another blood curdling scream and began flailing her arms in all directions. Dodging her fists, Gunter grabbed her and tried to subdue her while I tried to see what was wrong. I thought perhaps some terrible thing had gotten inside her clothing, but she broke Gunter's hold and I barely ducked a couple of solid roundhouses.

Then to my surprise, my gray-haired friend from the theater joined the fray. Together, he and Gunter managed to wrestle the poor woman to the floor. I tried to get her to tell me what was wrong while I frantically searched her clothing for the source of the pain but she was too incoherent to answer.

Gray Hair leaned toward me and said quietly, "There's nothing in the blouse. She's either psychotic or has DT's."

I looked up at his green eyes and saw in them far greater vitality than I found in most of the old homeless here. Also, his body seemed more muscular than it had appeared when I had watched his bent, shuffling walk. In that strange way that you sometimes perceive things when you are filled with the adrenaline of an emergency, I locked in on a vivid closeup of his gray hair. It had brown roots.

The woman screamed again and I looked back at her. Her eyes seemed large, unseeing, and sort of glazed. I had never seen anything like it. She was not seeing anything in this room, and she was without doubt, mortally terrified.

Instinctively I ran my hand through her hair and spoke soothingly. For a split second her eyes seemed almost to focus and she darted a momentary look at me. Then she was gone again, a wild thing, absolutely unreachable. I felt shaken just seeing what could happen to the human mind.

Gunter's gaze took in me and Gray Hair and I realized that once again, my impulsive response to a situation had led me to charge in rather than think about the consequences. There was no doubt that Gray Hair had noticed me but Gunter had been preoccupied giving orders to the security people who had arrived on the scene. As security took over, I exited discreetly and took a chair near another homeless guest on the other side of the counter.

By the time EMTs arrived the woman was no longer screaming, but was sobbing, a most soul-touching cry. Many of the residents were obviously disturbed by the scene and mumbled quietly as the paramedics took the woman away. The office workers, however, seemed to take it in their stride and were using the moment of confusion to have a coffee break. I guess such scenes were not that unusual to them.

Dorica was talking quietly with Gunter. In my first view of her from a distance, I had thought that she was quite a beautiful woman. Up close, I saw the hardness rather than the beauty. Two deep lines, like a set of parentheses, enclosed her mouth. They looked as if they had grown there by the pressure of constant anger or tension, or perhaps by the vigilant guard over anything her mouth might say. When she spoke, her mouth opened cautiously at the center but was almost immobile at the corners emphasizing her effort to tightly control every utterance. Her jaws bulged like overdeveloped biceps. She must have spent each moment, waking or sleeping, with her jaws tightly clenched. Her body looked as if it had never been indulged with a single ounce of extra flesh and her posture was as straight and as rigidly controlled as her face. A momentary smile almost succeeded in erasing the image of emotionless control, until you noticed her eyes. The smile, as controlled as everything else about her, stopped at her nose. Her eye lids were partly covering her eyes. As she spoke with Gunter, I realized she had good reason to shield those eyes. Only in her eyes did any excess show. Rather than shining with human warmth, they glittered like the eyes of an eager and voracious bird of prey.

Gray Hair moved out of the office and worked his way back into the crowd. I was considering doing the same when I noticed the way Dorica stared after him. I wondered what connection was there and if he would be reporting to her later.

I watched to see if Dorica followed him. Instead she picked up a file folder from the desk in front of her and held it over her mouth as she whispered something to Gunter. He looked up in time to see the bent, shuffling form of Gray Hair disappearing into the crowd. Gunter nodded and grunted disinterestedly. Dorica said one more thing to him and then went back into her office.

NINE

Gunter ran one hand through his greasy hair and began to reestablish order. "Okay folks, party's over. Let's get back to work."

A neat young woman in a business suit who had been sitting at the desk with the screamer said, "Gunter, that woman was my typist. I'm going to need a new one to continue the interviews."

"Well," he said, "can't you type it as you do the interview?"

"Ah, no sir, I don't type."

"You can't type? Aren't you the college whiz kid who's here on an internship?"

"Yes sir."

"And they don't teach typing in school these days?"

"My degree is in public administration, not secretarial services."

"My *degree*? Shows you just how fuckin' worthless a degree is. Okay, listen up, folks. "Hey, quiet down and listen. I got a deal for ya here. Who can type? I got a six-week work fellowship for anyone who can type."

My hand was up before I thought about it.

"Okay, you, come here and sit down and type sumthin' for me."

I sat at the old manual typewriter and pecked out the first typing exercise everyone learns, "Now is thee time for all good men to come to the aid of their courntry." I made two errors in one sentence but Gunter wanted to prove a point.

"See," he said, "even this old bag off the street can type. You got a *degree* honey?"

I shook my head.

"Good," he said and turned to go into his glass office. The young college intern watched him, her cheeks red with anger. She ran her hands through her neck-length brown hair and then turned to me.

"I'm sorry he called you an old bag," she said. "Well, let's get to it. My name is Tina McIntire, what's yours?"

"I'm Betty," I answered. "And he didn't bother me. I'm just glad to have the work."

She put a card in the typewriter and began typing to show me how to fill in the blanks. I decided it was best not to notice she could type quite well.

"Betty what?" she asked.

"Betty Bag . . . Baggetti," I stammered. She looked at me dubiously and I spelled it out, "B a g g e t t i." She typed it on the card and, *voila*, I had a last name.

"Social Security number?" she asked.

Remembering Walter's instructions I said, "Ah, I can't remember it but I could get hold of it if I could call back to Ohio."

She nodded and left that blank. With a glance over her shoulder to Gunter's cubical, she turned the typewriter over to me. We went on to the rest of my stats and a little background. By the time we had my card filled out, she had also taught me my job.

When we had finished with me, she called the next person in line and we repeated the same process with him.

During the interviews, Tina discreetly checked arms and legs for needle marks, heads for lice, and skin for any runny sores. In general, she seemed to give them as good a once-over as you could without a real physical. I wondered what class in public administration taught that.

She was also skilled at the art of interrogation and extremely tricky at getting to the truth. Listening to her, I realized how lucky I was not to have been questioned more fully. When she finished with her subjects she had them sign a large black register and sent them on to the next station. I began to recognize a pattern.

Those who were habitual, had lived on the street for years, admitted current substance abuse, or admitted staying in the hostel before, were sent on with no chit for a room. They reported to the Desk of Opportunity Assistance. That turned out to be a wonderful euphemism for figuring out which government office to send them to. It also occurred to me that Dorica had zinged in another of her acronyms, DOA, as in Dead On Arrival. Quite a sense of humor this Dorica had.

Those like the Cannons who seemed to be just momentarily knocked on their ass by life were screened a bit more carefully. If they passed Tina's gentle yet deceptively rigorous interrogation, they were granted a six-week stay in the hostel and were referred to the Desk Of Occupational Preference for a job assignment. DOOP. Could this be Dorica's spelling for dope or perhaps dupe? At the DOOP desk they were assigned to either in-house or outside work, depending on their skills and past jobs.

The third group was small but choice. Twice during the morning when Tina found a couple who seemed intelligent and able to communicate well, she referred them to Dorica's office. These chosen few came out of the mahogany door with a scholarship to Dorica's real estate school and only part-time work. This would leave them with time to try to use Dorica's secrets of how to buy foreclosure property and make their fortune.

By midmorning, when I was just settling comfortably into my job, Tina gave me a surprise. She turned to ask a question of the man at the DOOP desk and called him "Mac." I took a closer look at him. "Mac" was the name of the guy who had tried to warn the Cannons that the game was rigged. After that, I found myself listening partly to him and partly to Tina.

He was heavy set, beginning to gray, and did not look like he ever saw the inside of a gym. With a kind and patient voice, he interviewed his subjects and was resourceful in trying to find a helpful niche for each case. He sounded, however, like he had seen too much to waste energy on false hopes. He had reached what my Dad used to call, "The alignment of expectations with reality."

When Tina passed him a young man who really just needed short-term assistance, I got a glimpse of a totally different Mac. His blue-gray eyes, which had been passive throughout most of the morning, seemed to suddenly gleam with enthusiasm. In those eyes I saw the soul of an idealist who burned for a cause. I could see why such a person would warn the Cannons not to waste their time. But why would he be working here in the first place? I would definitely have to talk with Mac.

Gunter's annoying voice interrupted my thoughts. "Tina, haven't you had any specials for me yet?"

She shook her head.

"Not one? Let me see your cards. These can't all be such upstanding citizens. What are our total numbers for this month?" Tina handed Gunter a log book and pointed to the figures as if she didn't trust herself to speak to him.

While Gunter studied the book, I sat idly looking around the room. When I looked at Mac, he was staring back at me as he talked on the phone. It was not that blank look people get when they are just looking past you. He was studying me intently and taking notes from his caller. I looked back down at my typewriter.

Gunter handed the book back to Tina saying, "I want you to find me at least two real deadbeats before lunch."

I looked at Tina. I was now confused. Having watched her sorting process, I thought that the "specials" she was screening for were those who were sent to real estate school. But Gunter was hunting for another type of "special." A real deadbeat. Why?

I was about to ask her when Mac got up from his desk and came over to Tina's. "I don't believe I've met your new typist, Tina."

"Oh, sorry, Mac. This is Betty Baggetti and she is doing a very good job. I have hopes that we can get her ready for an outside job by the time her fellowship is up."

Mac grunted the appropriate responses but his attention was focused on reading my enrollment card. When he finished, he stared at me far longer than would normally be considered polite and I began to squirm inwardly. There was something powerful and slightly familiar in those eyes, but I couldn't quite identify the association that nagged in the back of my brain. Then he stepped in close, intruding into that eighteen inches of personal space we Americans consider socially correct, and said, "Well, Betty, we should have a talk about your future." Somehow it sounded more like a threat than a promise.

For the next few minutes I was distracted by my thoughts about Mac and forgot to ask Tina about Gunter's specials. About three souls later, Tina evidently found what Gunter was looking for: a guy who had drifted in from the desert over the summer, spent most of the summer panhandling at the county courthouse and sleeping in the little fenced off section of shrubbery next to a freeway on-ramp. He was now going to make his way back to Tucson for the winter. He had no job, no relatives, and wanted no part of any assistance program. Specifically, he wanted nothing that brought him in contact with any part of the government. He just wanted a couple nights' lodging and the twenty-five bucks he was told he could get for signing the LA LA Land register. And if possible, he wanted a new coat for the winter.

Tina drilled him harder than anyone. When she seemed satisfied, she pushed the buzzer to Gunter's desk. Gunter came out of his office and read what I had typed on the guy's card. Pulling a small digital camera from his jacket pocket,

Gunter took the guy's photo and said, "So you need a coat, huh? Come on in here and we'll see what we can do."

I could hardly type the next card for trying to watch and eavesdrop on Gunter, but it was useless. I couldn't hear a thing. I did, however, watch the drifter sign three things. Two seemed to be some kind of form on a tablet of forms. The other was a small green ledger.

I typed mechanically after that as my mind was busy trying to figure this one out. I used a lull in the process to ask Tina, "What was so special about that drifter that Gunter wanted to talk with him?"

"Oh, he's one of Gunter's stats for a new grant he's trying to get from the feds. He believes there are individuals, maybe two percent of the population, who are totally anonymous. He's trying to dig up a way to get more dollars for dealing with them. If there's an angle, Gunter will find it," she said in disgust.

That could explain his interest but it sounded like a cover. The guy had already signed the big register out here. What was the little green ledger and what forms had that guy signed?

I was pulled out of my reverie by a familiar voice.

"Walter," he said, "my name is Walter Johnson."

Walter had changed character. He was now much more shuffling and bungling. He gave a very good impression of someone barely literate and only temporarily sober. The tidy appearance he had at our first meeting was exchanged for one that would have made a good match for my Bag Lady Betty. "So," I thought, "Walter is a pretender, too."

He claimed no connections, no relatives, wanted no government programs, and he was heading out of town soon. Walter had the profile down pat. In a few minutes, Gunter was called out and stood looking suspiciously at Walter.

"You say you haven't been here before, huh?"

"Na, I ain't."

Gunter went back into his office and got the little green ledger and brought it back out. He searched through the book a few pages and then said, "You sure your name isn't John Morgan?"

"Na, it ain't. I'm Walter Johnson."

"Well, Walter Johnson, you got a twin that was in here about five weeks ago."

"Is zat right? Well, I'll be. They say everybody has a twin somewhere.

Imagine mine being here in L.A. Too bad I won't get to see him, 'cause I'll be headin' outa here soon. Umhum."

Gunter laughed. "Okay `Walter,' you come on in my office, but I'd better not find you got a triplet, understand?"

"Oh, yeah, I hear ya," answered Walter as he shuffled off to Gunter's office.

So Gunter didn't care if he had a few frauds in his little green ledger.

As Walter was getting up to leave Gunter's office, I quickly asked Tina if I could have a break.

She looked at her watch. "Oh, yes, I worked you right through break time. Go ahead and take lunch. Be back here about 1:30. You did very well this morning, Betty. Keep it up and stay straight and we can find you a real job when you finish your fellowship. Would you like that?"

"Sure," I said with little conviction. She looked truly disappointed.

TEN

I joined Walter in the cafeteria line.

"Okay, Walter, how come you played it so different from the way you told me to?"

He smiled. "All depends on what you want. I figured you'd like to stay in a clean bed for a while. They need your Social Security number if they gonna collect on you. If you give it to 'em right away, they sometime just send you on and write you down anyway. If you tell um you need time to get it, they more likely to keep you. You did okay, didn't you? You got a nice soft job, in the office yet. Now didn't I tell you right?"

"How did you know all that?"

"Well, I got eyes, girl. So do you. You an' me, we watch people and we see what we really seein'. Umhum."

I smiled at him. The old fox had probably made me when we first met in line. We finished filling our trays and went to sit down.

"Walter, why didn't you want to stay in a clean bed for a while?"

"Oh, I do, but by tomorrow I can qualify for the church home again and they don't care if I been there before. I been here twice before and they do care. So I just thought I would get my twenty-five bucks and have a good shower before I go to the church home."

"I see. What was it you had to sign in Gunter's office?"

"A little book."

"What's in the book?"

"Just names. Just names and place you born and your birthday."

"But you also signed forms on a tablet. What was that?"

He smiled. "You see that too, huh? You got eyes, girl. Now that's how they really makes their money on me. I figure they turn in them names and collect welfare or something. Ol' Gunter, he's real serious about that paper. The only ones that get to sign that paper are ones who don't collect Social Security or welfare from nowhere else."

"How do you know that?"

He looked at me slyly. "If you're livin' on the street you get friends and friends talk. It's good to know stuff so you can be prepared."

"What is it he has you sign, Walter?"

"Oh, he never lets you see exactly what you're signing neither."

"What do you mean? Don't you see it when you sign it?"

"Nope. There's a long piece of paper with a shorter piece of paper over the top of it. On the short page it say you received some clothes or them twenty-five dollars. What you sign is the longer paper under that and you can't tell what it is. Ol' Gunter, he keeps a paper clip on the pages and gets real nervous if you try to lift that paper."

"Doesn't that worry you? Aren't you afraid you'll sign something that will harm you in some way?"

He looked at me as if I were a bit daft. Of course it didn't worry him. It wasn't his name anyway.

"The other times you were here, did you ever stay?"

"Sure, first time."

"Did you ever try to go to the Dorica school?"

"Now don't get stupid on me, girl. You really think somebody's goin' to let the likes of me work a real 'state deal? Na. They put me ta work tearin' out old tile and linoleum outa an old house somebody else bought. That's about as close as I'm likely to get to a real 'state deal."

Walter and I were sipping a second cup of coffee when Mac walked in, took a lunch tray, and brought it directly to our table. "Hello, Betty Baggetti," he said with sarcastic emphasis on my name. My stomach clinched. His tone and the challenge in his eyes left no doubt that this was an official visit.

"Hello, Mac," I answered meeting his eyes.

Walter looked from me to Mac and back to me. Without a word he stood, picked up his tray, and made a fast exit.

Mac smiled insincerely and said, "Betty, you seem to be doing well at Tina's desk, but then we aren't always exactly what we seem to be."

Even if I hadn't remembered my words to Ben and Mary Anne, the way he almost spit them out would have been sufficient to get his message across. No doubt he had made me. The only question was, what would he do about it? How good a company man was he? After all, he had tipped off Ben and Mary Anne.

"They call you?" I asked.

"The minute they got to Bluff Beach."

"They told me you had warned them that the game was rigged and that they would not get the property they were working up."

He grimaced as he realized that the Cannons' information-leak drained in both directions.

"How did you know that, Mac? Does it happen all the time? Are these hopefuls just dupes doing Dorica's leg work?"

He stood up, lunch untouched. He kept his face masked in a phony smile, and the volume of his voice low despite the anger that radiated from every pore. He leaned over me with his face only about two inches from mine. "Look, Betty, people who have nosed around here have ended up in a gutter, beat to hell. One hint to Gunter and that could be you. I don't need this. I don't need Mother's careless, ill-informed private dicks nosing around and messing this thing up. This one's too dangerous and too important. Now you go back to my Mother and tell her to butt out before you and I both end up hurt."

I repeated stupidly, "Your mother?" Then it hit me. "Your mother! . . . Robby?" The last pictures I had seen of him, he had been a young man. Since then he had put on a lot of weight and was aged far beyond his forty-some years. But those gray eyes. Now that I knew, I wondered how I hadn't seen it before.

As Robby registered my genuine surprise, he realized his own error. He looked away from me a moment. When he looked back his anger was less intense but his message more desperate. "Please, just leave by the nearest door and tell her to back off. Let me handle this one."

"Maybe you could use some help."

"And have you reporting back to the Black Widow? I don't think so."

I was surprised to hear him use that term. "I could hold all reports until you're ready. You said it was dangerous. You may need backup." As he hesitated, I urged, "Give me a day . . . think on it."

ELEVEN

"Lecture" would be an inappropriate word to describe Dorica's real estate pitch. She could show Ed Sullivan a "really big show." It was part carnival sideshow, part revival meeting, part motivational seminar, and all choreographed to a laser light and band spectacular. The classic old theater had probably not seen anything like this in decades.

The old orchestra pit was occupied by a man with a huge assortment of electronic synthesizers, keyboards, and amplifiers, pumping out an incredible variety and volume of sound.

Backstage was crowded with stage crew and guest speakers who dined on wine and hors d'oeuvres. The place could have passed for a celebrity charity affair instead of the once a week shill show that it was. Heat from the mass of bodies forced one of the technicians to open the outside door. I made note of the easy access for future reference. I also found that a clipboard I had appropriated was the only badge I needed to wander around backstage unchallenged.

The auditorium filled up with a crowd of people from all over the L.A. basin. These were not homeless. They were hopefuls, brought in by the age-old promise of something for nothing. I spotted Jenny in the audience, then watched as a few folk I had seen at the hostel were ushered in, en masse, by one of the office staffers and were seated together in the reserved front row.

I watched the show from the wings. I told myself that I wanted a vantage point from which I could see the audience, which was true, but I was also debating whether or not to sneak back up to the office and have a look around while everyone was down here.

My internal board of control debated the wisdom of that action. The cautious one argued with the one who always runs headlong into everything. There was a time, while I was trying to make things work with my ex, that I tried very hard to tie and gag this foolish, wild, headstrong member of my board. I learned, however, that while she may at times lead me into trouble, she is also brave and resourceful. I can't gag her, because she is an important part of my strength. I just have to be careful about what she gets me into. My board members hadn't made up my mind yet, but I was standing where I could exit without being noticed.

I also spotted Gray Hair sitting alone about two thirds of the way toward the back exit. Was he also sitting where he could watch audience reaction or was he poised for a quiet retreat?

Dorica actually had an opening act, a comedian, no less, to warm up the audience. The guy wasn't bad and his material was filled with class strife, which also succeeded in subtly raising everyone's anger at being victimized. With millions of folks being dumped on the street by the unregulated excesses of Subprime lending, his jokes hit nerves.

Then to make sure everyone got the point, Gunter took center stage and pounded in the message that we were all victims of the greed of the few and it was time to take back what was justly ours. This guy, despite his repulsive personality in the office, was larger-than-life on stage. With make-up and stage lights the audience didn't see his pocked face. Dressed in casual slacks and a white shirt with the neck open and the sleeves rolled up, he looked like an ordinary guy ready to go to work. He spoke to his audience with compassion for their problems and reserved his nasty anger for *them*, the amorphous bad guys who caused all this trouble. Subtle he wasn't. Effective he was. By the time he finished his bit, everyone was seething with hate and rage at the injustice of *them*.

Then came the testimonials, some live, and others on video, presented on a large screen. From flashy dressed, self-proclaimed millionaires to dowdy little ex-homeless housewives, the message was that Dorica walked on water. She was salvation personified.

I felt as if I had stepped into a remake of Orwell's *1984*. First, we have a half hour of hate of "them." Then we have a half hour of love of Big Brother or in this case, Big Sister. Finally the magic moment arrived.

The screen in center stage parted in the middle and the two halves moved silently to each side. Projection never stopped but divided into two parts filling both sides of the screen with video of beautiful homes, cars, furniture, pools, tennis courts, golf courses, furs, airplanes, beautiful women, and handsome men. In short, it was a cornucopia of all the heart's desires. The music rose to a crescendo and all lights dimmed except a single spotlight aimed at center stage.

Between the two screens that flashed pictures of dream fulfillment, Dorica rose on an elevator straight up through an opening in the stage floor, dressed neck to toe in a gleaming white dress molded to her slender frame. Light caught and sparkled in faceted gems, which covered the dress. By some trick of light or backdrop, it appeared that she was actually encircled by a radiant halo. Even from the short distance of the stage wings, she was magnificent.

The audience, already manipulated to an emotional frenzy, exploded in ear rupturing applause. The clapping, yells, and shrill whistles were sustained for a full minute and died down only when the applause signs went off. Dorica waited a dramatic moment before she began to speak.

Dorica's "lecture" was short and inspirational and contained no real information. With the buildup she had, I would have thought she was prepared to release the financial secrets of the universe. Instead, all she really did was set the hook. Financial salvation was here. All you had to do was cough up $2500 bucks. It seemed that the Saturday night lecture was "free" as advertised. If you wanted any real information you had to buy into her week-long real estate school.

I wanted to barf but the audience wanted to believe. Dorica gave her audience no time to get cold. The minute she finished her spiel, an army of assistants marched out with Prussian proficiency into the audience from both front and back of the auditorium. Armed with contracts and credit card machines, they stood at the end of each row of the theater like church ushers and signed up each of the suckers as they exited the row. What efficiency!

Fascinated as I was, I might have stood there and tried to figure out what percentage of the sheep got fleeced. My attention was taken, however, by a hard, urgent look on Dorica's face. As she spoke quietly to Gunter, she pointed to the back of the theater.

I looked where she pointed. While the audience was involved in the process of signing contracts, one lone individual was making his way rapidly toward the back doors of the auditorium. Gray Hair.

Gunter took a disinterested look toward Gray Hair, then gave Dorica a disbelieving look and shook his head. Dorica again spoke quietly but insistently and Gunter reluctantly shrugged and gave in to her demands. He turned to leave the stage, and as he passed I shrank back behind some of the stage hands milling around in the wings. Gunter made his way down the stairs at the front of the stage and started up the aisle toward the back doors. From the look on his face, it didn't look like Gray Hair was on Dorica's trusted employee list.

I watched as Gray Hair turned right and headed toward the stairs that would take him up to the hostel floor. I would have bet that both Dorica and I knew where he was headed. He was on his way to take a look around the office before this shindig broke up. He would have no idea that Gunter was on his heels.

I wasn't sure who or what Gray Hair was but I was now certain that he was not plain clothes security for Dorica. I had to go upstairs and help somehow. I wasn't sure what I would do, but I knew something would come to me.

TWELVE

As I headed across the backstage area toward the stairway, I spotted a bottle of Chardonnay on the refreshment table. Inspired, I grabbed the wine, set down the clipboard, and headed up the stairs at a run. Opening the top door cautiously, I peeked out. The glass door to the office was still swinging. That had to be Gray Hair going in, because there hadn't been enough time for Gunter to get here. The trouble was, he would arrive before I could get to the office, grab Gray Hair, and haul him out. We were sure to get caught. I would need a bit of subterfuge.

I stepped into the third floor hall and as I did I caught a glimpse of Gunter peeking around the end wall, then drawing back quickly.

I set the bottle of wine down on the floor of the hall in plain sight and then made an elaborate show of straightening my clothes. I licked my hand and used the spit to try to straighten my messy hair, then said in a loud stage whisper, "Honey, you here?" When I got no response I put my hands on my hips and complained, "That S.O.B better not stand me up." Then I picked up the bottle and headed for the office.

The swinging glass door opened silently and for a moment I stood there watching Gray Hair bent over his work. He had a set of lock picks and was trying to open Gunter's office door. I soft-shoed it across the floor and stood behind him.

"Didn't your mama ever tell you lock picks are illegal?" I said quietly.

I had to admire his cool. If it had been me, I would have jumped out of my shoes. He didn't flinch but turned toward me with cool deliberation.

I set the Chardonnay on the desk near us. "Gunter followed you and is out in the hall now."

His hard, appraising look shifted momentarily from me to the door.

Signaling silence with one hand, I slowly reached out and put an arm around his waist. I then took the lock picks that dangled from his hand. As he started to resist, I added, "You might be searched." I dropped them in the waste basket where they slid heavily beneath loose paper.

In a slightly louder and huskier voice I said, "Come on, honey, did ya get the protection? I got the bottle just like I promised." I wrapped my arms around him and planted a long closed-lip kiss on him. He was stiff and resistant but I persisted. We heard a slight squeak from the floor and he tried to look, but I pretended to run my fingers through his hair, my hand preventing him from turning his head.

I could see out of the corner of my eye that Gunter stood in the shadows just inside the office. I kissed Gray Hair again and then put my mouth right next to his ear and whispered, "Pretend."

"Okay, baby," he answered, as he began to caress my back and shoulders and return my kisses. He seemed to get the idea a little too well and his hands began to roam.

I decided we had put on enough of a show for Gunter to see what he needed to see, turn on the lights, and kick us out. But he didn't. He just stood there in the shadows, enjoying the show. I pulled back and said, "There's a nice women's room for the staff on this floor. It even has a couch."

As soon as we tried to disengage and leave, Gunter snapped on one small light over the office door. "What the hell's going on here?" he barked.

I was tense enough that the startled little yelp I let out was not pretend. Gunter walked over to us leering at me. I started around him, heading for the door, but he yelled. "Stay right where you are."

I glared defiantly at him and continued on my way.

The backhand blow aimed at my face came so quickly I couldn't have ducked in time, but Gray Hair's arm was in the air and caught Gunter's arm before the blow could fall.

Gunter roared. He turned, and with his other fist planted a solid blow in Gray Hair's mid-section. It should have doubled Gray Hair in two, but he just grunted slightly and lunged at Gunter. And then all hell broke loose. The lights snapped on and Dorica entered with the two security goons in tow. In short order, Gray Hair and I were firmly in custody.

Dorica methodically examined the whole office. No one said a word until she finished. When she could find nothing out of place, she turned her attention to Gray Hair and me. I tried to look meek and homeless, but she didn't look like she was buying it.

"Two of them?" she asked Gunter.

"Yeah, but they just snuck up here to have a little fuck. I told you it was nothing."

"Yes, Gunter. Everyone in our little hotel chooses the office for such activities. Did you search them?"

With a lascivious grin, Gunter grabbed my arm said, "I was just about to."

Dorica stopped him. "Not now, Gunter. I'll find someone to tickle your tattoo later. I don't need more trouble."

"Tickle your tattoo" was a new expression to me. It was clearly a sexual reference, but it evidently had a personal meaning to Gunter. The phrase made him so angry I thought he was going to hit Dorica. She, however, wasn't the least bit afraid. She stood nose to nose with him, her eyes half lidded and a smug smile on her lips. These two seemed to be well matched.

Then, as she turned and grabbed my arm, her long nails bit into my skin. I was thinking that I would have to get my rabies shot, but I kept my mouth shut. I still had to get out of there with my cover intact.

I was taken to her office and given the most thorough strip search I could imagine. There was no place she didn't look, and she was so rough I was certain she enjoyed giving pain. The bitch was a sadist.

She took my clothes and left me sitting in her office naked. As she went out, Gray Hair was just coming back into the office with Gunter. He was buttoning his pants and I assumed he had also been searched.

I could hear Gunter and Dorica in some sort of argument but only caught a few words. Then Gunter raised his voice to a shout, "You're goddamned paranoid, Dorica, and they don't like your nuttso attitude in bond!"

In bond? There was definitely an implied threat in Gunter's voice, but the phrase seemed meaningless. What the hell kind of bond would Dorica have?

I heard her hush him and then more argument. Dorica suddenly turned on her spiked heels, and as she clicked across the floor toward the door I heard the sweetest words I had ever heard.

"Okay, Gunter, but I want it known whose decision this is. Get them out of here tonight, this minute. They are not to go to the dorm or get anything. Walk them from this door to the back entrance and toss them out. Post their photos at all entrances and make sure they never get back in here."

A few moments later, Gunter walked into Dorica's office with my clothes in one hand and his digital camera in the other. Naturally, he took the photo first, then tossed me my clothes.

THIRTEEN

We walked in silence for about a block, just wanting to get the hell away from LA LA Land. He finally broke the silence. "I'd say, I'll show you mine if you'll show me yours, but after the search we just had, it's obvious neither of us have I.D. on us."

"I'll take your word for it. Who the hell are you?"

He reached for a handshake as he said, "Nelson Langly, Independent Documentary Investigations. And you?"

"Betty Baggetti, I'm a private consultant."

"Betty Baggetti?"

"Something wrong with my name?"

"No, it's . . . alliterative."

"Well, my mother liked alliteration."

"Say, I really owe you one. I'd have been caught if you hadn't come in. Thanks."

"You're welcome, I guess." I was thinking about how much saving his ass had cost me. Kicked out my first night. I wasn't sure what the hell I was going to tell Maude. I asked, "What is Independent Documentary Investigations?"

"We're a small television company. We specialize in investigative documentaries."

"Really? Done any I might have seen?"

"Most of our bread and butter work is on product liability. Not stuff the public sees.

"Right."

"How about you? Who do you work for?"

"Oh, I couldn't say. You know how the client confidentiality thing works."

"Right."

We studied each other in doubting silence. He broke first.

"Are we going anywhere in particular or just away from that place?"

As we strolled down the street, I had been considering just what I should do with him. I still didn't know who he really was or what he was really up to, but I wanted to see what he might know. "I feel dirty after Dorica's strip search. You want a shower and a swim?"

I saw his hesitation and read the slight glint in his eye. Quickly I added, "Separate showers, public pool."

He smiled. "Sure. Where and how do we get there?"

"Right there," I said, pointing to the El Pueblo Athletic Club.

He whistled. "You really think they will let in a couple of bums like us?"

"Oh, I think so. I'm a member."

At this time of night there was no one on duty but the desk clerk, and to get in I was going to have to rent a room. That is an extravagance I didn't often allow myself, but after my last twenty-four hours I believed I deserved it. The trick was how to get into the El Pueblo as Betty Baggetti without someone calling me Diana Hunter. I casually said, "Have a seat, Nelson, I'll get us checked in." I wanted Nelson seated as far away from the registration desk as possible. Of course, he refused my offer and walked right up to the desk with me.

As I approached, the clerk recognized me and started to say hello. Before he could say my name, I announced, "Good evening, Danny, I'm going to need a room for the night. Betty Baggetti, a single. You're keeping a small athletic bag at the desk for me. Remember?"

His eyes darted quickly to the gentleman who had come in with me. Without the slightest hesitation, even on the name, he replied, "Why yes, Ms. Baggetti. Your bag is right here." He reached under the desk and pulled out my nylon bag. I took out my membership card, face down, and handed it to him. No doubt about it, Nelson was doing his best to take a peek at the card.

As Danny finished the registration I asked, "Could you do me one other favor? Could you open up the gift shop and get my guest a pair of swim trunks and add them to my bill?"

He smiled conspiratorially and said, "I'll be happy to. Have a good night, Ms. Baggetti."

FOURTEEN

The woman's shower at the El Pueblo Athletic Club is more like the powder room at the Ritz than any locker room I've ever seen. I was definitely not born to this kind of luxury and first experienced it during the four years I was the trophy wife of Martin Corman. The fact that I was not suited to that wifely roll was an unfortunate fact Martin and I both learned just a few months into our short marriage. I guess we both dealt with it by indulging in our own brands of deception.

I secretly went to work for Niles Investigations. To hide this activity from Martin, I bought a membership here in my maiden name and used the place as my office and "phone booth" to change wardrobe and character.

And for his little indulgence, Martin embezzled a couple billion dollars from his aerospace firm and disappeared. Of course, I was under suspicion and watched constantly by the FBI. When they finally determined that it was his secretary and not me who had been his partner in crime, they took me off their watch list and settled for seizing everything we ever owned: the cars, the plane, the home in Beverly Hills, the beach house in Seal Beach, even the small household bank account I lived on. If it hadn't been for a special case I did for my friend, Richard Barton, I would have been on the street then.

I managed to keep this membership because it was not in Martin's name and was overlooked in the government seizure of property. None-the-less, I always feel like I've just sneaked in and they might catch me and kick me out any minute.

I hung my LA LA Land clothes in the locker I kept at the club and took out my swimsuit. After a long hot shower, I put on the suit and headed for the pool. No lights were on, no sign of Nelson, but just as I flipped on the lights, he arrived with a bottle of scotch and two glasses with ice. How, I wondered, did he accomplish that?

As he walked down the pool side, his slender, muscular body bore no traces of the bent, old man I had seen exit the theater. His hair was now a soft, wavy light brown with a bit of gray at the temples.

"I take it you found the bar," I said.

"Yeah, just as the bartender was closing. God, what a view of the city, and it rotates no less. Private consultants must do okay."

I smiled. If my last client hadn't doubled my fee I would never have made the annual dues. The chances of my continuing to maintain this luxury were slim."It's a legacy from my late husband," I said. "He bought the membership. I just keep up the annual dues and pay my bar bill." Using "late husband" rather than "ex" shortstops questions, and this is a subject I discuss with no one.

"Speaking of which, I'm afraid I had to add this to your bill," he said. "No cash. But I'll reimburse you for it tomorrow." With eyelids half masking his sideways glance, he added, "The bartender must be new. He didn't seem to know your name until he called down to the desk clerk."

Oops. This was a smart guy. He was watching for a telltale response but with a smile I said, "Don't worry about reimbursing me. This was a great idea."

He poured and we each drank the first quickly. I dived in and began swimming laps. Soon he was in the next lane, pacing me.

As we swam, we began a type of verbal fencing common to information purveyors of all sorts. The trick is to give information that is common knowledge or worthless and hope the other guy will drop something really useful. If both parties know and understand the rules, it's a wash, but once in a while you get a pleasant surprise.

We swam eight laps, our verbal *assaut* never scoring a single *touche* on either side. I was getting tired and decided to toss a small bit of news as a *seconde intention*. I turned on my side and began doing a slow side stroke. "Well, there was something fishy about this one old guy we checked in this morning."

He turned to face me and his green eyes were fully alert. The color looked less cloudy and the whites were no longer bloodshot. I'd bet five dollars he had worn contacts before to give him that old wino look. I would have to have Richard find out where I could get those.

"From the interplay between Gunter and this old guy named Walter, I was sure that Walter had been there before under another name. Gunter knew it, but he played along with it. So I went and checked out the old guy. You know what he told me?"

We had reached the shallow end of the pool on our tenth lap and Nelson stopped swimming and stood still. "What?" he asked, not even trying to disguise his eagerness.

"He said that he thought all they wanted was his name so they could collect some sort of welfare or Social Security on him. What do you think of that?"

Disappointment registered clearly on his face. I could see his mental tabulations as he dismissed me as an information source. "Na," he said, and started the next lap. "The feds suspected that and have had their guys all over that operation. They check every detail with a fine-tooth comb. They have never found as much as a comma out of place."

"Well, I guess I came up with nothing then. How 'bout you?"

A chuckle began to rumble from deep in his chest and grew to a full laugh. His voice seemed to echo around the walls of the indoor pool. "Well," he said with a mischievous look, "there was one thing that seemed to be confirmed by something Dorica said tonight. We had heard a story that we thought was apocryphal, but maybe not. Did you hear her crack about tickling his tattoo?"

"Yes, it seemed to really piss Gunter off."

"Well, the story goes that when Dorica and Gunter first got together, Gunter was into a little mild S & M. Liked to be tied spread eagle and take a little light whipping. According to rumor, one night they got to kidding about branding each other. Dorica had Gunter tied securely and proceeded to personally tattoo his balls with her initials. No matter how much he yelled and screamed, she just kept sticking the needle to him, literally."

"Having met them, I can believe that story. It fits them both. Do you suppose it was kinky sex that brought them together or some other attraction?"

"We don't know for sure but we think Gunter set out specifically to move in on Dorica's operation. Gunter entered her life when she had a pile of lawsuits and judgments. He took over, declared bankruptcy and cleaned the slate for her. They've been a duet ever since. Now it's hard to tell who really runs things, but whoever's in charge, it's a squeaky clean operation."

"She sounds like a model citizen. Maybe she really did turn over a new leaf. I'll tell you, whatever else she does, after one night on the street I was truly grateful for a shower, clean clothes, a bed, and a meal. If the operation looks so clean why do you suspect her?"

He stopped at the end of the pool again and studied me a long time before answering.

"Look, Betty, you're a very nice lady and you saved my ass tonight and I owe you so I'm going give you the best advice I can. You're in way over your head. Get out. Tell your client you couldn't find any signs of fraud and go on to the next case. You may think we got rough treatment in there tonight. In fact, we were lucky to get out alive. These are really not nice people."

I looked steadily into his eyes and said, "If you're trying to tell me that Dorica and Gunter are capable of murder, you're going to have to give me more than that. What do you really know about these two?"

As I watched his eyes, I could see the hesitation and the evaluation of me. When he made his decision he gave me a big smile and a playful splash of water in my face. I was wiping the water from my eyes when he said, "Hell, for all I know Dorica may really have turned saint and is making real estate tycoons out of all those street bums."

His facetious statement hit me much harder than the water and I was glad I had my hands over my face so he could not see my expression. I took a deep breath, dived under the water and swam the length of the pool. I thought about his statement: Dorica may really be making real estate tycoons out of street bums. He had inadvertently given me the key. The homeless were strawmen to hide the assets.

When I came up at the other end of the pool I was back in control. Inwardly, however, I was so excited that I could hardly contain myself. I was sure I knew why Walter's name was in the little green ledger and I could also make a good guess about what else he signed.

Nelson swam up beside me. "Hey, anything wrong?"

"Nothing except that I'm worn out. It's been a rough twenty-four hours."

"So are you planning on going back for more?"

"No. Whatever else they are, I know from personal experience Dorica is a sadist and Gunter is a lech. I have no desire to tangle with them again."

"Good!" he said. But he sounded doubtful.

I asked him if he needed a taxi or a room and he declined both. I gathered up the scotch and glasses and said good night at the pool room door.

After showering again and changing into sweats, I retired to my plush room on the twelfth floor and stared out the window as I sipped on a second scotch. The city looked so incredibly beautiful from up here. Street and building lights sparkled and twinkled and the strings of red and white car lights moved constantly along the freeways. Here, you could tell why the city could be referred to as a jewel.

What a shocking difference from the dark, lonely, frightening, stinking streets of my previous night in this city. Here I was surrounded by comfort, luxury, and elegance, while others holed up like animals in cement burrows down on the street. Unbidden, the vision of that mother and two children formed in my mind. I closed my eyes as if that would shut out the sorrow. This is not the America I grew up in. The ideal of free enterprise was supposed to be the rising tide that would lift all boats, but it seems that only the greedy and immoral floated to the top. Somehow somebody had changed the rules.

That made Dorica's scam feel more like true evil rather than simple illegality. She cunningly preyed on everyone: the helpless taxpayer, the hopeful suckers, and the hopeless poor, all unknowing pawns. No wonder Robby was interested in nailing her. So was I.

I wondered what Maude would think of that cause. Did she secretly approve? Is that why she hired me? I doubted that. Her opinion of the less fortunate was that if they were more productive, they wouldn't be less fortunate. And, if they couldn't be more productive? Survival of the fittest was best for the human race. No, she didn't hire me for humanitarian reasons.

Did she hire me just to keep an eye on Robby? Why? She had others to do that. She knew where he was and what he was doing. Or did she? What was it she said? That I was good at paper chase and that was what Robby was doing. If that was why she hired me she wouldn't care that I was no longer at the school to watch Robby. She would simply want me to follow the paper trail. Or maybe she would just want to brush out the tracks.

FIFTEEN

I awoke at four a.m., my three hours sleep painfully insufficient, but my brain was too restless to let me sleep any longer. I was sure I knew what Dorica and Gunter were up to and what it was that Robby was after. I just needed to figure out how to document it.

It was nice driving back to Bluff Beach—quiet, dark, and no traffic. I called Jenny's answer machine and asked her to meet me for a bike ride along the river at first light.

By the time I got home, collected my bike, and rode to our rendezvous, Jenny was already there, nursing a thermal cup of coffee. She reached into a cloth bag that hung from her handlebars and silently she poured another from a larger thermos and handed it to me. She smirked as I set it in the cup holder in my "old lady"handlebar basket, but her disapproval didn't stop her from using the basket to stash her bag and thermos. With a superior sniff, she threw a leg over her eighteen-speed racing bike and pulled out ahead of me as I pushed off on my one-speed beach cruiser. We headed down the bike path without a word because we have a long-standing agreement that I never talk to Jenny until the first cup of coffee is finished.

A short ride down the bike trail, the San Gabriel begins to look like a real river. You no longer see the cement bottom, water flows deeply, and the banks are covered with greenery. Cormorants, pelicans, gulls, herons, egrets, ducks, terns, and sandpipers all congregate there. Sometimes you even see red fox trying to catch a duck for breakfast. It's one of the few places I almost feel the kind of peace I find in the wilderness.

"Well?" Jenny said as soon as she had downed enough coffee to be coherent. "You know I'm dying to hear what happened at the hostel."

She listened without questions until I finished the whole story.

"So, who do you figure the mystery man is? Federal?"

"Maybe. He seemed to know a lot about the federal investigation, but he seemed sort of removed. It was like he was talking about the feds as 'them' instead of 'us.' He may really be the investigative journalist he claimed to be. I don't know, but he's not important now."

"You're sure about that, huh?"

"Well for now I have more immediate questions."

"Okay. So, you said he gave you an idea of what Dorica is doing. What?"

We paused long enough to pour the rest of the coffee into our cups.

"This is going to sound crazy, but hear it out. What Nelson said was that maybe Dorica really was making millionaires out of those homeless bums. What if that's how they are hiding their assets?

"We know that the people who come through the hostel fall into three groups. First there are those who get rejected at the door or are put on government programs and sent away. Second are those who are recruited for short-term work or real estate school. Then there are Gunter's 'specials,' people who totally fall through the cracks. No relatives, friends, or government programs. If the paper that Gunter has them sign is a deed for property, that asset could sit in the bum's name forever without any chance of the guy trying to claim it. These guys would make the perfect anonymous straw men."

I could see by her expression that Jenny wasn't buying it.

"But how would she make money from it? If she rents or sells it, isn't the check made out to Mr. Street Bum?"

"I don't know yet, but whatever else Mr. Bum signs must give Dorica power to collect the profits."

"Why bother? Why not just be a real estate tycoon in her own name?"

"I don't know that yet either, but I'll bet my bottom dollar that somehow using those straw men to hold the property maximizes her profit and minimizes both her taxes and her liability. What did you find out in the school?"

"Not too much yet, but there are sure a lot of people combing through a lot of information on distressed foreclosure property. She has an army of free labor making phone calls and contacts per her *Method*."

"That's what the Cannons did, but in the end someone else got the property they had worked up. What if that someone else was a straw man?"

"Okay, let me see if I've got this. You think they take the property that the free labor in the school finds and puts it in the name of some anonymous wino, right?"

"Exactly! Dorica identifies pieces of property lost in foreclosure and purchases them under the names of the anonymous souls who sign the green ledger. One of the documents they sign must be a blank title document and the other a power of attorney or some such."

"Sounds like a stretch, Diana."

"Maybe. Next I check out the assets and see if I can find a connection to prove my theory. What I would give to get my hands on the little green ledger."

"You're not going to try to get in there again are you?"

"And give Dorica another shot at me? Not on a bet. I have two of the names that Walter/John used. When I go back to the apartment I'll see the Cannons and get the address of the property they worked on. I'll start by running these through the Recorder's index and see what kind of deeds and transfers I can come up with. In the meantime, you keep up the school and see if you can find any other leads."

We had some breakfast in Seal Beach, then peddled back to pursue our separate assignments.

After a shower I went next door to see the Cannons and was disappointed to find Ben was no less suspicious or hostile than he had been at LA LA Land. It wasn't that I wanted him to be knee-bending grateful, but I had thought that once he saw I was for real he would be a bit more friendly. I made small talk with him until Mary Anne came into the room and rescued me. Ben retreated to a chair on the far side of the living room.

"Hello, Betty," she said. " Thank you so much. This apartment is . . . I don't know how to . . . ."

"Hey, it's no problem." I felt just as uncomfortable with her gratitude as I did with Ben's hostility, so I jumped right to the point.

"Mary Anne, I wonder if you could do me a favor."

"Anything I can."

"You know that property you worked up that someone else bought?"

"Yeah, what about it?"

"Could you give me the address?"

"Sure, it was in Sun Heights at 9717 West Wagon Road."

Ben was immediately out of his chair and over to Mary Anne's side. "Just what do you need that for?"

"Ben!" said Mary Anne, as surprised as I by his surly tone.

"I thought I'd look at the property records. Why? Is that a problem?"

He looked like it was, but after a moment of indecision he said "No." No explanation, no change in attitude. Mary Anne was embarrassed and I made a quick job of thanking her and leaving.

I went back to my apartment and sat by the phone, organizing my thoughts. I had to figure out how to put the best light on the fact that I got kicked out of LA LA Land the first night there. Finally I dialed Maude on the confidential line she had provided. The phone rang four times before she answered and then she said, "One moment, please." I could hear her ending a conversation with someone else and then closing a door.

"Yes, Diana?"

I guess I had my very own private line to her. "Hello, Maude, ah, things are moving rapidly. I saw Robby and he seems to be all right." I paused for response.

"Yes?"

"I've decided to put someone else undercover in the school so I can be free to pursue the paper trail. I have some reason to believe that the place could be dangerous, and I was wondering about Robby . . ."

"You've found something to 'pursue' already?"

"I won't know for sure until I check it out."

"Well, what do you think you have found?"

"It might sound kinda crazy."

"Try me."

"I don't have details yet, but in a nutshell, I think Dorica may be using a series of straw men to buy and profit from real estate purchases. I have three leads I intend to check out today."

There was a long pause as she considered this. "That's interesting. Let me know how it checks out, will you?"

"Of course. About Robby . . ."

"Call back when you have something, Diana." She hung up.

SIXTEEN

By 8:30 a.m. I was cooling my heels at the Recorder's office waiting for the doors to open. Being first in line gave me a chance to grab a microfilm reader that actually worked.

Before I left my apartment, I ran the address I got from Mary Anne through my online data base and learned that the man who bought the Cannons' property was named Chester Alejo. At the recorder's office I checked the names John Morgan, Walter Johnson, and Chester Alejo for ownership, and within an hour I had copies of multiple title documents on two very expensive properties.

I read and reread the documents, checking every detail. There was no mistake: my friend, Walter, under his John Morgan alias, owned an office building worth more than 5.7 million dollars. Chester Alejo owned a light industrial complex worth over 6.4 million dollars.

No wonder Ben was pissed. If he had succeeded in buying this property on the "no money down" terms that Dorica promised, the rents would have provided the Cannons with quite a comfortable living.

I pictured Walter as he walked up to me that day, stiff legged and dignified, setting up his little three-legged stool. I chuckled to myself as I thought about running out and finding Walter and telling him the good news, but I realized I still had more research to do.

I found the papers that Walter and Chester had signed when they signed the green ledger. The first document was a Trust Deed. A German bank called the Bankhaus Von Kleimur had loaned John Morgan 5.7 million to buy his office building. The same German bank had loaned Chester 6.4 million to buy his industrial complex. Not bad for a couple of guys who were bumming quarters for coffee.

As I suspected, the second paper they signed was a power of attorney giving Gunter the right to act and sign for them. In effect he took the property right back away from them by setting up a California Limited Partnership and assigning their rights to that partnership. Then the partnership assigned its rights to a corporation.

Well, there went the fortunes of poor old John and Chester. Gunter didn't have them sell the property. That would change the ownership name. He just had them assign their rights away "for valuable consideration received." The irony of that phrase got me. The "valuable consideration" they received was twenty-five bucks and a winter coat. I suppose it could be argued that they got what they asked for.

Anyone looking up property ownership would come up with John's and Chester's names. Any necessary business such as taxes, rents, etc., would probably be handled by a management company chosen by Dorica and Gunter.

With this set-up income taxes could be paid by the phony corporation at corporate rates, which would be much lower than the rates ordinary individuals pay. Dorica and Gunter could pocket all the profits from rents, management fees, or other proceeds without having to show any personal income. As long as the corporation kept its nose clean, no one asked any questions. So this was why Robby had been checking out the law in regards to real estate fraud. He was trying to figure out what he needed to turn this whole thing over to the authorities.

If only we could get our hands on the little green ledger, we could look up the property records on all of Dorica's holdings. But then what? How would we prove the owners were bums? I considered telling Jenny to ask Robby to copy the ledger. Remembering my narrow escape in the office, however, I dismissed that idea as too dangerous. Besides, any further contact with Robby would take a lot of explaining. He might disappear again, and Maude would have fits.

I decided to find out how Dorica and Gunter had convinced a German bank to give financing to a couple of homeless bums. Maybe the Bankhaus Von Kleimur would be grateful to find out about the fraud and swap a bit of useful information.

I drove three blocks up Bunker Hill and pulled into the underground parking of a major bank. In the international banking division I was greeted by an immaculately dressed and groomed woman with gray hair, black eyes, and a crisp British accent.

"Good morning, Miss, may we be of assistance?"

"Well, I hope so," I replied. "My employer has received a prospectus for a project from a foreign bank. He's not familiar with the bank and sent me over to see if you have any information."

She hesitated a moment, then asked. "What's the name of the bank?"

"Bankhaus Von Kleimur."

"Ah, a German bank. That would be Mr. Franklin's desk. Down this hall to the left and then the third office on the right."

"Thank you," I said, as I breathed a sigh of relief at sneaking past the door guard.

Mr. Franklin was a short, thin man with straight black hair, blue eyes magnified behind coke bottle glasses, and huge ears at right angles to his head. He greeted me politely in a heavy German accent.

As I repeated my cover story, he listened politely; however, his facial expression and body language told me that he was a very busy man and that I was intruding on important business. When I gave him the name of the bank, his small pale lips compressed in what came close to a grimace. He nodded recognition of the bank name.

"Ya, the Bankhaus Von Kleimur is a private commercial bank which has opened within the last few years. I'm not sure the date. They now offer 7.79 percent interest, and with the current crisis in the world financial markets it is one of the few institutions able to lure capital deposits."

"How can they offer such high rates?"

He hesitated a moment and then phrased his answer carefully."They report that their success is due to a wise and aggressive international investment program."

"I see. Would you have any other information? Owners' names, board of directors, address?"

He studied me a moment and then rather reluctantly produced a loose-leaf volume from the credenza behind his desk. Looking up the Bankhaus Von Kleimur he wrote out an address in Bonn, Germany. I tried to peek at the book to see what other information might be there, but reading upside-down was not one of my skills. He handed me the address with an air of dismissal.

I took it, thanked him, and asked, "I don't suppose they might have a branch in the States?"

With growing impatience he looked into the volume and produced an address in New York and another in San Francisco. Again I thanked him and asked one more question, "Does that book say who the owners or directors are or anything about the kind of investments they do?"

He shook his head and shut the book. "I am sorry but that information is available only to other banks. If your employer would care to have his banker call us we would be happy to help you further." He folded his hands over the book and, like a video game character, ceased all animation. His eyes stared blankly and registered "Game Over." I had my quarter's worth.

SEVENTEEN

I drove slowly down the narrow roads within Chester's industrial park on West Wagon Road. It was nestled in a small quiet corner at the north end of the county and occupied the last flat space at the foothills of the San Gabriel Mountains. It was one of those efficient little complexes where small manufacturers can lease units that have an office in front and a garage-like manufacturing area in back. It looked well maintained and most units were occupied.

I saw nothing noteworthy until I spotted the name and address of the property management firm: "Mono Hano Property Management, Inc., One Avenue of the Stars, Suite 2700, Los Angeles, CA, (213) 555-7676."

Bingo! There was the tie to LA LA Land. As Jenny had discovered, Founder's Trust owned the LA LA Land building and Simboyd N. A. owned Founder's Trust. The mail drop in Hawaii told me that they shipped all of Simboyd's mail back here to One Avenue of the Stars, the same address as the company that managed Chester's property.

I drove back to town and out Wilshire to 5400 Midtown Place. This nice office building was the property that had been put in the name of John Morgan, the previous alias Walter had used. Here too, the property seemed prosperous and almost fully leased, a good trick in today's market. It was no surprise that the manager was Mono Hano.

Turning south on surface streets, I drove to One Avenue of the Stars to have a talk with the folks at Mono Hano.

I knew this place would be in the high rent district, but I was surprised when my turn into the parking lot was blocked by a limo with motorcycle escort. As I watched from the distance, I saw a thin, older man emerge from the limo and enter the building. The walk looked familiar. I couldn't be sure, but I thought I had seen that walk on TV in places like the White House Rose Garden and going aboard Air Force One.

While I was waiting impatiently for the parade to clear so I could park, a side street parking place opened up. I decided this must be my lucky day.

The plush lobby had four different banks of elevators and uniformed, armed security everywhere. I walked over to the directory and found the office number for Mono Hano. Simboyd was not listed. I found no listing for past presidents, but in my search I did spot another familiar name, which began to ring all kinds of bells: George B. Simpson.

The grant deeds for the two properties were signed over to the homeless paper tycoons by the TRI SUM LP. The officer signing for that corporation was George Bernard Simpson, Senator George B. Simpson, retired. And he was doing business on the same floor as Mono Hano. Well, well, well. I tried to remember what I had read about him. It wasn't much. All I really knew was that he was a powerful senator from some southwestern state. He had recently retired, quite unexpectedly, with all sorts of rumors as to his reasons for retirement.

"May I help you?"

The voice belonged to a tall, middle-aged, heavily built man in uniform. He had a 1950s crewcut in shades of gray, fat red cheeks, and cold blue eyes. His tone was not the least bit helpful. It said, "What the hell are you doing here?"

Since I had jumped guiltily at his voice, I smiled as sweetly and innocently as possible. I decided that asking about the guy in the limo was not a good idea. "Oh, thank you, no. I found my party." With that, I hurried over to the elevator and headed up to the twenty-seventh floor.

I would have made the doll at the desk as a receptionist no matter where I saw her. She had the uniform: elaborate make-up, long red acrylic nails, and the hauteur that comes from petty power.

"Good morning. I need to speak with someone about the possibility of leasing space in one of your office buildings."

"Do you have an appointment?"

"Do I need an appointment to bring your company business?"

"Who referred you to us?"

"Your billboard-sized sign on the side of the office building referred me to you."

"Which building?"

"5400 Midtown Place."

"Your name?"

I pulled out one of my "consultant" business cards and presented it to her silently. She studied it with distaste. "What kind of space were you looking for, Ms. Hunter?"

"Just a small office with enough room for me and a secretary. Look, isn't there someone here who just handles rentals?"

"Most of our prospective tenants call before coming in so we can set up an appointment with the most appropriate placement advisor. I need to know enough about your requirements to know who to refer you to. One moment, please."

She picked up the phone, and with those inch-long acrylic nails she tapped out the extension for someone in an inner office. "Mr. Gardino, I have a walk-in here who wants a small single in the Midtown. Have you time to see her this morning?" She listened a moment and answered, "Consultant." This word was said in the same tone one might say "smelly dead cat." She hung up. "You may sit down. Mr. Gardino will be with you in a few minutes." There must be a receptionist school somewhere that teaches them all the same tricks of the trade.

It was twenty-five minutes before I was finally ushered into Mr. Gardino's office. He was a short, rotund fellow of about thirty-five or so. His round baby face and exuberant, damp-handed welcome had all the sincerity of a time share salesman, but that was an improvement over the receptionist.

"Well, I understand you are interested in our Midtown office tower. Would this be for yourself?"

"Yes, just me and my secretary."

"And I see you're a consultant. That must be interesting work."

He was fishing and didn't know how. "It's like any other job."

"Yes, I know what you mean. Well, tell me, what makes you choose this particular building?"

"Is there something wrong with that property? You don't seem overly eager to lease it."

"Oh no. No, nothing, except, ah, the only thing we have available in there at this time is a corner office on the top floor and a large suite which I am afraid would be more, ah, more room than you require."

So he didn't think I looked successful enough to rent in his building? And I'd gone to all the trouble of getting into my best suit today too. "Well, it's a great location, close to my clients."

He nodded his head but kept watching me and waiting as if he expected something further.

I decided I had better dive in and see what I could learn. "Actually, I was kind of interested in that particular building because I had heard that my real estate teacher has an interest in it. Maybe your company handles another of her buildings which might have a small space for me. Dorica June Grizel. Do you manage any of her other buildings?"

There was no doubt that Mr. Gardino knew the name. But the response wasn't exactly what I had hoped for. His face went totally blank. He registered that expression people get when they are trying desperately to show no emotion and no response. It has, of course, quite the opposite effect. It always reminds me of the Star Trek episode with androids that went blank and shut down when their systems were overloaded with confusing data.

When this android came out of it, he was stammering for an appropriate response. "I, er, I, did . . . Who told you that Ms. Grizel owned that office building?"

Whoops, I thought, maybe that was the wrong thing to say. Now it was my turn to stammer. "I, ah, I guess I heard it at the school."

Mr. Gardino was thumbing absently through a bunch of papers as if some answer to his dilemma might be found in them. Then he abruptly rose from his desk saying, "Excuse me, I think there is someone else you should speak with."

He went out to his secretary's desk and I followed as far as the door to her office so I could listen. I heard him give her an instruction to call someone on the intercom, and I thought I recognized the name. When the answering voice came over the intercom, there was no doubt. I knew that nasty voice well. Gunter. "Oh, shit," I muttered.

I looked around the room for another way out. There were two other doors. I opened the first one and found it led to a small washroom and closet. To my relief, the other led to a hall. I went back to the chair I had been sitting in and grabbed my purse and started to leave through that hall, but then I saw Gunter at the other end. He had just come out of an office, but with his face turned toward the door as he shut it, he had not seen me.

I backed into Gardino's office, pulled the door open, and left it that way. I then went through the only door left to me, the washroom, a dead end.

I heard Gardino come back into the room and heard his muttered, "What the hell?" About that time, Gunter entered from the hall. "Okay Gardino, what's this all about?"

"Did you see her?"

"Did I see who?"

"That woman. She had to have gone out your way because she didn't come past me."

"What woman? What the hell are you talking about?"

"There was a woman came in here on a walk-in saying she wanted to rent in the Midtown. Then she says somebody told her Dorica owned the place."

Gunter's shout exploded through the room. "You stupid fuckin' bastard! What the hell were you doing? Why did you let her in here anyway? What did you tell her?"

Gardino yelled back. "Hey, she walked in saying she wanted a rental! What the hell was I supposed to do? How was I supposed to know? The minute she mentioned Dorica I called you."

"Jesus, Gardino! Wait a minute. What did she look like?"

"Good-looking brunette. About 5'6, maybe 130 pounds. Big tits."

"Janet," Gunter called to the secretary. "Call downstairs and tell Floyd to lock the doors and let no one out unless he knows them. Tell him to send Webber and a couple of other guards up here to the twenty-seventh floor to me. Then get me Dorica on the phone and hurry it up."

I looked around my small cell. They would be searching for me as soon as the guards arrived. I heard Gunter again. "Dorica, you know that broad we found in the office last night? Yeah. Run downstairs and get the picture we have on the hostel door and fax it to me. Now! Just do it! Don't argue!"

I looked desperately at the one small, high window. I tied my purse to my belt and climbed silently onto the counter next to the wash basin so I could look out. There was no convenient fire escape or even a death defying ledge to crawl out on. The window didn't even open.

There was no other exit.

EIGHTEEN

I heard the fax beep and then begin to sputter, spitting out my naked photo. "Is this the bitch who was here?"

"Yeah. She looks a little rough in this fax but that's the same woman."

Janet's voice came over the intercom. "Gunter, the guards are here,"

"Gardino, you know what she looks like. Search every office on this floor. Guards, go with Janet to the copy room and get copies of this picture for every guard in the building. I'll go down to the main entrance and make sure she doesn't get out of the building. If anyone asks tell them . . . tell them we caught her going through a secretary's purse. Go."

I heard the door shut and then silence. Quietly I climbed down from the bathroom counter and cautiously peeked out. The office was empty. I couldn't believe my luck.

As I crept out through the reception area into the main hall, I could hear voices and the sound of the copy machine coming from somewhere down the hall. In the same direction I spotted an exit sign and an "IN CASE OF FIRE" sign. The question was, could I make it to the exit before they came back out of the copy room? I slipped out of my high heels, ran to the exit door and prayed, "God, don't let it be alarmed." It opened with only a small click and I slipped out. Gently I shut it again so that the only noise it made was the quiet wheeze of the hydraulic door closer.

Standing for a moment in the quiet of the stairway, I closed my eyes and took several deep breaths. I knew the doors downstairs would be guarded and my photo would be circulating. If I couldn't get out of the building, maybe I could hide long enough for Gunter to think I'd left. At the very least, I had to get caught where there were other people. Maybe that way I could arrange to just be arrested, not killed.

I heard a door open somewhere below me and then heavy footsteps.

Guards or office workers? Most people in a high rise use the elevator. I had to climb up away from whoever was on the stairs and hoped I wouldn't end up trapping myself. I passed exits to two floors and then hit a dead end at what seemed to be the final exit. With nowhere else to go, I opened the door and peered out. To my surprise, I saw a lovely rooftop patio with tables draped in white linen and decorated with fall-colored floral arrangements. An elaborate ice sculpture rose from the center of a buffet table that was mounded with food. Formally attired waiters circulated around the patio with wine and hors d'oeuvres. The guests at this afternoon soiree were elegantly clad from their picture-perfect California coifs to their highly polished Italian shoe leather.

I slipped back into my high heels, untied the purse from my belt and draped it over my shoulder, then moved casually into a small group of business types. From a passing waiter, I gratefully accepted a glass of wine that not only served as a good prop, but satisfied a strong desire for a drink. I barely resisted the urge to drain the glass in one gulp.

Smiling and nodding, I moved to the far side of the cluster of people. From this angle I could watch the door I had come through without being seen.

Two men emerged from the exit. They were without doubt security, but not in uniform. They were dressed in dark suits and each had an earphone. As they stood in front of the exit talking, they surveyed the patio with the alert manner of professional security but they didn't seem to be actively searching the crowd and they didn't have my picture.

Moving further away from them, I walked to the hors d'oeuvre table and nibbled my way around it. This allowed me to get discreet 360 view of the patio. There was one main exit/entrance that came off the central elevator lobby, and four fire exits, one at each corner of the building.

To my dismay, two plain clothes security officers stood at each corner, plus the two at the main door. Now this was too much. How could Gunter possibly have this many men to chase one little woman? If he had this many on the top floor, how many must he have in the rest of the building?

I backed into someone and turned to apologize. He was a tall, well-dressed man with no hair, a jowly, red face and a rotund body.

"Oh, pardon me."

"Not at all, my dear," he said. "Glad you could make it today. So nice to see you again."

Again? He did look vaguely familiar and for just a moment I thought maybe we really had met before.

He shook my hand with practiced ease and rehearsed sincerity.

"Oh, it's lovely to be here, thank you, sir."

With that he brushed right past me and went on to the next ever so sincere greeting. As he did, I remembered who he was. It was Senator George B. Simpson, in the flesh. Lots of flesh.

Two uniformed guards showed up at the main entrance and began talking and showing papers to the plain clothes security. How embarrassing! Next Gunter would run my photo on milk cartons and billboards.

The security guards were shaking their heads and there seemed to be some disagreement as the uniformed guards tried to get into the party. Then it hit me. The plain clothes security didn't know anything about me. They were here for the party security. Of course. Why? Because the senator was here?

If I were a cartoon, a light bulb would have gone on over my head. No. The security was for a guest, the one I saw arriving earlier by limo. He was probably waiting somewhere else in the building until all was in place for his grand entrance. How stupid of me to think these guys were all here for me.

The uniformed ones at the door, however, were here for me. Judging by the body language at the door, they were being very insistent. Twelve guards in all. In just a moment they would all be alerted to an intruder. That bit of intelligence would demand attention because it was just moments before a famed guest was to arrive.

I walked around to the far side of the hors d'oeuvre table and peeked over a mountain of fruit and vegetables. As the uniformed guards were allowed in and began to circulate, I knew I'd had it. My only chance would be to throw myself at some plain clothes officer and claim Gunter was a white slaver or something. With the picture he had of me, that might work.

Then I finally saw the obvious. In my near panic I had almost missed it. I had concluded that there were only five exits and all guarded. How silly of me.

It is a fact that people in work uniform tend to become almost invisible as long as they look like they belong where they are. I had been watching waiters come and go from a service entrance for fifteen minutes without really seeing the entrance. But how was I to use that entrance? I was not a waiter and would not be invisible if I went out that way. There was no guard there, but there was a formidable looking maitre d'.

I thought frantically. It was time for some creative thinking, but I was fresh out of ideas. I was too scared for ideas.

The uniformed guards had brought copies of my x-rated photo to each of the door security teams. While one man stayed at the exit, now much more alert, the other joined in a discreet but thorough search of the crowd.

Nervously, I gnawed on a bite of carrot and reached for another. I looked down at the vegetable mound and saw something there that struck me as funny. My mind does work in strange ways. I picked up another vegetable and walked purposefully toward the maitre d'.

He was about my height and I was able to look him straight in his condescending brown eyes. I stood almost nose to nose, so there was no doubt about my aggression. "I'm Champs O'Shanassy from the Senator's staff and I assume you are the maitre d' of this disgrace?" Without premeditation my voice came out in a high, nasal West Texas drawl.

"Madame?"

"Don't madame me," I said, shaking a small sprig of broccoli in his face. "Do you have any idea what this is?"

"It appears to be broccoli, madame. Is there something wrong with it?"

"Something wrong? Is there something wrong?" I placed my hand firmly on his chest and shoved him backward toward the service door. "I'll tell you what's wrong, but not out here where it is so public." He gave an inch or two and I shoved again saying, "You have no idea what a stupid faux pas this kitchen has made, do you? You have no idea who the guest of honor is today, do you?"

"Yes, of course, madame, but . . ."

"But what? I believe his opinion of this green substance is well known."

"But, madame . . ."

I was on a roll. I shoved him back again and now was completely within the service entrance. "I don't suppose you have set out his branch water yet, either. It should have been delivered by 10:00 a.m. Did you receive the delivery?"

"I don't know, madame."

"You don't know? Well, I think we had better find out. Don't you?" I put both hands on his shoulder and turned him around and then placed my hand in the crook of his elbow and started walking. "Take me to your delivery entrance."

We took the service elevator down to the first floor and then walked back toward the delivery entrance. I kept up a patter the whole way but by the time we almost reached the delivery bay, I could see that the wheels in his brain were beginning to turn.

He interrupted my chatter to ask, "But wasn't it Johnson who drank branch water?"

It's always a mistake to give them too much time to think. Seeing things begin to unravel, I smacked my head as if I had just remembered something critical. "Oh, my God, we left the broccoli upstairs on the table." I looked at my watch. "He's due any minute. Run back up and see to it that every bit of broccoli is removed from the table immediately. I'll tend to the water."

He hesitated. "But I thought it was Bush senior who didn't like broccoli."

I summoned up the commanding tone Gunter had used earlier on Dorica. "Now! Do it! Don't argue!" He turned to go and then hesitated again. I was already running for the entrance and just waved him on. The last I saw of him he was stepping onto the service elevator shaking his head.

NINETEEN

Out on the street, I ran for my car, started it up, and pulled out into traffic as soon as I could get an opening. About a block down the street, I realized I had a parking ticket stuck under the wiper blade and pulled to the curb to grab it. Twenty-eight bucks for an overdue meter. Well, the day could have turned out worse. My car could have been in the parking structure at Gunter's building.

Away from the building, I leaned back in the seat, taking long, deep breaths and trying to calm the adrenaline overload. Events of the morning played in my mind and suddenly, unbidden, I saw that pompous maitre d' and the silly look he had when I shook the broccoli in his face. I started to laugh, but the laughter was more hysterical than true humor.

As I was getting myself under control, my attention was caught by a large gray limo stopped at the light. It was like any other limo except for one little thing. I knew the license plate: HMS INC. The joke was that it stood for Her Majesty's Service, but in fact it stood for Herman McCallvoy Systems Inc. I saw Maude's car every week when she came to get her hair done at Richard's. As I watched in the side mirror, her stretch limo made its way down the street and, as I expected, turned into One Avenue of the Stars.

I put the T-bird into gear and continued toward the freeway. There was no way to know if it was Maude in the limo because she often used her car for various VPs on company business, and I certainly wasn't going back there to check it out.

On the cell phone I dialed Maude's private number. No answer. I dialed her secretary and was told Maude was out of the office for the rest of the day. Would I like to leave a message? I said no, I'd call back.

Of course, One Avenue of the Stars was a big and prestigious address. Hundreds of attorneys and businessmen had offices there, so whoever was in the limo could be seeing anyone on any business. Even if it was Maude, and even if she was on her way to the party, so what? She was the largest individual contributor to

Republican politicians in the country. She would naturally be invited to any major Republican shindig in the area. But I still didn't like the nagging suspicions it raised. All the way home I chewed on the problem. By the time I got to Bluff Beach I had decided that leaping to a conclusion would be unjustified, but it wouldn't hurt to keep my eyes and options open.

I had looked forward to getting home and relaxing, but all the way up to the eighth floor Merle, my crazy elevator operator, was mumbling under her breath. Something about, "They can't do this to me. They think I don't know. They'll find out."

My nerves were already frayed and I couldn't take her craziness. I yelled, "Merle, for Christ's sake, quit talking to yourself,"

She let out a startled yelp and stared at me like a frightened child. I felt like a total jerk. "Oh, shit, I'm sorry, Merle. I'm just a little grouchy tonight." I tried to reach out to give her a consoling pat on the shoulder but she drew back from my touch. She jerked the elevator to a sudden stop and threw open the door. She was a good foot below floor level, but from the look on her face, I wasn't going to get any closer. I shook my head and said, "Thanks, Merle," and climbed out. The closing door almost caught my foot.

Inside my apartment, I poured myself a scotch and flopped down on the couch. My "apartment" is a rough conversion in an old office building. In fact, it's actually a large one-room loft, divided by bits of furniture rather than real walls. The kitchen corner is walled off by an old oak china buffet and hutch and a small bookcase. These help hide the stove, sink and refrigerator, which are haphazardly plumbed into the corner. The bedroom/bathroom is at the far end and is hidden by a "wall" of plywood which isn't even close to code. My office is a square in front of the windows on the north wall, defined by tall cheap bookcases and furnished with a desk, computer, file cabinet, fax, and microfiche reader. The living room is sort of everything in the middle, furnished in early St. Vincent de Paul.

Most importantly, on the wall above my desk is a photo of Danny Kaye as Walter Mitty. Next to it is my motto which reads, "PHANTASIA CAMBIARE REALIS." Translation: FANTASY CAN CHANGE REALITY.

There have been times when my clients could find no justice in either civil or criminal remedies, that I have used a bit of creative subterfuge that changed the appearance of reality in order to change reality. Some uncharitable folks might call this a con. I call it evening the odds against the bad guys. Walter Mitty is my patron saint.

Ex-friends who knew me when I was married and lived in Beverly Hills, would pity me if they saw my present abode. I doubt I could explain to them why I like this place. When I was a kid growing up in isolated mining camps, one of my greatest joys was constructing my own secret hideouts. I made a woven brush wickiup among the pines in the Sierra mining town of Allegheny, and I hollowed out a cave lodge among the eroded, castle-like sand cathedrals near Pioche, Nevada. In Idaho I crammed blowing tumble weed into the corner of a fence, covered the top with a tarp, the floor with an old carpet, then added a bit more fence and tumble weed. No one ever guessed that it was anything other than a pile of tumble weed. Hideouts were stocked with items necessary for comfort during long days lived in fantasy worlds, and only special, trusted friends were invited in. Like those hideouts, I created this loft by myself and on very little cash. It is my small secret kingdom.

With the close of the short fall day, the apartment was growing cold as well as dark. I finished my scotch, changed into a sweat suit and tennis shoes, and was about to listen to my phone messages when it dawned on me that Yeabot was nowhere in sight.

"Yeabot?" No answer. My stomach did a flip.

I turned on the main lights at the wall switch, as well as the kitchen and office florescent, checked the locks on all of the windows on the north wall, and lowered all of the blinds. Mentally eliminating the possibilities, I searched every corner of the apartment. There was no sign of forced entry, and the robot could not let himself out; at least I didn't think he could. If anyone had tried to pick the lock on the state-of-the-art door Sam had installed, it would have set off an alarm. Sam was very protective of Yeabot, because if anyone exposed his handiwork, his past employer would not be pleased.

I went to the phone to dial Sam's number and found a tacky note from him attached to the receiver. "Look kid, if you insist on living in this pit, you're taking a real chance on getting hit. (Hey, I made a poem.) I'm doing a few refinements to Yeabot's security program. He'll be back this evening. S." Even Sam disapproved of my place.

I had a little time to kill before meeting Jenny to compare notes, so I sat down at the computer to run Senator Simpson through a few databases. I found he had been a U.S. senator for more than twenty years and had recently resigned under a cloud of federal investigation. His career was bracketed by two major mortgage meltdowns, and he allegedly had unsavory ties to the more fraudulent activities of both disasters.

Simpson had been a part owner in a savings and loan in Texas that went broke due to bad, some said, fraudulent investments. The government stepped in, took over all the bad investments using taxpayer money and also paid off the FSLIC insured saving accounts after FSLIC went broke.

Simpson then created a huge hedge fund called TRI SUM LP. When the government agency, the Resolution Trust Corporation, sold off all the bad S&L assets, Simpson's TRI SUM LP was one of only five hedge funds allowed to buy these properties for ten cents on the dollar. He made billions of dollars on both ends of this disaster.

One Texas reporter claimed he had hard evidence against Simpson of fraud and criminal conduct. That reporter was found dead in his car after it ran off the road. Dallas sheriffs called it accidental and made no further investigation. The congressional investigation into Simpson was quietly dropped.

Total losses due to savings and loan failures in the 1980's amounted to more than 500 billion dollars. For its time it was the greatest bank robbery in history. I came across a political cartoon that said it all: An S & L president was drawn sitting at his office desk watching masked bandits robbing the teller at gun point. He says, "Such amateurs."

Now it was happening again with many of the same big hedge funds as active players. The profit-driven inflation of the real estate balloon combined with unregulated and usurious subprime mortgages sold as unregulated securities, had all come crashing down, resulting in a world wide financial crisis. Once again people like Simpson made money as the balloon went up and were free and clear of the deal by the time it popped. And once again the taxpayer was stuck with paying the bill. And if my guesses were right, once again, Simpson and his ilk lurked in the wings, gobbling up the rapidly deflated property, getting set to make a second fortune off the misery and loss of others. Will we ever learn that *regulation* is not a dirty word?

Dorica and Gunter were definitely nibbling around the edges of this financial carcass, scooping up foreclosures at huge discounts. But Simpson's involvement meant that something much bigger was happening out of sight.

The phone rang. I considered letting the machine get it but thought it might be Jenny.

"Hello."

"Is this Diana Hunter?"

I don't know what it was in his tone or question, but the hair on the back of my neck stood up. "Yes. Who's this?"

Dial tone. I sat holding the phone a minute then hit the dial-back code. Seven ringy-dingys, then someone picked up and hung up. That was his mistake, because the call would now show up on my bill. I made a note of the date and time and then went back to the computer.

The phone rang again. I jumped at the sound. This time I did let the machine get it and this time it was Jenny. I picked up and we agreed to meet and trade information over dinner at the Ocean Way Grill.

I put on my windbreaker, stuck my stun gun in my pocket, and gave serious thought to bringing my Walther .32 but I was still more afraid of getting caught carrying concealed than I was of getting killed.

Bluff Beach is very walkable, only about two-and-a-half miles long and three miles deep. The grill was only eight blocks away, so I headed there on foot. In a place this size, you can get to know everyone you deal with on a first-name basis, because, despite the fact that it is part of the L.A. sprawl, it's really a small town on the waterfront. The two main streets are a delightful mixture of thrift shops, used book shops, 60s-style coffeehouses, excellent restaurants, and artist lofts. I dread the day it gets as popular as Pasadena Old Town or Santa Monica Promenade. Not only would that change the tone of the place, but then I wouldn't be able to afford it.

As I walked through the dark streets, my mind wandered and I found myself thinking about the longevity of this habit of meeting Jenny to share news. We had been doing this, on and off, since I was eight and she was nine. Our friendship had even survived my nomadic childhood as we kept in touch by letter.

When we first met, we both lived in a small town up in the foothills between the Verdugo Mountains and the San Gabriels, and even though it was part of the city, we found "wilderness" to play in. We used to slip into the storm drain on Paddlemyer Avenue, and in darkness, follow the drain until we reached the sandy wash in the Verdugo foothills. That wash was our "desert" when we played cowboys. We had to walk bent over because the drain was shorter than we were and we had to straddle the small stream that seemed to always run down the middle of the pipe. Our precautions included taking a walking stick to beat the air in front of us for spider webs and pound the bottom of the pipe to scare away the rats. Sometimes we had the luxury of a flashlight. In addition, we always checked to make sure it didn't look like rain, at least not where we were. It never occurred to us that rain up in the San Gabriels could wash down this drain or that the flood control folks might release water from one of the reservoirs. The fact that we were not drowned or bitten by rabid rats proved we had guardian angels.

From the wash we would follow a small creek up into the foothills where we had built a hideout concealed in dense chaparral. Not until we got to our "fort" did we talk about the latest adventures on our pretend horses, King and Midnight. Even at that tender age we had learned to guard our secrets.

The swordfish and salmon at the Ocean Way Grill were a bit of an improvement over the nuts, candy, and crackers we squirreled away in our fort, and the wine was a definite improvement over the creek water. Yet, as Jenny reported on her day in Dorica's real estate school, I lingered in the nostalgic memories of secret meetings in hidden places. As she gave me the details, I watched the way she talked with her hands and thought of how little had changed and how much had changed. Maybe it was the third glass of wine, or maybe since I had taken a sentimental trip, I wanted her to join me. When she paused I asked, "Do you suppose that old carpet and tent could still be up in the Verdugos where we left them."

She looked at me like I had just spoken in Martian. "What?"

"Remember that old carpet we carried and dragged up into the Verdugos to put down as a floor for the tent we . . ."

"Yes, I remember. What on earth brought that up?"

"I don't know. I just got to thinking about it on the way down here tonight."

We both sat silently evaluating each other's state of mind. Finally, Jenny shook her head and answered matter-of-factly: "I doubt it. If someone hasn't already built a house on the site, it was probably burned up in one of the fires. Now, did you get what I was saying, or should I go over this again?"

Back to business. I quoted her last three sentences verbatim to show I had been listening.

"Right, well to sum it up, everything Dorica taught was legal. It was just slimy and extremely risky, especially for a novice. Misused, it also lends itself very easily to fraud against the unsuspecting public. One woman, who was already a successful realtor, told me she could see that this wouldn't work. She demanded a refund and left."

When my turn came, I told her about my narrow escape at Mono Hano, and we had a nervous laugh over the gag I pulled to get out of there. Then I told her about the Simpson connection and, appropriately, she played devil's advocate.

"Wait a minute. Do you really think these two slime balls are mixed up with a former U.S. senator?"

"Well, look at it. We know his company sold both the office building and the industrial park that were put in the names of the homeless."

"So? He might not know anything about that."

"He also has his office on the same floor in the same building as Mono Hano."

"Okay, so it's a strong coincidence. We better have a lot more information before we go making any allegations, even to Maude. A senator could be powerful stuff."

"Agreed."

"Did you know I served on the committee to get them grated up?"

Now it was my turn for confusion. "What?"

"The storm drains." She smiled. "Jerry was just about a year old and I was a worried new mom when I read of a kid being drowned in one of those drains. I guess I was afraid he might take after me, so I yelled and hollered until the flood control people covered all the entrances with permanent grates." She giggled. "A picture is worth a thousand words. What finally sold them was when I showed them the old flash pictures of you and me inside the drain."

We both laughed, definitely therapeutic to the recent tension in our friendship.

"By the time Jerry was old enough to find ways to kill himself we had moved to the beach. I had to worry about skateboards and rip tides. It's amazing that kids get to grow up."

In the silence that followed I knew I had to fill Jenny in on one other problem. "There's another concern I haven't told you yet. As I was leaving, I saw Maude's limo turn into that building. I don't know if it was Maude or one of her staff and I don't know if she or whoever it was went to the party, but I did learn in my research this afternoon that Maude was Simpson's largest financial backer. It's getting to be a little too much coincidence."

Jenny paused mid bite and put down her fork. She made no comment.

Dealing with bad guys is part of the business. In my case, I learned early how to keep my distance while doing my job, using quiet, sub-rosa investigation instead of direct confrontation. It's not only safer, it's mostly legal and usually more successful than macho frontal attacks. Having a double-dealing client, however, is a danger that is hard to skirt around. Not only can it put you at personal risk, it can transform a legal investigator into an accessory to a crime.

I signaled our waiter and ordered two espressos. We sipped our coffee in silence.

"What are you going to do, Diana? You going to ask Maude about this?"

"No. I'm just going to continue the assignment, carefully. You remember the first law that Lacey taught us when we went to work at the *Bluff Beach Gazette*?"

She smiled and then we said in unison, "Nothing is ever what it appears to be, nothing."

TWENTY

I was full, sleepy, and had just climbed eight flights of stairs. Merle quits work at five p.m. and residents are not permitted to run the elevator themselves. I was looking forward to a good night's sleep in my own bed, and the last thing I wanted to see on my doorstep was Mary Anne. She sat on the floor, leaning against the wall, her face red and puffy from crying. I cursed myself for moving them into an apartment so close. I wanted to help them, not take them to raise. First, I felt guilt for my selfish thoughts, then anger because Mary Anne made me feel guilty.

With little sympathy I said, "What's the matter, Mary Anne?"

"It's Ben."

"What about Ben?"

"I don't know what he's going to do. He scares me these days. He didn't used to be this way, you know. He was the kindest man before we . . . it's all the things that have happened. Coming so close to being on the street, it just . . ."

With increased impatience I said, "Mary Anne, you're rambling. I understand that what you have been through could warp anyone. I don't blame Ben for being short with me this afternoon, if that's what you're worried about."

"That's just part of it. After you left we had a huge fight about me giving you that address. He said we couldn't trust you or anyone else. Then he slammed out of the apartment and was gone for most of the day. When he came back he took all the money Jenny loaned us for job hunting." She started to cry again and through her tears said, "He wouldn't tell me what he was going to do."

I started digging into my purse. "Don't worry about the money. I can give you more. What did . . ."

"No, don't. It's not the money. It's Ben. He said he needed to steal a car for him and Mac. He said they were going to 'get' Dorica."

A moment passed as I digested that bit of information. "What did he mean by that? How were they going to 'get' her?"

She buried her head in her hands and sobbed, "I don't know, but I'm afraid. He was so angry."

With my own anxiety growing, I pulled her to her feet. Mouthing reassurances I didn't believe, I tried to calm her as I walked her to her own door, but the sympathy just increased her sobs. I grabbed her wrist before she could open her apartment door. "You can't go in there crying. You might wake the kids. They don't need to see you this upset."

That worked. She put both hands to her mouth as if to stop her crying by force, swallowed a few muffled sobs, and brought herself under control.

"Now," I said, "Ben took the money and left here saying he was going to steal a car for Mac? Is that right?"

She nodded, not removing her hands from her mouth.

"How long ago?"

She took a deep shuddering breath and moved her fingers to her chin. In a weak but controlled voice she said, "About three hours ago."

"Okay. Now listen. I know Mac. I don't think he would do anything foolish or lead Ben into anything illegal, so don't worry. I'll go into town and check on them. Your job is to take care of those kids and let them have a nice quiet night with no worries. Okay?"

She folded her arms across her chest as if holding herself, and nodded agreement. I opened the door and sent her into her apartment with promises that everything would be okay. As I headed downstairs to my car, I tried to give myself the same reassurance.

The freeway was wide open so I pushed the speed up to eighty and got into downtown in twenty-four minutes. As I pulled into the lot across from the back entrance to LA LA Land, I wondered why I had been in such a hurry. What could I do? I sat in my car and watched. There was no one on the street, not even the homeless. I held my watch to the street light. It was 9:15.

The light was on in the narrow hallway that led up the back stairway, and I knew a sleepy guard would be sitting behind the iron gate halfway up the stairs, but I couldn't see him. Besides, I knew from experience he wouldn't let me in. The large office window on the third floor was illuminated only by the dim night lights of the interior hallway. No one seemed to be in there.

After a few more moments of inactivity I started the car and drove around the block. I checked LA LA Land from every angle but saw nothing unusual. For lack of anything better to do, I took up my parking spot across the street again. Nothing had changed.

I got out of the car, checked the seven other vehicles in the almost empty lot, and found an older Chevy with a broken wing window and dangling ignition wires. Looking through the windows, I tried to focus on the interior, which was unevenly lit by the slanting light of the street lamp. I opened the door for a closer look at a small dark object on the passenger seat. It was an empty gun case lying next to a partly empty box of shells.

"Shit!"

I looked back over at LA LA Land, wondering what I could do. Then I saw it: a small light, like a flashlight bobbing in one place behind the office window. If my guess was right, that location was the door to Gunter's glass office. A second flashlight came on. The lights bobbed together and then apart and then closer to the window. They were into Gunter's office. I knew, as surely as if I could see into the dark, who was there and what they were doing. Robby Mcallvoy and Ben Cannon were after the little green ledger. I stood still, hardly breathing, a distant partner to their stealth.

The office lights blazed on and I could see Robby and Ben turn toward the office door. Then the lights went out again. I started trotting toward the back entrance without any conscious idea of what I could do. As I got to the edge of the parking lot shots rang out. "Oh no," I cried and broke into a full run, across the street up the stairs two at a time. The guard was looking away from the gate and toward the direction of the shots. When I hit the gate and started rattling it, he jumped and turned a frightened face toward me.

"I'm a police officer," I lied. "I heard shots. Let me in." The startled old guard turned to obey me without question, but as he unlocked the gate, someone half ran and half stumbled down the stairs toward us. Ben, gun in hand, shoved the old man aside and burst through the gate, knocking me down the stairs. I bumped down on my back, head first toward the street, and Ben stumbled down the stairs just behind me. I came to a thudding stop at the bottom, but I could see that Ben had too much momentum to stop, so I rolled to the side just as his foot landed where my head had been.

"Ben!" I shouted. The name made him stop, turn, and point his navy-issued pistol directly at me. "Ben, what happened up there?" I think he really saw me for the first time and recognized who I was.

He lowered the gun and in a voice cracked with emotion he said, "They got Mac." Then he turned and ran toward the car.

I stood, ignoring the protests of my bruised body, and shouted at him again. This time he didn't stop. When I tried to run after him, my right leg wanted me to lie down again. With effort I stayed on my feet but was reduced to a limping walk. As I reached the edge of the street, I heard another shot inside the building. "Robby," I mumbled and turned back toward the building. I forced my legs to take the stairs two at a time, the complaints of my bruised body numbed by the adrenalin. The old guard stood hugging the wall, giving me all the room he could.

Inside, the night lights had been turned off and the hall was dark. Cautiously I walked toward the office listening. Faintly, I heard whispered voices down the hall. With one hand out, feeling my way along the wall, I followed the whispers, hoping desperately that one was Robby, still alive. But who would he whisper to? It had to be Gunter and at least one of his goons. If they were whispering, they were hunting for Robby, so there was hope.

I knew I was nearing the office because street lights shone dimly through the office windows, but the voices were moving on down the hall. Then with my next step the game of blind hide and seek came to an end. Stumbling over something on the floor, I fell with a crash. I listened to see if the seekers heard me and were coming back my way. Silence. That meant they probably did.

I reached out to see what I had stumbled over and touched a foot which lay protruding from the women's restroom door. I entered the restroom and pulled out the little pen light attached to my keys. In the narrow beam of light I could see Robby's blue-gray eyes open and staring. His shirt was soaked with dark blood. Cautiously I pulled aside some of the torn fabric and found myself looking at a huge bloody exit wound in his chest. Knowing it was useless, but still absolutely necessary, I felt his neck and wrist searching vainly for a pulse. Of course there was none. As I lifted his wrist I could see that his hand still clutched the torn corners of green ledger paper.

"Oh, Robby!"

Footsteps and whispers in the hall, very close. Pen light off. The only exit from this room would put me right in their gun sights. I went into one of the stalls, leaving the door hanging slightly ajar. I climbed cautiously onto the toilet seat, hoping my shoes wouldn't slip, and crouched low like a hen on a nest, praying they wouldn't think to look in. The bathroom door squeaked open. The wall switch clicked and light flooded the room.

"I told you we got him."

The voice belonged to one of Gunter's henchmen who had captured Nelson and me in the office, the short, thin fellow with pocks from bad acne.

"Yeah, you stupid fuck," said Gunter. "Be sure and tell the police that, will ya."

"Well you said . . ."

"Shut up. Get the body down to the office. Then you personally clean up every spot of blood between there and here."

"Why put him back there? Why not just dump him?"

"Because one of them got away, you stupid bastard. The police will be here any minute. Now do what I told you. I've got to think of a cover."

I heard Gunter walk off and heard the scuffing sound as the other one dragged Robby's body toward the office. Quietly I climbed down from my perch and crept toward the door. Peeking out, I watched as he walked backwards to the office, struggling with the body.

The office lights were blazing. Gunter would now be initializing control measures. It was now or never. I slipped out of the restroom and ran toward the back exit. The guard was standing at the top of the stairs peeking in. I stopped, looking from his face to his hand and his gun. He met my eyes, then backed up to the wall again, giving me space to pass. I walked past him, down the stairs, but looked back to see if I was about to get it in the back. Instead I found the guard was right behind me. He followed me out, and the minute he hit the sidewalk pushed past me and ran like a rabbit to a car parked across the street. He was no dummy.

I started to follow suit but couldn't resist one last look up to the office window. My mistake. Two men stood at the window. Gunter was at that moment looking down and checking the street. When our eyes met I saw recognition register on his face. Though I couldn't hear his voice, I had no doubt about what he was saying. His goon would be on me in a heartbeat. I turned and ran for my car.

TWENTY-ONE

When I first peeled out of the parking lot, my only thought was to distance myself from pursuit, and so I took a wandering path through the mostly deserted streets of Los Angeles with no conscious plan. My outward focus was limited to a heightened awareness of other cars as I made sure Gunter's goons had not gotten downstairs in time to follow me. Inwardly, I began to feel the horror and sadness I had shut off earlier.

When I realized my preoccupation with Robby's murder had just caused me to run a red light I pulled over to the curb and just sat there for a long time. I couldn't cry. I just stuffed my emotions back in a box and began thinking analytically. I was in South Central Los Angeles. It had never fully recovered after the Watts riots, and many of the buildings were empty or boarded up. Not a good place to sit alone in the middle of the night, and there was no chance of finding a working public phone. I didn't want to use my cell phone because the number would be identified on the other end. I started up the car and drove south on surface streets until I reached a twenty-four-hour coffee shop just north of the 405 freeway.

At the coffee shop I used the pay phone to call WE TIP. I gave them as complete a report as I could, then headed home. It was 10:45 but it felt much later.

For the second time that night I walked up eight flights to my apartment. It was now after 11:00 p.m.; my legs were shaky and weak, and all the bruises and abrasions from my fall down the stairs had started to throb and burn.

I dragged myself up the last flight and went straight to Ben and Mary Anne's. The door stood open, the light on. One tiny child's sock lay in the hall. They hadn't had much more than the clothes on their backs, so it didn't take much for them to flee. I turned to my own apartment door. My head was aching and I was beginning to feel nauseous.

Leaning heavily against the door, I pushed my thumb to the doorbell to open the locks. I had left no light on and I was standing in the doorway feeling for the wall switch when someone powerful grabbed me from behind, one large hand over my mouth and the other pinning my arm in a hammer lock. With the weight and momentum of his body, he shoved me into my apartment.

I bit his finger and held on, my teeth sinking in and drawing blood. He yelled and then began twisting my arm until I was sure he would break it. When I loosened my teeth, he pulled his hand away and I began to scream, but he covered my mouth again and shoved me forward. In the dark I stumbled over a small table and we both went crashing to the floor. He fell, dead weight on top of me, and I couldn't breathe. I thought I must be passing out because I heard this strange mechanical little voice saying "Intruder alert, intruder alert."

The voice was no hallucination. It was Yeabot. I tried to look in the direction of the voice but the guy on top of me was now trying to get his hands around my neck. I fought to prevent a choke hold.

Suddenly a very bright light shone directly in my eyes. My assailant was as startled as I by the spotlight and paused long enough for me to twist around and reach for my stun gun. Without pulling it out of my pocket I planted it on his side and squeezed the trigger. He yelled and pulled away from me before I could give him enough of a zap to incapacitate him. I rolled free and got to my feet.

The spotlight was coming from Yeabot's head. He moved the light from me to my assailant saying, "This is Mother. This is intruder." My intruder paused, cocked his head to one side like my dad's old retriever, and stared dumbly at Yeabot. A critical mistake. Yeabot turned and his arms came up from his sides. Two small projectiles appeared at the ends of his arms, and as he finished his turn, he shot two taser darts with complete accuracy. My assailant yelled and fell writhing to the floor.

I stood there, staring stupidly, trying to figure out where in the hell the taser came from. Then I remembered Sam's note. This must be Yeabot's new security program. I'd have to remember to tell Sam it worked.

The robot continued to circle the intruder repeating, "Intruder alert, intruder alert."

"End program, Yeabot." I stifled an illogical urge to reward his action with praise and a pat on the head. He turned off the light, retracted the taser darts and said, "Mother, you have no messages. Would you like a scotch?"

I moved cautiously to the door, turned on the apartment lights, peeked outside, and then shut and locked the door. I sank down weakly on the couch and took a good look at the now still form on my living room floor. "No thank you, Yeabot. I'm going to need a clear head."

I found some cord and tied the guy up. He was about 6' 2", 200 pounds, and I had seen his face before. He was the tall slender guy who had stood beside Gunter at the office window.

A frisk produced a nine-millimeter semiautomatic pistol, a copy of the nude photo Gunter had taken at LA LA Land, my "consultant" business card, and an ID card that said Paul Kennedy, Special Agent, Federal Bureau of Investigation. My business card didn't have my home address, but it did have my postal box and phone number on it. This guy obviously didn't have much trouble finding me. I thought back to the mystery caller earlier in the day.

I walked eight flights down and broke house rules by taking the elevator up myself. After dragging Kennedy's unconscious form into the elevator, I took him down to the street level and dragged him to the trash can in the alley. I kept his ID, unloaded the gun, wiped it, and returned it to his shoulder holster. Then, I leveraged him to the edge of the dumpster and shoved him in head first. At a corner pay phone I called WE TIP for the second time and told them where to find a suspect in the murder of Robby McCallvoy.

Too tired to climb the stairs again, I took the elevator back up, threw a few things in a suitcase, and gathered up all my notes on LA LA Land. Pulling my Walther out of the gun case, I shoved one clip in and chambered a round. I stuck the Walther and the spare clip in my fanny pack and put a box of bullets in my suitcase. After locking the apartment, I returned the elevator to its proper place in the lobby and walked to the parking garage. Tossing the suitcase in the passenger seat of my car, I climbed in. I had no clear idea of where I was heading, but I knew I was going to have to disappear for a few days.

As I drove out of the parking garage, I realized I had to call Sam. I looked at the cell phone but decided to play it safe and head for downtown Bluff Beach and the row of phone booths in the San Marcos Hotel lobby.

Headlights from another car made the first two left turns with me. I pulled to the curb and stopped. The other car, a yellow Grand Prix driven by a tall guy in a hat, drove straight past me. I went around the block, stopped in front of the San Marcos and parked in the twenty-minute spot.

As I was running into the hotel, I saw a yellow Grand Prix come around the corner, and my stomach clenched. It drove on by. The driver was a short woman with long hair and a scarf around her head. I decided I was just being paranoid.

From the wooden phone-booth inside the hotel, I called Sam. His J. Edgar answered. J. Edgar is the father of Yeabot. I have no idea what he is programmed to do and I would never ask. With Sam's skill and background, it could probably run a small Latin American country while making the perfect cup of espresso.

"Sam, if you're there, for God sake pick up. It's important." There was a long pause and then Sam spoke into a speaker phone.

"What's up, Diana?"

"I have a problem and I need your help. I don't have time to really explain, but it's very important that you come over and get Yeabot right away."

"Why? Something wrong with that new program?"

"No. In fact the program works great. But somebody saw it, Sam."

"Whada ya mean?"

"Somebody got into my apartment and saw Yeabot. In fact, Yeabot zapped him with his new taser darts."

"Damn it, Diana, I told you to move out of that dump. It's a bad . . ."

"No! It wasn't a burglar. It's a case. The guy who broke in was probably a hit man. If he doesn't come back they'll just send someone else. They'll break into the apartment and find Yeabot. You've got to get him out of there and to safety."

"Diana, I don't like the sound of this. What are you into?"

"Thanks, Sam, gotta go."

I hung up. The minute I settled that receiver into its cradle I thought of one tiny problem. I watched the second hand on my watch while my mind tried to sort through all the other possible problems and see if there was anything else I should tell Sam. Sam had his phone rigged to detect incoming callers' numbers years before the phone company offered such services, and his technology still has far greater abilities than Ma Bell's. I knew it wouldn't take long for him to call back. Even though I was expecting it, I jumped when the phone rang.

He was trying to sputter out something when I picked up the receiver but I talked over him. "I thought of another problem."

Sam tried to interrupt and I shouted him down with a bit of panic in my voice. "No, Sam, listen! The guy who broke in had some ID. I mean . . . I don't really believe he really is . . . I guess he could be . . . but if he's messed up in this case . . . and he has to be because he had my picture. He had to have gotten that from Gunter, so I don't think the ID could be real, but just in case . . ."

"Diana, calm down. You're babbling like one of Lily Tomlin's characters. What ID did this guy have."

"FBI."

An FBI agent saw Yeabot? Jesus. What the hell are you doing messing around with the Feds?"

"Now you got the picture. That's why you got to clean up my apartment."

"Where's the Fibby now?"

I paused. I knew he wasn't going to like my answer. "In the trash dumpster behind my apartment. But it's okay, Sam, I'm sure he's not really FBI."

I hung up the phone. It started ringing before I could get out of the booth. Funny, I could have sworn that the ring itself seemed angrier and more persistent than it had before. The amount of imagination I have is a dangerous thing.

I started to leave and then I thought about Jenny. I stopped at the next booth, dialed her number and got her machine. "Jenny, it's Diana. Stay away from my place. Don't call, come by, or leave a message on . . ." Before I could finish and escape, she picked up the phone.

"What's the matter, Diana?"

"I can't explain now, just keep your distance and don't . . ."

"Don't give me a shut out. I want to know what's wrong."

The phone I had used to call Sam was still blasting the quiet lobby with steady ringing. Any minute the desk clerk would come to check it. "I've got to get out of here. Just stay away from me and from Dorica's school. I can't . . ."

"No! This is going to stop right here. Either you tell me what's going on or I'm through. I mean it. I am sick and tired of you playing me for the puppet dummy. Either you make . . ."

"I can't! I've got to get out of here. Be careful." I hung up and headed for my car, hoping Jenny would heed the warning.

No matter how much he hated it, Sam would be forced to take care of things at my apartment. He would also be furious and be on my tail faster than anyone else.

Wonderful! I had Gunter sending hit men after me, the police would probably want to talk with me, my client's son was murdered on my watch, my best friend was ready to walk, and my special ops mentor would probably never speak to me again. My body felt battered, bruised, and exhausted and to ice the cake, I had gotten a huge parking ticket. Other than that, I was having a swell day.

TWENTY-TWO

As I pushed the combination lock buttons on the door, I looked around in all directions. No sign of the yellow Grand Prix. If I hadn't been directing my attention away from my car, it might have registered that the door lock did not process through all its reassuring clicks. I opened the door, jumped in, and started the engine.

I was just pulling out from the curb when a hand fell heavily on my shoulder. I stifled a scream, slammed on the brakes, and tried to turn to see my assailant. A familiar voice said, "Good evening, Diana. Didn't your mama ever teach you to look in the back seat before getting into your car?"

"Jesus, Nelson. You scared the hell out of me. This Bird doesn't have a back seat." His head and shoulders appeared in my rearview mirror but the rest of him was wedged into the trunk through the hole left by my incomplete remodeling job.

"Perhaps true, but with the modifications you have on this one, it is quite easy for even a big person to lie in wait. If I scared you it serves you right. If your mama didn't teach you any better, I'd have thought Sam would."

My antenna went up. "Sam? Sam who?"

"You know Sam who. He's left three messages on your cell phone in the last three minutes. I'd tell you what he said but *my* mama taught me not to use language like that. What did you do to set him off?"

So Nelson had been playing my cell phone messages. "Didn't your mama also teach you not to eavesdrop on other people's messages?" I reached down to turn off the phone.

"No, leave it on. When Sam calls again, I'll answer it. Sam can give us a proper introduction and maybe you and I can begin to be honest with each other."

"What?"

"Hold on a minute." He opened the passenger door and half crawled, half fell out of the car. Tossing my suitcase into the back, he climbed stiffly into the passenger seat. As he settled in, he turned to face me and found himself facing my Walther. He didn't even jump, just studied it a moment.

"How long have you been in my car?"

"About fifteen minutes, since you went into the hotel."

"Was that you in the Grand Prix?"

"Yes."

"Why were you following me? How did you find me and how did you know my name?"

"Everyone knows your name now, Diana, ever since you flashed your card around Mono Hano. You really need taking care of, Betty Baggetti. And I was following you because I'm the one who was lucky enough to get assigned the baby-sitting duty."

"Baby-sitting!" I blushed hot with anger. "Oh, you're supposed to be protecting me? Then I would say you're a failure. Where were you when that FBI guy was in my apartment trying to strangle me?"

His face went blank. "What FBI guy?"

With my left hand I reached into my fanny pack and pulled out Paul Kennedy's ID and tossed it at Nelson. He looked more surprised by the ID than he had been by the Walther.

"Paul was in your apartment?"

"You know him? Is he really FBI?"

"Not anymore. But he used to be. You could say he's now a freelance agent. He had a bit of a disagree . . ."

The phone rang. Nelson pushed the speaker button and said something in some Asian language. There was silence and then Sam's voice came over the speaker. For once he sounded truly surprised. "Langly? Is that you?"

"It's me, Uncle Sam. Thought you were in a padded cell somewhere, ol' man."

"Yeah, well, we can catch up on the small talk later. Is Diana with you?"

"Yes, or rather I'm with Diana. Look, to get right to it and then get off this unsecured line, Diana and I have been working a parallel course that has converged a couple times. I gather from your previous messages you are aware that she has tied into a rather large tiger."

"Has she gotten messed up with something The Group's on?"

"Yes, sir."

"Shit, Diana!" roared Sam. "Get your butt home and stay out of this. Whatever it is, it's too big to mess with. You'll just . . ."

"Hey, Uncle, wait a minute. I'm afraid she's already out front. She's known and is now playing the rabbit."

Sam's voice took on a commanding tone. "No, Goddamn it! You use her that way and you'll just get her killed."

"Hey, Sam, give me credit. I know that. I didn't use her. In fact, I tried to get her out of play before anyone knew who she was, but she doesn't listen very well and she does lie."

Sam sighed. "Yeah, I know. If you want you can bring her to me and I'll keep her safe until it's over."

"Will you guys quit talking about me as if I weren't here! I take it you're old buddies. Would you please let me in on what's going on?"

"No!" they both said in chorus.

"Look, Sam, she may not be with The Group but she's pretty damn good. If you want to know the truth, I think she has developed information that may be critical to a good play. I'd like to talk with her but I thought she might be a little straighter with me if you put in a good word."

"Okay, Diana, this kid is one of my best efforts. Don't ask any questions, because he can't answer them. But if you have any information that can help him, he works for some of the good guys. Okay?"

"Okay, Sam, if you say so." It crossed my mind to ask just who Sam considered "good guys" these days. I had gotten the impression he was cynical about all participants.

Sam and Nelson signed off with more Chinese or whatever it was. Then Nelson turned to me. He watched as I stuck my Walther back in the fanny pack. My hand was shaking.

"Why don't you change places with me, Diana? You can sit back and relax. I'll drive and you can tell me about Paul Kennedy and Dorica and Gunter."

The events of this night had hit me one after another, so fast I was keeping myself glued together with nothing but leftover adrenaline. With the night I'd had, leaving the driving to Nelson sounded like a good idea. I was also scared enough that I was glad to have someone to talk to about this thing. This someone had Sam's blessings.

Before I knew it, I was spilling my guts. Everything from the first meeting with Maude to Robby's murder to the attack in my apartment. Well, maybe not quite everything. Some perverse factor in my makeup made me hold back a few of my details. I must have talked for over an hour. He interrupted little and asked only a few questions. Thankfully, he gave me no sympathy. Sympathy always starts me crying. About the time I was finally winding down, he asked, "You hungry?" As he asked, he was in the process of pulling off the road.

I had paid little attention to where we were going or why. It was nice to have someone else worrying about that for a while. I was vaguely aware that we had driven north up into the San Bernardino Mountains, and when I looked around I saw we were in Crestline, a small village just above San Bernardino that caters to tourists and skiers.

He parked in front of a rustic restaurant and, as we got out of the car, he casually stashed my keys in his pocket; then, to my surprise, pushed exactly the right two buttons to lock the car. How did he do that? I had set that combination myself. And come to think of it, how did he get into my car in the first place? Sam had installed the lock set because he was tired of me locking myself out of the car. Because Sam had put it in, I had assumed that it would provide above average security. Either Nelson was an above average burglar or I would have to rethink my security.

We crunched across the pine needles to the restaurant. It was only the first of November, and no snow had fallen yet, but up here in the mountains the air was pleasantly nippy, smog-free, and scented with pine. The wind carried a fragrant promise of snow. The restaurant was almost empty at this late hour and smelled of good food and a pine fire. I couldn't have felt farther away from the trouble of the city if we had traveled a thousand miles.

TWENTY-THREE

We had a very pleasant dinner and then sat by the fire, enjoying a coffee and brandy. He had whisked me away from trouble, taken me to a safe, cozy haven, and with Sam's blessing, proved to be someone I could confide in. This was definitely a Lois Lane/Superman moment. Funny how many of us independent women are suckers for that movie hero magic of quiet cloaked strength. Someone on my internal board of directors was whispering a warning that my vision of this man might be a bit skewed by my roller coaster day and that I was feeling an intimacy not justified by our two brief meetings. An answering voice said, *Go away, be quiet.*

"So, you think Paul Kennedy is the one who killed Robby McCallvoy?" I asked.

As he thought about his answer, he picked up the poker and prodded the dying embers to flame. His hands, matching his tall frame, were large and long fingered. As he moved, his shoulder and arm muscles revealed strength without bulk.

"It's very possible. Since he was kicked out of the FBI he's been suspected of being a hired gun."

He laughed, a wonderful, warm, deep-voiced laugh expressing genuine humor. Then he turned those crystal bright green eyes and enchanting roguish smile on me and touched my cheek tenderly. "When the word gets out that you tossed Paul in a garbage dumpster, he may have a hard time getting his next job. Some tough guy."

To my total surprise, I melted like a school girl. I hadn't felt such a stomach clenching attraction to a man since I was about sixteen. In fact, I thought I had outgrown such reactions. What was it about him that was so appealing? His voice dipped musically into a deeper register on some words, adding a unique humor to his delivery and I suddenly realized that his voice was the sexiest thing about him. I had only heard a voice like that once before. I had been fourteen, he was sixteen and was the boy next door. He was my first and worst crush—and he had rejected me.

After a long silence to recover my equilibrium, I said, "When I first saw Paul's ID I was afraid Gunter had told security people at the rooftop patio party some story and I really did have the FBI after me. But the way Kennedy jumped me, I couldn't believe he was really federal. Say, what did Gunter tell those guys anyway? Do they all know who I am?"

Nelson laughed again. "No, Gunter told them you were a Hollywood hooker who got mad when you got stiffed. He said that you came to the office to steal somebody's wallet."

"A hooker! That son of a . . ."

"Well, how else was he going to explain that nude photo? The one who really got pissed was that Gardino guy who ran the management office. Gunter made him say he was the one who didn't pay you."

We both laughed. "How do you know all that, Nelson? Who do you work for?"

"Now, Uncle Sam said no questions, remember?"

"I figure it's got to be federal level. Otherwise you wouldn't know things like what Gunter told the Secret Service and what investigations had been done on Dorica and that Paul used to be FBI. For that matter you probably wouldn't know Sam. But Sam said you worked for the good guys. From what he has told me of his experience, I didn't think he believed there were any good guys. That's why he got out of all that. So who do you work for?"

Instead of answering me, he leaned closer and kissed me gently on the lips. I knew he was just avoiding the question, but it was a pleasant kiss. He said, "I'll be right back."

He went over and spoke quietly to the innkeeper. As he walked back, the old fellow turned on a radio and Frankie Sinatra crooned romantically out of the little box as Nelson asked, "Care to dance?"

He had read my mind. He reached for my hand and drew me up to him, folding his long arms around my body. It felt wonderful to lay my head on his well-muscled shoulder. When the song ended he kissed me again, and we returned to our drinks by the fire. We sat closer and he kept a strong protective arm around my shoulders.

"So where do we go from here?" I asked dreamily.

"Actually, I was thinking about a cabin out back of this place."

I laughed. "Well, that might be nice too, but I was referring to the case. I still have to face Maude and figure out . . . Oh my God! I wonder if she even knows Robby's been killed."

"Don't."

"What do you mean *don't?*"

"It's two in the morning. You don't want to call Maude at this hour to tell her Robby's dead. You're exhausted. You're emotionally drained by a night that would put most people in a padded cell. Just forget everything for tonight."

That sounded like wisdom but I couldn't help feeling that it was also irresponsible and cowardly. Maude was my client. No matter how alienated their relationship, her son had been murdered. I had a responsibility to her. Here I was, miles away, pretending it was prom night. Who would tell her—how, and when? My mind replayed the vision of Robby's eyes staring lifeless up at me, and the mood Nelson had worked so hard to create evaporated like a morning mist. Escape time was over. The pain I had turned off threatened to overwhelm me, and my relaxed body, no longer buoyed by adrenaline, gave in to weighty fatigue. I felt weak and sick.

"I have to get back to town, Nelson. I don't know what the police did with my WE TIP information. I must see Maude."

"Hey, will you quit already? Time out. Kings X. Get some rest first, okay?"

I looked at him for a long time and weighed the wisdom of rest against my anxiety for Maude. "Okay, but let's make a plan for early in the morning and then maybe I can put it to rest."

"All right, Diana. Tomorrow's plan is this. By morning there will be somebody here to keep you safe. With the help you have given us on this deal we should be able to wrap up the Los Angeles end of things in just a couple more days. You've done a great job of developing information on this, by the way. You really are very good. There are just a few other connections to make on this thing and we will have the whole cabal. Then we can pop the lid and let the various law enforcement agencies do their thing. After that it will be safe for you to come back down to the city."

He leaned over and put his lips very close to mine. "And then you and I will be able to take a little R and R together. How does that sound?"

How did that sound? Like I had been a silly fool. He really was just baby-sitting, and I got sucked in like a sophomore. I managed to smile, but I didn't quite trust myself to come up with an answer. He saw my hesitation but had no idea yet how much trouble he was in.

"Or, if the city doesn't sound too good, you could stay right here and I could come back up. It's a great place, isn't it?"

"Yes, it's a great place. And when you drove up here, you weren't just driving aimlessly, were you? You knew exactly where you were headed. You were getting me out of harm's way, weren't you?"

He took this to be gratitude rather than accusation.

"Well, I promised Uncle I would take care of you. Besides, I have my own reasons for wanting to make sure you're safe."

He kissed me and I responded rather mechanically. I couldn't decide which one of us was the bigger jerk, him for tossing the line or me for swallowing the bait. Nevertheless I smiled at him and snuggled in a little closer. I asked one more question. "You told Sam I was 'playing the rabbit.' What did that mean?"

"That meant that you were right out there in front, running ahead of the hounds. They knew who you were and they were all chasing you. It exposes them and could help The Group, but as Sam said, that's a good way to get you killed. So we had to get you out of play for a while."

"I'm really a lucky girl to have two such capable men to take care of me." He was so full of himself he didn't even hear the sarcasm that slipped into my voice.

He stood and drew me up to him. "Let's dance, Diana, and forget business for a while. I want to hold you in my arms again."

I made no reply as I wasn't sure I could control my anger. I simply stood up and let him shuffle me around the dance floor. My brain was working rapidly.

I have learned to cope with the fact that emotions such as embarrassment and anger can interfere with my thought processes, and I have developed a little litany to help me stay clearheaded: "Emotion floods the intellect."

Now it may be sexist, but I have observed that women tend to suffer this emotional lapse more than men. Men, on the other hand, have another response which can act as a great equalizer. I have observed that when a man is sexually aroused, he suffers a similar loss of clear thinking. With that thought clearly in mind, I worked diligently on the lovely romantic involvement we had begun. As we danced, I plastered my body to his and began to kiss and nibble. When I knew I was beginning to arouse the required response I asked, "Have you talked to the man about the cabin?"

"Not yet. I needed to know if we would want one or two." I love the male mentality. He was sure that I was too emotionally exhausted to think or talk about my client, but not too exhausted for a little roll in the hay.

"I'm sure one will be plenty," I responded in a husky voice. "I need to go to the ladies' room. You check on the cabin and I'll see you back at the table in a few minutes." He gave me that wonderful self-satisfied smile men get when they know they have won the sexual duel. I smiled sweetly back at him and gave him a parting kiss.

I was out the back door and around to my car before he had time to say "one large double bed." Of course, Nelson had my keys tucked away in his pocket, but I had an extra set in the glove box. I punched the buttons and climbed in, grabbed the spare keys, and was headed downhill before Nelson had time to draw his credit card. At that moment I didn't have any idea what to do about this tragic mess. I just knew that I would not allow Nelson and Sam to bench me.

As I drove and thought, I realized that Nelson was right about one thing. Everyone knew who I was. It would be nice to pop into Rick's and get a disguise special, but he was miles away and I didn't have time. Realizing that, I was forced to admit that Nelson had been right about one other thing. I had to make the final connections to wrap this case up, turn it over to the authorities, and get the hell out of it. I didn't know what "parallel course" Nelson had been on or what organization hid behind the "The Group" Sam had been talking about. I did know that Gunter and his goons would have to kill me. I was probably the only witness to Robby's murder. No. Ben was a witness too, but where was he?

I considered finding Ben and going to the police, but I gave that up. They could have gone anywhere in that stolen car. I couldn't call the police and ask them to find them. I didn't know how the cops would handle it or how Ben would react. In his frame of mind, and with his service revolver . . . no. That could lead to another tragedy.

I had to get enough evidence to show the true motive for Robby's murder. If I was going to make the police listen I would need the evidence that Ben and Robby were after in that office. How to get it without getting myself killed was the question.

The bank was the key to this thing. If I tipped them off about the scam Gunter was pulling, I might get their cooperation in exposing this whole operation. And, the bank was one of those little bits of information I had perversely withheld from Nelson. With the bank's cooperation I could take this thing to the authorities, put the heat on Gunter and Dorica, and distract them from me. Then somehow I would have to find Ben so the two of us could make sure Kennedy or Gunter was charged with the murder. Murder! I was a civil investigator. How in the heck did I let myself get mixed up in murder?

From my cell phone I called the Ontario airport and found I had missed the last flight to San Francisco, so I checked into a motel and crawled into bed exhausted and emotionally drained. I would get up early in the morning and be on the first flight to Frisco.

TWENTY-FOUR

I slept like the dead and upon opening my eyes the next morning, looked around the room in confusion, not sure where I was or why. Sleep cleared slowly from my foggy brain and full memory returned.

When I saw that my watch read 10:15, I held it to my ear to see if it was ticking, a silly act preserved from ancient habit. It's battery powered and doesn't tick. The clock on the night stand confirmed the midmorning hour. I mumbled a curse as I tumbled out of bed and headed for the shower.

I got to the airport by 11:00 a.m. With the flights available, it would take me at least until 1:30 to fly to San Francisco, rent a car, and drive into the city. If the Bankhaus von Kleimur was one of those banks that closed early or if I ran into bad traffic I might miss the branch manager and lose the whole day. To avoid checking baggage I put my wallet and things I needed for the day into my shoulder bag. My suitcase and fanny pack with the Walther would have to stay locked in the car.

Having little cash on me, I paid for the ticket with my credit card even though I knew that would allow Sam and Nelson to track me. Besides, I would only be there a few hours. I picked up a newspaper and headed for the plane.

My purse was on the security conveyer belt and I was stepping through the metal detector before I thought about the stun gun. My Walther was safely in the car but the stun gun was, as usual, in my shoulder bag.

Assuming a pose of bored nonchalance, I watched my bag come through on the conveyer belt expecting the security guard to ask me to open my purse. The two security officers behind the conveyer belt were deep in conversation about the upcoming strike and paid scant attention to the x-ray of my bag. I picked it up and headed for my gate, somewhat unnerved. I know I'm not a terrorist but it makes you wonder who else they let on the plane.

Settling into my seat by the window I opened my *Los Angeles Times,* glanced through the front section, and turned to the local news. Under the headline

MURDER SUSPECTS SOUGHT were two pictures. One was a picture of Ben in Navy uniform, and the other was a head shot taken from my naked photo. I looked around to see who else might have an *L.A. Times,* and then pulled mine up in front of my face.

With growing alarm I read the story. Gunter's version of the last night's events went something like this: Ben was a disgruntled and mentally disturbed veteran who had been housed at LA LA Land temporarily. The hostel had tried to assist him in finding a job, but he was too violent to be employable. He had demanded a second six-week stay in the hostel and when he was refused, he angrily threatened the staff. He then returned to the hostel at night to try to steal money. Caught in the act, he had wounded one security guard and had shot and killed a volunteer, Mac Murphy. A woman who called herself Betty Baggetti had also spent a night in the hostel and was spotted waiting for Ben on the sidewalk. It was believed that she was an accomplice and had driven the get-away car.

They were still referring to Robby as Mac Murphy. Did Maude still not know?

There were two sidebars. One described Ben's Navy career in the worst light possible and made him sound like he could be a crazed killer. The other was on private investigator, Paul Kennedy. On staff at the hostel, he had been viciously attacked when he attempted to locate and speak with the woman accomplice.

As I read the next paragraph, I sank further down in my seat, cramming my knees against the tray in front of me and trying to disappear into the upholstery. Hostel sources reported that the woman, identified as Diana Hunter, had entered the hostel the previous night under the alias of Betty Baggetti. She had been caught, after hours, sneaking into the same office where the attempted burglary had taken place. Paul Kennedy speculated that Hunter had been in there planning the burglary.

No mention of my PI license. They must still be working from my consultant business card.

For some time my mind was so disordered by panic that I couldn't think at all. When I pulled myself together, I considered all the possibilities. I could call Maude, call Sam, call the police, call my lawyer, call Jenny. No matter which action I considered, it all came back to the same thing. In order to vindicate myself and Ben, I still had to prove what Dorica and Gunter were doing and why they would have a motive to kill Robby.

TWENTY-FIVE

While I waited for my rental car, I called Maude from a pay phone. She picked up on the first ring and said, "Just a minute."

When she had evicted whoever was in her office she returned. I talked over her first question. "Maude, please, just listen. I have no time and a very painful message. The man the paper identified as Mac Murphy was . . ."

"I know who he was," she said shortly and without emotion. "Where are you?"

I ignored her question. "Maude, I'm working a lead and I swear I will get the evidence to put the real murderers in jail. I just . . ."

"Diana, stop. Right now. Just stop. I'll take care of things from this end. Do nothing more."

I considered this for a moment. Was she in shock? Somehow I doubted that. Maybe she just didn't understand what I was trying to tell her and what I needed to do. "I can't do that. I was there. I saw it. I know who killed Robby and why."

"Diana, your assignment is ended. You are no longer retained in this matter. I demand that you stop, instantly!"

Several thoughts went through my head at once, including giant questions about Maude's motives.

The PA system blasted a flight announcement and Maude picked up on it. "Diana, what are you doing in San Francisco? What *lead* are you working? You must simply stop."

I repeated, "I can't do that, Maude," and hung up the phone.

Why was she so insistent that I quit? Was she worried about me—or what I might discover? As I drove into town the vague doubts I had about Maude's motives grew into a generalized paranoia. I had been so focused on Dorica and Gunter I hadn't taken time to look at the big picture. Who bankrolled the properties they found? What roll did Senator Simpson play in this deal? Was Bankhaus Von Kleimur a victim or one of the players?

After the S&Ls were deregulated Simpson took his S&L in Texas on a fraudulent spending spree which squandered investors' savings and made himself a fortune. Maude was his largest political contributor.

In the current subprime scandal, mortgage banks were deregulated and made loans to anyone with a pulse. Many loans had worse terms than you could get from a loan shark. The banks made a fast profit on the sale and quickly sold off the mortgages bundled as *securities*. Investors around the world bought them. After all, what could be safer than a loan guaranteed by the old homestead. When property owners couldn't pay, and the loans went bad . . . the mortgage banks were free and clear. Was Bankhaus Von Kleimur a mortgage bank or an investor or was this a whole new scam?

When Simpson's old S&L became insolvent, the government seized it, paid off insured investors with FSLIC funds until they went broke. Then congress voted to pay the rest with taxpayer dollars. Then the government sold off the property holdings through the Resolution Trust Corporation. The RTC would only sell S&L properties in huge bundles. The only buyers who could afford to buy into the game were five or six large hedge funds including Simpson's TRI SUM LP. The hedge funds got billions of dollars worth of property for ten cents on the dollar. I guess their only problem was how to sell the properties and cash out.

Was that the hidden link? Had Simpson and his cabal created the mortgage securities so they could cash out of their S&L property and not worry about servicing the long-term mortgage? Even if there was such a conspiracy, what difference would it make? Once this racket was set up, everyone up and down the real estate food chain had hopped on that band wagon. With deregulation they probably hadn't even broken any law you could nail them on, yet they robbed everyone and made billions.

I gave up this line of thought and went back to Dorica and Gunter and their little racket of buying foreclosure property at a bargain price. Was it their little racket or were they fronting for bigger fish? Were the hedge funds buying up distressed property again? Was Bankhaus von Kleimur a conduit for the hedge funds?

It was 1:55 before I walked into the office tower that housed Bankhaus von Kleimur. By then I was doubtful that an open approach was a good idea. I checked the directory and headed for suite 1417. After being trapped in the midtown building, going up in another high-rise made me a little nervous. I carefully took note of all exits and even checked the stairs to make sure the door wasn't alarmed.

The receptionist at Bankhaus von Kleimur was an absolutely striking young man. He had pale blond hair cut to medium length on the top and shaved to a sharp clean line at the neck and above the ears. His blue eyes were framed by dark brown lashes and brows which contrasted sharply with his light hair. The colors, however, were all quite natural. His high cheekbones, small nose, and full sensual lips gave him a beauty that one expects to see only in magazine models. As he spoke, however, the sharpness of his personality detracted from his good looks.

"Good afternoon. May we help you please?" he said with a heavy German accent.

I looked around the reception room. Not a teller window in sight. "Ah, I'm not sure. I thought this was a bank."

"Of course it is a bank, an investment bank. What is your business, please?"

"I was told to speak to the branch manager. What is his name, please?"

"That would be Mr. Leonard von Kleimur II, but he is not available at this time. Perhaps I could be of assistance."

I hesitated as I considered whether there was anything else of use to me here.

He interpreted my hesitation as determination to see the manager. He shrugged his shoulders. "I assure you, Miss, that I would oblige you if it were possible, but Mr. von Kleimur will not be taking appointments today. He is preparing for a very important dinner conference tonight."

That sounded promising so I said, "Oh, that is probably what my boss sent me to ask about. Is it the one at the, ah, oh, that big hotel, you know the . . ."

"The Palace Garden Court," he said and was about to add more when the inner office door opened. Heinrich drew himself to attention. I could almost hear his heel click. Standing in the doorway was a short, heavy set man with straight black hair, a gold-tipped walking stick, and a very expensive dark-blue pinstripe suit. He looked first at me and then at Heinrich for an explanation.

My young blond friend's light complexion blushed red as he hastily explained, "Sir, I have explained to this lady that you are too busy to see her today and . . ."

Von Kleimur held up one hand to his assistant, instantly silencing him. He was a round little man, no more than my height and perhaps an inch shorter. The way he carried himself, however, made it clear that stature had nothing to do with the amount of power he was accustomed to. He stared at me longer than was necessary and his small dark eyes held a look of acute appraisal. My neck tensed.

"Well," said von Kleimur with only a pleasant hint of an accent, "it's not every day I have such a lovely woman call upon me." He gave me a smile, but his eyes were cold and eager as he asked, "What did you say your name was, dear?"

I began backing toward the outer door. It was probably only my own paranoia . . . all the thinking I had been doing on the way here, but there was something about this fellow that rang my escape button.

"I'm so sorry but I've got the wrong office." I smiled at Heinrich. "My boss's meeting is at the Hilton. Sorry to bother you." My back touched the door. I reached for the handle to let my self out and ran, not walked to the nearest elevator.

TWENTY-SIX

I retrieved my rental car from the underground garage, then drove aimlessly around the city, trying to navigate San Francisco traffic and think at the same time. Why did I react so to von Kleimur? What had that aborted interview done to my purpose in coming all the way up here? What should I do now?

Between the crowded, confusing traffic of the city and thoughts that distracted from my driving, I almost had an accident—twice. After the second near-miss I concluded that I'd better ditch the car and find a computer. My plan was to drop the car at the Avis office on California Street and take a bus or cable car to the nearest branch library where I could get to the EDGAR site and look up the SEC filings on Bankhaus von Kleimur. On the way to Avis, however, I spotted something much more interesting: the Palace Hotel. I had eaten there once with my ex-husband Martin, and had been captivated by its elegant old world charm. Now it held a more immediate fascination. The Palace was where Heinrich said von Kleimur would hold his dinner meeting. I could spend a couple hours on the computer in their Business Center, then see what I could see when von Kleimur and friends showed up.

I called the hotel, booked a room, and verified the nature of the dinner being held that night in the Garden Court. It was a private dinner meeting of the International Investment Bankers Commonwealth. Then I headed for a second-hand store I knew about from past trips. They had great resale items and a large costume section.

I parked a few doors down from the shop in front of a combination bookstore and coffeehouse and paused at the door. The wonderful aroma of fresh roasted coffee mingled with damp, sea-scented air. It was one of my earliest memories of this city. Martin used to bring me here to stock up on deep-roasted Fog-Lifter coffee and brick-oven sourdough bread. For me, San Francisco was always more of an amusement park than Disneyland, complete with E-ticket rides on the cable cars.

Unfortunately those memories pulled up other embedded memories: the happiness I had felt when I first married Martin; the crushing pain I bore when he disappeared, leaving me to answer to the FBI. Unexpectedly the pain of that sudden recall was as sharp and devastating as it had been four years ago. I try to never think or talk about that part of my life. I had buried it, but the smell of coffee and sea conjured it up unbidden. I turned away from the coffeehouse, turned off the memories, and headed for the second-hand shop.

By the time I arrived at the Palace Hotel I was wearing a neck length dark-blond wig, nothing showy or attention getting, just a different color and length than my long brown hair. I finished off the look with a pair of clear-lens glasses. Not a disguise that would work for close-ups, but effective at a distance. After the uneasy feeling I had gotten in von Kleimur's office, I wasn't planning on any close encounters, but I had bought an evening dress that would work if I needed to be in the same dining room. I would probably be observing from the lobby. It helped that the dress was irresistible and a tax deductible disguise. It was a cocktail-length black dress, softly shaped and delicately beaded on the bodice. I was sure it would have been at least five hundred dollars new and I bought it for only one hundred. Shoes, evening bag and a small wheeled-suitcase came to another forty-two bucks.

I pulled my little suitcase through the magnificent three door entry under a triple glass canopy and headed toward the registration desk. Checked in, room key in hand, I headed for the second floor room to stash my stuff, then to the third floor where the desk clerk said I would find the Business Center.

The Business Center was empty at this hour and I signed in on a computer to do the kind of investigation that kept the bad guy at a distance. I pulled up the EDGAR site which posts all documents filed with the US Securities and Exchange Commission, the SEC. All companies, foreign and domestic, are required to file registration statements, periodic reports, and other forms electronically through EDGAR. Anyone can access and download this information for free. To study all the recent filings by Bankhaus von Kleimur would require a serious investment of time. But in just forty-five minutes I knew what I needed to know for now. Both Senator Simpson and Maude McCallvoy held positions on the board of directors of Bankhaus von Kleimur.

On the way back to my room I spotted something called the French Parlor and couldn't resist peeking in. It was a beautiful private dining area which hung like a balcony above the Garden Court. Though it was currently empty, it was set for what appeared to be a small wedding party later in the evening. I looked out of the windows of the French Parlor and found I had a magnificent view of the spectacular Garden Court where von Kleimur would hold his dinner.

The room had once been the courtyard entrance for horse drawn carriages arriving at the hotel and was now a huge room with a lofty ceiling of iridescent glass three stories up. During the day sunlight filtered down giving the room a warm amber hue. At night it was lit with magnificent crystal chandeliers which hung elegantly from the lofty ceiling. Lush green plants throughout made it truly a garden setting. The linen-covered tables glittered with china, crystal and silver. This room lived up to the hotel's "Palace" name.

Once in my room, I opened the suitcase and took out the things I would need for the evening. Upon closer examination I realized the cocktail dress was a Paris original. Raising my estimate of the original price from five hundred to five thousand, I began to handle it much more carefully. It would undoubtedly be my only Paris original.

I showered, dressed, did makeup and wig, then transferred evening necessities, including my little stun gun, to the small thrift shop handbag that attached conveniently to my wrist. Then, with no certainty that this would be of any real use, I headed downstairs to find a surveillance position from which I could observe unobtrusively.

TWENTY-SEVEN

Seated in a comfortable chair across from the grand Garden Court dining room, I watched guests arrive. I had noticed that the very civil and deferential maitre d' who greeted guests spoke to the de facto leaders of each group, making sure they were there for the IIBC dinner, but he did not insult them by checking every individual's invitation. That made it too easy to resist. I waited for a large group of a dozen or so folks, then I stepped quietly up and joined the group on the left side, away from the maitre d'.

The woman I stood next to gave me a once over. I returned the look with a knowing smile.

"Nice place for the dinner, isn't it," she said in a somewhat awestruck tone.

"Yes, it's nice but not quite as nice as Geneva last year," I responded, pulling up something I had read on the computer about their last annual meeting.

Her eyes widened a bit and she nodded and said, "Oh, I'll bet that was nice."

As our little party was allowed in, I found myself walking close to two men engaged in a quiet conversation. A low urgent male voice insisted, "But not a damn thing has changed. There's no regulation. The U.S. Government hasn't done a thing." I couldn't hear the other's response.

The group split, taking two tables, all with name tags. I moved in the direction of the voice, took up a standing position with my back to him, close enough to hear what else he had to say.

His dinner partner was saying, "I know. I mean, I'm glad that the threatened pay cut and bonus loss didn't really happen, but how long will this last? All the banks I have checked are still selling unregulated derivatives. Where is that fundamental reform everyone said we needed?"

The first voice answered, "I'm telling you, we better have a bunker to crawl into and soon. If industry risks are not addressed, there is going to be a much bigger crisis and it's not decades away, but a very few years. And the senior partners in my firm are still saying, don't worry, the market can handle it. We don't want regulation."

I left the worried bankers and wandered through the room hearing snatches of conversation and checking out name tags. Most names meant nothing to me. The head table was still empty so I was able to check out the name tags. I saw von Kleimur and Senator Simpson, no surprise, but then I saw the name I hoped would not be there: Maude McCallvoy. I headed away from the table knowing I dare not be close when any of these folk arrived.

I was watching the room from a quiet corner near the side service entrance when a waiter stopped in front of me with a tray of champaign. He handed me one, which struck me as inappropriate. He should have allowed me to select one. However, I was thirsty, distracted and trying to hear a conversation behind me. I simply said a quiet thank you and then drank the champaign a bit too fast. My first reaction was that it was very poor champaign, and with this hotel and this group of bankers, it should have been first class.

The waiter had set the tray down on a table and turned back around, eyeing me with a toothy smile. I looked up and the waiter's face suddenly registered. I froze. It was one of Gunter's goons. I had only seen him once but I now recognized him from that night Nelson and I were caught in the LA LA Land office .

"Oh no," I mumbled. I realized I was getting dizzy. I grabbed for the chair in front of me but missed. I would have fallen but Heirnich had somehow materialized at my side. He took one arm and the waiter took the other as they half carried, half dragged me out of the dining room. I heard Heinrich explain in a sad voice, "Poor thing, never could control her drinking." That was the last thing I heard.

I had come to before, but the headache and tight rope tying me to a chair had driven me back to the escape of a drug-induced slumber. This time when I awoke, I still had the headache and the ropes were still hurting me, but I was now fully awake and taking in the view of a massive room. It had an atrium ceiling that rose three stories. The entire bay side wall, from floor to ceiling, was a window with a panoramic view set at just the right angle to perfectly frame the San Francisco skyline.

To the right of the city glowed the ghostly lights of the Golden Gate bridge. A low ocean fog was rolling in making the bottom of the bridge invisible. To my foggy brain the overhead spans looked like giants walking across the clouds holding a magic roadway.

I pulled my thoughts and observations back to the room. The furnishings told me it was an elegant private home. The view told me it must be across the bay from the city; where, I wasn't sure. The beautifully carved grandfather clock told me I had been out for hours. It was after one a.m.

I heard footsteps, then a door open, then Heinrich's voice, but could not make out his words. The footsteps came my way and seconds later Heinrich and Von Kleimur walked up behind me. The banker smiled down as Heinrich began untying the rope.

"Good evening, Miss Hunter. My, you are amazing. You look absolutely beautiful. What an elegant dress for you to find on such short notice. But then you seem to be very good at finding things. Come. It's time for you to meet my other guests."

He grabbed me just above the elbow while Heinrich took my other arm and together they propelled me out of the room and toward a great stairway. A cold chill of fear ran down my spine as I belatedly realized he had addressed me by my name, Miss Hunter. It confirmed my worst fear, the fear that he had known exactly who I was the minute he saw me in his office.

As we started up the stairs, I tried to pull away but they tightened their grip. "Hey," I said, "you're hurting. Let me go." They ignored me as they moved me up the stairs. "If you don't let me go I'll scream." Now that has to be one of the dumbest things I have ever said, and I couldn't believe that it really came out of my mouth.

Von Kleimur looked me right in the eye and with a vile grin said, "Really? Some of my guests would find that quite entertaining."

If he was trying to scare me, it worked.

We reached the top of the stairs and went down the hall to a heavy wooden door. Heinrich knocked a couple of times and I could hear a bolt being slipped open. Von Kleimur entered, pulling me in after him. "Let me introduce you, my dear, to Gunter Hengst and . . ."

Gunter smiled as I looked from him to his two goons and sucked in my breath.

Von Kleimur heard my sudden intake of breath and said, "Oh, how wonderful, I see you already know my other guests."

I turned and tried to run back out the door. The tall muscular blond who had opened the door grabbed me by my hair, and with just an open-handed slap to the side of my head hit me hard enough to knock me to the floor. My ear rang from the blow and my mouth bled all over my one and only Paris original.

I looked past him toward the open door. In response he shut the door and slammed the bolt closed.

Looking around for any other exits I saw the room was about thirty by forty feet and filled with various musical instruments. French doors led out onto a balcony that looked out on the bay but was several floors above the rocky shore. Gunter was seated on a small couch in front of me. One of his men stood behind him while the blond stayed at the door. Von Kleimur took a chair over by the French doors, leaving center stage to Gunter. I sat still on the floor, not really daring to move.

TWENTY-EIGHT

"Good evening, Betty Baggetti," said Gunter. "As you can tell by that little love pat, my friends here have a fairly heavy-handed way of expressing themselves. But Von Kleimur says you should have a chance to tell us what we want to know. One chance is all you get. If you don't talk I'll turn these two loose and they will take great pleasure in beating you until you either tell us or are not able to tell anyone, anything, ever. Is that clear?"

I nodded.

Gunter nodded to the guy at the door and another blow fell, this time on my back. It was still an open-handed blow, but he was so powerful that it knocked the wind out of me. I coughed and gasped, trying to get my breath back.

"Miss Hunter, when I ask you a question, you answer me 'yes' or 'no,' not a shake of the head. Understand?"

Between coughs and sputters I spit out a weak, "Yes, yes."

The fear I had felt when I first entered the room was now locked away somewhere in the back of my brain as my analytical side took charge. As part of my mind listened to Gunter, the rest was focused on my situation.

"With his bare fist he could actually split your skull. You know that?"

"Yes," I answered quickly before he decided to demonstrate.

What I was thinking wasn't very hopeful. The bank was in on everything and Von Kleimur must have known exactly who I was the minute he saw me in his reception room. They must have brought me here to kill me.

Another small detail suddenly took focus in my thoughts. When Nelson and I had been caught in the hostel office, Gunter had said something to Dorica about her attitude not being liked in *bond*. I had wondered at the time what sort of bond he could have been talking about, but my conscious mind had dropped that small curiosity. Now I knew. He didn't say *bond*, he said *Bonn*, and he was talking about the bosses in Bonn, Germany.

"Miss Hunter. Is your ear ringing?"

"Yes."

"You want to try for stereo?

"No."

"Have you ever been really beat up? Really in pain so you would rather die than take another blow?"

"No."

Von Kleimur must have called Gunter the minute I left his office. But why was Gunter trying so hard to scare the shit out of me? Why didn't he just have these goons kill me?

As if in answer to my question, Von Kleimur said, "Gunter, just get on with the questions."

They needed answers before they killed me.

"Okay, first question. No lies. Who are you working for?"

I didn't know yet what they wanted, but I knew I would not give them the truth. "*The National Tittle-Tattle.*"

"You mean the tabloid? You're a reporter?"

"Yes."

"What story are you working on?"

"I was checking out this story we got from a young couple who were once homeless and stayed at the shelter."

"What's their name?"

"They gave me the name of Contreras but when I tried to check it out, it was a phony."

"I told you what would happen if you lied, Miss Hunter."

"It's true, don't hit me. My editor said he had heard three more stories just like theirs and wanted it checked out."

"Who's your editor?"

I gave him the name of a tabloid barracuda who had recently been in the news when he beat a libel suit. Von Kleimur winced. Good. He knew the editor's name too.

"So what was this story?"

"Mr. Contreras said he and his wife had gone through the real estate school and had worked up this piece of property. They thought they were going to really score big, and then somebody else got the deal. They believed there was some sort of fraud involved."

He studied me coldly.

"I'm not lying, Gunter. I have no reason to lie. This whole thing's turned into a mess and I just want to get out and to forget it."

"What were you looking for at the Midtown office building?"

I shrugged. "I hadn't had time to find out. I just followed you there." Gunter looked uncomfortable at that and glanced quickly at Von Kleimur.

"Who's tipping you? Who told you about the bank?"

"Oh, nobody told me. I found that myself. I just looked up the title documents on the property and the bank's name was there as lender. I figured that if I put the bank wise to something fishy in their deal, there might at least be a buck or two in it for me. Reporters don't make a lot, you know."

I looked at my hands and toyed with my evening bag, which was still attached to my wrist. I considered the stun gun and dismissed the idea. There were, after all, four of them. I decided now was as good a time as any to try my briar patch ploy. "Look, Gunter, I'll do anything you want and tell you anything, but I got to ask you one favor."

"Oh ho, you want favors, do you?"

"Please, Gunter. Please don't let my editor know I blew this story. This is the third investigative story he's tried me on and I've flubbed every one so far. Three strikes and I'm fired. I'll be back to writing puff pieces and obits for a throw away weekly paper. Please, keep this whole thing a secret. I'll just report that I found nothing and it will be over and done with. Think about it. If I disappear, my editor will have to find out why. If I tell him there's no story, it's over. In fact, I could even take one of your successful people and write a rags-to-riches story that would be a real inspiration."

Again the eyes went to Von Kleimur for silent consultation.

Gunter asked. "What were you doing at the hostel, Diana, and who was your little pal in the office?"

"My first plan was to try to get into the real estate school and see how it worked. When I didn't make that, I just tried to find out what I could, wherever I could. That tall guy seemed to know something, so I was trying to get him alone and romance it out of him. He turned out to be a loss, though."

"What do you mean, a loss?"

"He didn't know anything about the real estate deal."

Gunter nodded to the goon hovering over me. He raised his meaty hand and I moved across the floor as fast as I could and threw myself at the banker's feet.

"I'm telling the truth, Mr. Von Kleimur. Honest, he didn't know a thing about the real estate deal. He was working on something else." Now that got everyone's attention.

"What was he working on?" asked Von Kleimur. First question out of the ol' boy.

Sitting on the floor, looking up at Von Kleimur gave me a different perspective than the rest of them, and as I started to answer his question, I saw something out the French door behind him that almost broke my concentration on the story I was weaving. A giant Morton Bay fig tree grew outside that window. A man was lying prone on a branch, cat-like, hidden in the dark leaves, and I caught a brief look at the face before he hid it again. It was Nelson.

I had to get everyone looking back toward the inside wall. Relapsing into another coughing fit, I stood and walked to the coffee table and poured myself a glass of water.

As I drank it, I got a fix on who was where and looking in what direction. The only one still looking toward the French doors was the blond hovering over me. I set the glass down and moved in very close to Gunter, changing the guy's direction.

"Look, Gunter, I'll tell you the truth. But I swear, I'll never breathe a word of this to anyone else." By now I was very close, almost rubbing my body against his. He took me by the shoulders and shook me as he asked, "What was it? What did he have?"

With apparent reluctance, I said. "He knew about some welfare fraud. He said you guys were collecting money from all over the place, city, county, federal, and that you were just using the school as a front to get all this benefit money." The relief on Gunter's face was so obvious I could hardly keep a straight face. I didn't have much time to try.

Suddenly the French doors burst open and Nelson came flying into the room. Then all hell broke loose.

As the little banker tried to stand, Nelson gave him one swift blow which laid him out cold. Then both of Gunter's goons converged on Nelson. I had already experienced a tiny bit of their power. I was terrified that Nelson would never survive both of them.

Gunter grabbed me by the hair, yanked me toward him and pulled a small revolver out of a shoulder holster. Nelson and Gunter's men were trading blows and kicks and crashing into the furniture and musical instruments like some martial arts movie, only it was real and much too close. Gunter held me by the hair while trying to take aim at Nelson.

Now, I thought, is the time for my stun gun. I quit resisting Gunter's hold and threw my body next to his, putting my head on his chest as if I were ducking for cover. This was sufficiently confusing to distract Gunter for a moment.

With my hands behind his back, I pulled out my stun gun. With my right hand ready to zap him I got my left ready to grab the cylinder of the revolver. With the shock of the stun gun Gunter might squeeze off shots and hit Nelson or the stun gun wouldn't work fast enough and Gunter could still shoot me. I stepped back so my body was no longer touching Gunters, then pulled the trigger on the stun gun at the same moment I put my hand on the cylinder.

As Gunter shook from the shock, I felt the cylinder try to turn in my hand. I squeezed as hard as I could because, theoretically, it's supposed to be possible to prevent the cylinder from turning. I was not at all that sure I had the strength to do it, so I pulled downward on the pistol to deflect any shots into the floor and at the same time kept up a constant pull on the stun gun trigger. After what seemed an eternity, Gunter's hand loosened and the revolver fell into my hand. His body seemed to go slack and he fell heavily on me. I moved to the side, kicked his legs out from under him, and allowed him to crash down on his face.

Not taking any chances, I stood straddling him and hit him with the stun gun again. When I was sure he wouldn't get up, I sank to the floor, my body trembling. Blood pooled on the floor where his nose had hit. The amount of pleasure I got from watching Gunter bleed shocked me. It was a startling insight to realize how fast a relatively peaceful person like me could turn nasty.

The piano crashed and I looked up to see the blond goon lying across it. I had the uncomfortable feeling he was not just unconscious. Nelson still fought with the dark-haired guard in one of the most incredible scenes I have ever witnessed. Nothing I have seen in movies prepared me for seeing what was taking place in this room. This kind of brutal power was awesome and fascinating, but not up this close.

There was pounding at the door and I heard Heinrich's voice and one other person. Nelson landed one last cracking blow and Gunter's guy fell to the floor and did not get up.

Nelson turned on me. The look on his face was so fierce that I was afraid he might beat me next. He looked toward the door, which sounded about to break, then in a soft, controlled voice he said, "I've taken enough bruises for you tonight, Diana. Get up."

I stood without a word, holding my stun gun in one hand and the revolver in the other. My little black thrift-shop bag still dangled from my wrist.

Nelson reached down and took the revolver from me, and I tucked the stun gun back into the bag. He released the cocked hammer and stuck the gun in his waistband. "Come on," he said. We took the only exit available, out through the French doors and down the fig tree.

TWENTY-NINE

As we climbed down the fig tree, I could hear my dress catching and ripping, but since I could also hear wood-splintering blows pounding the door upstairs, I didn't worry about the dress. All things are relative.

From the lowest limb, we jumped to the ground and ran across the lawn. Shots popped and bullets whizzed past us just as we reached the end of the yard. Nelson grabbed me and threw both of us to the ground, rolling us over the edge of a steep drop off. We landed heavily on a carpet of ice plant and rolled most of the way to the sandy shore.

Before I even had time to catch my breath or regain my equilibrium, Nelson grabbed my hand and yanked me up. We ran to the right, around the hill, so that we were no longer visible from the house balcony. Once out of sight, he pulled me out onto a boat dock and checked the small boat for a key. No such luck. We could hear voices and knew our pursuers were climbing down the embankment after us.

"Into the water," whispered Nelson, "but quietly." He lowered himself like a gymnast performing a graceful routine and then helped me slide quietly into the icy water beside him. We swam under the dock and listened as our pursuers followed us down the ice plant.

Nelson whispered, "We need to swim underwater across that cove in front of the house."

I nodded and looked, then shook my head. "Too far."

"If you have to come up for air, keep the back of your head toward the house. Don't turn your face toward the house lights. Don't come out of the water any further than . . . He stopped even whispering. Someone was on the dock. To demonstrate the rest of his sentence, he held his head out of the water just far enough for his nose to clear. Then he pointed downward, indicating we were to submerge.

Between the icy water, the fear, and the pell mell run, I found it difficult to take a deep breath, but I did the best I could and ducked silently under the water. While Heinrich and his friends chased around to the right of the mansion, Nelson and I swam underwater, across the cove to the left. I had to surface for air twice before I reached the point. Each time I surfaced I took a deep breath, trying not to swallow icy sea water, checked to make sure I was still swimming in the right direction, then submerged again.

Around the point we found another cove with a large private marina. From the shore it would have a locked fence and gate but from the sea it could easily be accessed. Nelson swam among the expensive floating playhouses until he found one that met his approval. As he started to climb up, I touched his hand and whispered, "Nelson, there's someone on board. The light's on."

His face registered impatience at either my ignorance or my presumption in questioning him. He yanked his hand free. "That's left on to dry the air," he snapped. He climbed up the back ladder and left me to fumble my way up after him.

As I stood there shivering, Nelson pulled out a pocketknife with multi-purpose tools and popped the lock on the cabin door. I gratefully took refuge inside the cabin, but I was so cold I could not quit shaking or even think clearly.

On the front berth Nelson found two rolled-up sleeping bags and tossed one at me. "Here, get out of your wet things and wrap up in this," he said curtly. I did so without even worrying about modesty. I was too cold to think of anything but the warmth of that bag.

I stripped, unzipped the bag and wrapped it around me, then sat at the galley dinette, shivering and wondering if I would ever warm up. Continuing his search of our borrowed quarters, Nelson found some clothing hanging in the back compartment and tossed jeans and a sweatshirt my way. I was too cold to bother getting out of my sleeping bag, but he slipped into a pair of jeans and a jacket which were cut for a much shorter, heavier man.

Then Nelson pulled out a coffeepot, turned on the water pump, filled the pot and set it on the propane stove to heat. Performing real magic, he located a bottle of bourbon, plunked two plastic cups down on the table in front of me, and poured a very large shot in both. He downed his at once and poured a second. When the water boiled he added it to the shots, creating a rather basic hot toddy. I nested the hot cup in my cold hands, sipped cautiously, and felt the delicious warm liquid trickle down my throat and warm my stomach. Though I had read that liquor is not the proper treatment at such times, I found that the bourbon triggered a flush of warmth throughout my body.

As we sipped in silence, I looked around the cabin cruiser. Like a small RV, it had a forward bunk, a central galley with a dinette that could make down into another bunk. Shower, toilet and closets were in the back. Perhaps not a yacht in style or size, but as my body began to warm slightly this little boat seemed like a true luxury.

I knew Nelson was glaring down at me. I stared at my cup and felt like I was a kid about to get a lecture from my dad. I didn't have to wait too long.

"How anyone as basically smart as you are can be as consistently stupid as you have been the last two days, I will never understand."

"Me either," I mumbled with no defense.

"First, you walked into a trap at Mono Hano and blew your cover. Then you ran away from me, even after I told you about the danger, and flew all the way to San Francisco to fall into another trap. Do you have a frigging death wish or something?"

I looked up at him and shrugged helplessly. "*Nolo contendere.*"

"What the hell did you think you were doing? Did you suppose that a man like Von Kleimur was just going to roll over and say, 'Okay, you caught me. I give up'?"

Finally, he gave me one small point I could defend. "I didn't know that Von Kleimur was in on it. I thought that if the bank knew they had a loan with a fraudulent name on it they might be willing to help me investigate Dorica. I mean, for crying out loud, if you can't trust your banker, who can you trust?" I considered that statement in light of the current financial crisis caused by banks and decided that was the second stupidest thing I had said today, clocking in right behind telling von Kleimur I would scream.

"You didn't know Von Kleimur was in? You're dumber than I thought you were. You still don't get it, do you? Jesus, Diana! This isn't about a little con like Dorica. This is an international financial cabal involving thousands of properties and billions of dollars. A team of very skilled, knowledgeable people has worked very carefully all over the world for more than two years on this case. Do you have any idea what you've done to our case? We were within days of busting it wide open. Then the Bluff Beach Avenger, with more skill than wisdom, blunders in. You have probably blown this case past recovery."

I jumped as he slammed his fist on the table.

"Damn! If I hadn't figured Sam would use my balls for racket ball, I'd have let them kill you. Then I could at least have gotten them for murder."

I was afraid I was going to cry, and not being able to control it was one humiliation too many for this night. Clutching my sleeping bag, I slipped out of the dinette and headed for the V-berth in the bow. With as steady a voice as I could manage, I said, "They told me they were going to beat me to death. If you want to finish the job, it will have to wait until I've had some sleep. I've had all I can handle for today."

I lay down, continuing to shiver and beginning to feel hot tears run down my cheeks. All things considered, it had been an unqualified shitty day.

He was silent for a while. Exhausted, I was already dropping off to sleep. Then he was beside me, his hand on my shoulder, his voice softened. "Here," he said, "finish your hot toddy. It will help make you feel better."

I considered just pretending I was already asleep, but the drink did sound good. I sat up and took the cup. I finished that one and Nelson made us both another. Then he sat down beside me. "I'm sorry. I guess you have had a pretty rough time of it." He reached out and gently touched my cheek. "You're going to have a magnificent shiner."

His understanding tone made me feel worse than his yelling. I pushed his hand away. It was icy cold, cut, and bruised.

"No. I screwed up and you took the worst of it. You were amazing in there and I didn't even thank you for saving my life. I believe they were going to kill me no matter what I told them. They just had to find out what I knew before they did. Gunter said they would beat me to death, and he described it in gory, bone-crushing detail."

"So what did you tell them?"

"I told them I was a reporter working on a story about a young homeless couple who had been in Dorica's school."

"They buy it?"

"Maybe."

"Just before I came in, Gunter was shaking you like he didn't believe you. What was that about?"

"Oh!" I laughed and then yelped at the pain in my jaw. "I have to remember not to laugh or smile for a while." I rubbed very gently on my cheek.

"That was about you. They wanted to know who you were. I told them I had met you at the hostel and was trying to get information from you. Gunter was shaking me because I was pretending to be reluctant to tell them what you were working on."

"What did you tell them?"

His voice had taken on a hard urgency. I realized that, as pleasant as he was being, he was actually in the process of "debriefing" me. Oh well, I owed him that much.

"I told them that you were working on some sort of welfare scam."

"Do you think they bought that?"

"Oh, I know they did. The relief on Gunter's face was almost comical. That is, until you came swinging through the door like a combination of Tarzan and Bruce Lee." The talk had helped me regain my balance after the fear and flight and cold. All of a sudden something dawned on me that I should have thought of earlier. "Wait a minute. How did you know where I was?"

"Sam found your flight to San Francisco on your credit card. From there it wasn't hard to figure where you had gone. Of course, Sam said you wouldn't be stupid enough to go to the bank. But that was the only connection to the case in San Francisco and I was sure that was where you had headed. A check with our surveillance guy up here confirmed it."

I was now very alert and beginning to think clearly again. "But, Nelson, I didn't tell you about the bank."

"I know, and that should have been my first clue. I should have known that you wouldn't have missed a lead like that."

I studied Nelson for a moment, carefully choosing my next words. Though I tried to control it, my voice was low and cold when I asked, "Then you already knew about the bank?"

"Of course we already knew about the bank. The bank is where we started this whole investigation. We started at the top with international finance; you started at the bottom with Dorica's street bums, and our paths converged somewhere in the middle."

"You knew about the bank and you said nothing."

"Diana, you were supposed to be out of it. How was I to know you would go running off, leaving me stranded in the mountains? Besides, I couldn't tell you. This was a secret operation, a team effort. Do you know what that means or do you only know how to play the Lone Ranger?"

I handed Nelson my cup and pulled the sleeping bag around me. "And only your team counts? You may not have noticed, but I had a team and a case too. If you had one bit of respect for the information I gave you, you could have given back a little. Then you wouldn't have needed to play the hero for me in there." I rolled away, not knowing how much of my anger was professional and how much personal. Either way, I felt stupid for having expected anything more. Turning my back on him, I closed my eyes to sleep.

Nelson sat silently on the edge of the berth. I felt him lay one hand on my shoulder and heard him draw breath to say something. He must have thought better of it because he simply patted my shoulder and got up. The last thing I heard before I drifted off to sleep was Nelson making down the dinette into a bunk.

THIRTY

My mind was trying desperately not to leave the pleasant dream it was in, but an annoying voice kept calling my name. I opened my eyes to darkness. There was a constant clinking sound, like poorly tuned wind chimes, then the creak of a board and the wash of a wave against the bow brought me back to real time and place. I tried to move and found that everything hurt.

"Leave me alone, Nelson. I need to sleep."

"Not now, Sleeping Beauty. It's going to be light in another hour and we need to be out of here by then. Come on. Get up and put on those clothes."

I lay there a few moments longer, allowing my senses to fully wake up. The chimes I was hearing were actually the lines on all the sailboats in the marina as they slapped around in the wind and clanged against the metal masts. They made a rather pleasant music. A damp, mildewy smell seemed to cloak everything, but one delicious aroma percolated above all. "Do I smell coffee?"

"Yes, but you don't get any until you're on your feet and dressed."

I raised my head and said, "Ouch."

"I also found some aspirin, but you don't get that either until you're up."

Reluctantly and feebly I sat up. Without bending over any more than I had to, I slipped into the jeans and sweatshirt. I looked up and caught Nelson looking my way. He turned quickly. He was once again dressed in his own pants but kept his borrowed jacket, which hung open. My gaze paused momentarily on his well-muscled chest, then searched around the boat for something else, anything else.

My lovely Paris original was hanging from a peg. It was shrunk and shriveled until it looked like it might make a mini dress for Twiggy. "Coffee." I demanded.

"Not until you have your shoes on."

"I, I think I lost them last night, the hill or the water, I don't . . ."

"Here, try these deck shoes. They may be a bit big."

"I can't bend my head over."

He looked at me and shook his head, then picked up a shoe and said, "Your foot, Cinderella."

My anger flared. "I'll do it," I snapped and grabbed the shoe. He looked perplexed. As I bent to the task, my head felt like everything inside was falling into my forehead and eyeballs. I groaned.

He held out his hand for my shoe. The look I gave him said, "Back off." It was bad enough that I had to be rescued by him. I wasn't about to be so helpless he had to put my shoes on. "Thanks, but I can put on my own shoes." I raised my foot to the bed so I didn't have to bend down so far. The minute I got them on, I helped myself to three aspirins and a cup of coffee.

Nelson turned to go out the cabin door, muttering some curse on liberated women. I followed glumly. He had already lowered the dinghy, and with his coffee in one hand he climbed gracefully down into the bobbing little boat. I followed clumsily, spilling my coffee. He fired up the outboard and headed through the morning fog and around to the next cove on the left.

We made our short jaunt in silence, lost in our own thoughts. A very grey morning was just beginning to light the sky when we tied up the dinghy at a gasoline dock. "My car is parked over there," Nelson said stonily and took off walking. I followed him past several small nautical shops and across the parking lot to a black car with an Avis sticker. He unlocked the doors and started to open the door for me, then hesitated and left it for me to open for myself. I guess wanting to put on my own shoes qualified me as a card-carrying bra burner.

As he drove back around the bay and headed toward the bridge, he dug his cell phone out of the glove compartment and dialed Sam's number. I wasn't allowed to listen in as they spoke the Asian language they had used before. Even so, it was obvious that at least part of the conversation was about me. Finally, Nelson handed me the phone.

"Hello, Sam."

"How you doing, Diana?"

"Okay. Considering. Better than I might have been."

"Yeah, and maybe better than you have a right to with that dumb stunt."

"Sam, please."

He was silent for a while and then said, "Listen, I had to tidy up your place a bit. You were right about someone trying to get in there. I took care of it and rearranged things a bit. Nelson's going to stay with you until this thing is shut down and no one's chasing you. Okay? Are you going to behave yourself and stay put this time?"

"Sure," I said vaguely. I thanked him and hung up the phone. "Sam said you were going to stay with me until this thing was shut down."

"That's right."

"Don't you have other things you need to do?"

"No. Not now." His voice was crisp.

"Nelson, square with me for once. Is the group shutting down the whole investigation?"

He looked into my eyes a moment and then back at the road. "I don't know yet, but it's likely. At least the L.A. end."

"But I got the impression that the part in L.A. was the key to the whole case. Why would you shut it down?"

He gave me a long look. "I think it's time you understood the whole thing so you have a little bit better idea what's happening here."

"I'd say it was well past time."

He gave me an angry look and as he opened his mouth I expected him to snap back. Instead, he returned his eyes to the road and began an explanation in a calm voice. "A little more than two years ago some people at a federal level, who shall be nameless, got information about some cash transfers. Big cash, I mean hundreds of millions were leaving the country illegally. After a circuitous route the money ended up as deposits in the Bankhaus Von Kleimur in Germany, which was paying 7.75 percent for passbook and a lot more for investment packages. Try getting that on a passbook or even a CD at your local bank today. That's what my group started to look at."

"Then you are federal."

"No. We're private and unofficial. We have clients who hire us to work a case when regulatory and police agencies don't have budget or manpower to handle it or when the press or political reality makes it difficult for a public agency to operate. When we have developed the case, we quietly turn it over to the appropriate jurisdiction for prosecution. We get the evidence. They get the conviction and glory."

"You must have some high-level clients."

"We do. The trick is to develop the evidence before either the press or the politically powerful can marshal interference and resistance."

His tone was matter-of-fact, not accusatory, but I could see the implications.

"When we started checking, we found a few instances where Bankhaus Von Kleimur was sneaking its money back into the U.S. through an attorney in Mexico City. The funds were deposited directly into escrow accounts."

"Why?"

"For several reasons, but to start with, to avoid the laws that say foreign companies must disclose their investments in this country. Then, when the escrow was for a property that was recorded in the name of a straw man like the homeless guys you found . . ."

"Oh, I see. By putting cash into escrow and then putting the property in a homeless guy's name, no one would know that the money came from offshore or that the owner was really a foreigner. Sort of the same scam I figured, only Dorica and Gunter aren't the only ones involved."

"Right, and that's not all. You traced the transfer of ownership from the homeless guy to the limited partnership to the California corporation. What you didn't know was that the California corporation then sold its securities to Simboyd N.A., which is a corporation in the Netherlands Antilles. Secrecy laws there do for corporations what secrecy banking laws do for numbered bank accounts in Switzerland or the Caymans. When these deals were handled right, everything was secret: the sources of the money, the owners/investors, and all corporate records. The U.S. collected little or no taxes and our regulatory agencies had no power."

"You know, Nelson, I was horrified at Dorica's greed, but this . . . Hidden money, hidden investment, hidden profits, no taxes. God, aren't the rich ever rich enough? That's more than illegal. It's immoral. Someone who can afford to buy a six million dollar building exempts himself from all responsibility, and the working stiff, who just barely pays a mortgage on a three- bedroom home, has to pay more tax to make up the loss."

We had crossed the bridge and gone through the city. Nelson turned toward the airport and was quiet while he merged with heavy traffic. Then he added, "You about got the picture, but there's also another problem. With this fraud, foreign investors avoid the laws that require them to report U.S. holdings. Terrorists might even buy a company in high tech or weapons manufacturing that they would never be allowed to buy if the true owners were known to the proper authorities.

And a drug cartel can turn dirty cocaine money into clean, tax-free U.S. real estate."

"Wow! The scope of this cabal is mind boggling. And now, with the mortgage meltdown, real estate in the U.S. is available at bargain basement prices. Bankhaus Von Kleimur can pay such high rates because they make profits far greater than an honest investor."

"And they can charge through the nose for investments which give anonymity."

Nelson did an unexpected lane change and pulled off the freeway. As he drove through a shopping center he explained, "I don't know about you," he said, "but that one cup of coffee just isn't doing the job."

"You read my mind. Make mine a triple shot latte with three sugars and an old-fashioned donut."

We used the drive-through and headed back to the freeway. As I sipped the wonderful hot coffee, I returned to our discussion of the case.

"So I guess it was Dorica's job to find good investments, and Gunter's job to find a bum's name to put the property in."

"Yeah. We figure that Dorica was already working this scam for her own investments before Gunter and the bank decided to move in on her operation. She got herself in so much hot water by not paying her bills, though, that the bank sent Gunter in to keep her under control."

"That's why her recent M. O. is so different from her actions in the nineties. What do you suppose Senator George Bernard Simpson has to do with this?"

"Where did you pick up that name?"

"The recorder's office. He signed for the seller's company when the property was put in the homeless guys' names."

"He did? You get more out of public documents than anyone else I know. This is such a leviathan of power and money, I've stopped being surprised by who all is involved."

His statement made my stomach churn as I wondered about Maude's real involvement in this thing."Well, if you know they're doing all that, why can't you turn your information over to the SEC or the IRS or somebody?"

"We intend to, but there are two things we needed to uncover first. We only found a few properties, and we needed some way to figure out what names the properties are in."

"Like Gunter's green ledger?"

"Exactly. So when you gave us the information about the ledger we were almost ready to move in."

"So why don't you?"

"One, we were going to hold off until we had the other key piece we needed."

"Which was?"

"How U.S. investors were getting their money out of the country and over to Bankhaus Von Kleimur."

"So, why shut down now?"

"You've forced our hand, Diana. When you went to the bank, your actions alerted everyone. If we can get the evidence we need today we will move ahead with the part of the case we have, but we may be too late."

His statement was accusation and verdict, and my face blushed hot. Part of me could see how detrimental my actions had been, and part of me raged at the injustice of Nelson's blame.

"So if your case fails, I'm the patsy? Well, when you're telling that to your client, be sure to tell him what would have happened if I hadn't rescued your ass as you were breaking into Gunter's office. If you have any doubts about the consequences, think about Robby McCallvoy. I don't suppose either of those incidents alerted anybody, did they? And if you'd been honest with me when we talked . . ."

He doubled his fist and slammed the steering wheel. "Damn it, Diana! You still don't get it, do you? I'm not trying to lay blame here. I'm trying to bring you in. I thought that if you understood what was at stake, you might be willing to join the team, not be such a damned Lone Ranger. What's with you anyway? Has everyone you've ever dealt with dumped on you or something?"

"Yes!" I shouted. As we both recoiled in silence I thought about my response and realized that wasn't true. Only one person had really betrayed me. Of course, I wasn't about to try to explain my ex-husband to Nelson.

The rest of the way home we avoided conversation and my thoughts returned to Maude. With growing uneasiness, I analyzed her actions and tried to determine her motives. Was she trying to protect her son, or was she protecting herself, her political minions, and her hidden, tax-free investments? Was I ending up Nelson's patsy or Maude's?

THIRTY-ONE

As I unlocked my apartment door and looked in I was surprised to find it quite dark with all the shades drawn. I was focused on the windows, trying to recall pulling the blinds, when I walked right into a chair and banged my shins. I cursed and then stared dumbly at the chair. It was too far toward the center of the room. I never left it there.

"Here, let me get a light on before you break your leg," Nelson growled as he followed me into the room.

I started to tell him that something was wrong with the room, but remembered Sam saying he had "tidied up" my apartment. I couldn't explain this to Nelson even if he was Sam's confidante. Yeabot was Sam's secret, and only he could disclose it to anyone.

Nelson turned on his "man in charge" mode and busied himself opening the blinds, checking out my apartment, and making sure no boogie men were under the bed or hidden in the closet. I stood silently wondering where Yeabot was. Had Sam repossessed him?

When Nelson finished his inspection, he walked up, put his hands on his hips, and asked, "Will you stay put or do I have to tie you up?"

I was flabbergasted. As I considered his question my first inclination was to laugh, but I could see he was quite serious. My second impulse was to tell him to go screw himself. But given the last twenty-four hours, I quickly reconsidered. Controlling my incredulity, my humor, and my anger, I replied flatly, "I have no plans to go anywhere today, Nelson."

He stood there for several moments watching my face as he appraised my answer. In a deadly serious voice he said, "Don't change your plans while I'm gone. I will make you very sorry."

As soon as he left, I turned my attention to the puzzle of the furniture arrangement. First I tried to shove the chair toward the inside wall but I realized that the couch was in the way. There was no room to scoot the chair over. I studied the room in confusion. I was certain that before, all this furniture fit over on the right-hand side of the apartment, leaving plenty of room to walk down the middle.

In a systematic search of the apartment I discovered my laptop and all my current files were also missing. On my desk was my old PC that I now used only to search the internet, and a printer I had never seen before. Reaching for the phone to call Sam I realized that my phone/fax was gone and in its place was an old message phone that had been in the closet. I dialed Sam's number.

"Sam, it's Diana."

"Well, hello there, darlin'. Everything okay?"

"It will be if you tell me you know where my computer and Yeabot are."

"Ah, you're in your apartment."

"Yes."

"You alone?"

"Yes. Have you got Yeabot?"

"No, you have. I want you to hang up the phone and then pick it up again. When you get a dial tone, dial S-A-M-#. Then you'll hear a different tone, then dial Y-e-a-b-o-t. Keep your eye on the inner wall."

"Okay," I answered rather vaguely. I followed Sam's instructions, and as I did I noticed something else different about my apartment. How could I have missed it? The whole inside wall was now covered in wallpaper with huge yellow roses. So much for my Sherlockian powers of observation.

I finished dialing, as instructed, and was staring at the ugly big roses when a door opened in the wall. I hung up the receiver and went over and peeked through the door.

"Hello, Mother. You have many messages. Would you like to hear your messages?"

"Hello, Yeabot. No, thank you. I'll hear my messages later." Looking around I saw that all of Sam's high-tech wonders had been transferred to a little room about four feet deep that ran the full length of my apartment. Sam had brought the inside wall even with the door which was recessed inward from the hall. Hanging over the desk was my framed motto, "PHANTASIA CAMBIARE REALIS." Fantasy can change reality. No wonder my living room seemed to have shrunk.

The phone rang, but I could only hear it ring on the living room phone. The phone/fax in the secret room had a new little light that blinked when the other phone rang. I answered and Sam said, "Well, what do you think?"

"It's like magic, Sam. How could you get all this done so fast?"

"I got a friend who builds sets for the studios, at least when he works. With all the things they can do with computers these days, things are a little slow, so he gave me a hand. It's all made with MDF so it's soundproof too."

"It's . . . it's absolutely amazing, Sam. Thank you."

"I don't recall your giving me any option." His tone changed to the sternest I had ever heard. "Which, by the way, was a lousy way to treat a friend, Diana. In our work the line between white and black and grey is often blurred. The only way to maintain your sanity and humanity is to keep a tight focus on the few true friends you have."

We were both silent a moment. "I'm sorry, Sam. I . . ."

"But, you're welcome. I love doing that kind of stuff. Oh, by the way, see that watch lying there beside your laptop?"

"Yes."

"Put it on and push the little gold button on the left."

I did and the door closed. I pushed it again and the door reopened. "That's incredible. Thanks."

"Take care of yourself, Diana."

"Right. Uh, Sam, Nelson brought me home and he will be back in a bit. I mean, what about Yeabot?"

"Nelson's a good kid, Diana, but Yeabot is still our little secret. Okay?"

"Of course."Actually I was delighted. Sam and I still had our secrets.

"Talk to you later, Beautiful."

"Wait, Sam." Too late, he hung up. I sat and stared at my little room and all its technological wonders. Aloud I said, "Clarke's third law. Any sufficiently advanced technology is indistinguishable from magic." I decided I would frame that and put it next to Walter Mitty.

"Okay, Yeabot, let's hear my messages." There were several calls from Maude, a few other client calls, and several hang-ups. Gunter and gang, maybe? All the calls were yesterday's news except one. Maude had called this morning. Her tone was strange and her message sounded as if she knew a great deal about my last two days.

"Diana, I know you boarded a return flight from San Francisco to the

Ontario Airport early this morning. I assume that means that you will be back in Bluff Beach by approximately 11:00 a.m. There will be a meeting at my home tonight precisely at 7:30 p.m. You are to be there."

That was it: no goodbye, just a command to attend. I listened to the message twice more, had Yeabot print it out, then studied and weighed each word.

What did Maude know? Everything? How much of it had she known when she hired me? I now knew for sure that she had been a partner in the financial conspiracy. Had she hired me to protect Robby or to find out how much he knew and protect herself? How far would she go to protect herself? A shiver ran through me as I wondered if she could have had Robby killed? Or, was his death an unseen consequence caused by clumsy and brutish pawns in the big game? Who would show up at tonight's little party? And of course the big question: if I showed up at Maude's tonight was I to be killed too?

Before seven tonight I would find a few answers. It was time for a little techno-magic.

THIRTY-TWO

Nelson returned an hour later with lunch and a perfectly foul mood. After one attempt at small talk I retreated into silence and concentrated on lunch. We sat on my old sofa in the living room eating hot sub-sandwiches and drinking cold beer. The only sound in the room was munching.

Finally, I could stand it no longer. "Well, tell me, damn it."

He set down his beer and finished his chewing as he mentally composed his answer. "We didn't get there soon enough. By the time we could form a liaison with our prosecution people, get the proper subpoenas, and go in, the green ledger was gone."

"Did they arrest Gunter and Dorica?"

He shook his head. "Not enough evidence."

"What about Mono Hano? They would have all the property records."

"When our people arrived with the subpoena the manager informed them that there had been a tragic computer virus which had destroyed all their computer records."

"Did they check?"

"Yep, pure garbage."

"And they claimed they had no backup?"

"Correct. Mono Hano was the picture of cooperation but said they were so sorry. It might take months or even years to reconstruct their records. By the time they have to comply, the records will have been sufficiently sanitized to be useless."

"What about Bankhaus Von Kleimur? It would have papers as lender . . ."

"We tried that road a year ago. Too much juice there. Just the suggestion that we take a peek at their records caused an international incident that went all the way to the top. And . . ."

He paused and I could see from the grimace on his face that there was more bad news. "I suppose you better know this too. Among those very powerful forces was HMS, Herman McCallvoy Systems. Your client may have been playing more than one role in this thing."

Not sure how to respond to that, I distracted myself by downing the last of my beer and going to the kitchen to get both of us another. Should I confess all my own misgivings about Maude? My small list of circumstances were wanting in hard evidence and I hadn't had time to work out things in my computer room before Nelson returned. "So what are you going to do?"

He shrugged. "Nothing to do. We have no evidence, case closed."

"That's nonsense! You can't quit now. You know what they've been doing and how they've been doing it. There has to be a way to develop usable evidence."

I didn't realize that I had been almost shouting until he shouted back.

"You tell me how! Every property is listed under a different name of a different unknown street bum. Without the ledger, or any other record, how do we build a case?"

"Gunter isn't going to destroy that list. They've just hidden it."

"Right. They've hidden it. Game over. We lose. We can start a new game. But that will take another year and thousands of man hours. With all the heat that people like Maude are now generating to cover their collective asses, I doubt seriously that our group will get another shot at this one. That's the trouble with a case like this. It's so political. They have so much juice. They can quickly and easily tie up all the little threads that we have worked all year to pull loose."

"Nelson, what I do best as a PI is find information for people, and this I know: real estate leaves a written, recorded trail. It's not like money you can wire to secret accounts or gold and jewels you can stash some place. There's got to be a way to find those records."

As he drew breath to answer, the phone rang. Someone asked to speak to Langly and I handed him the receiver, forgetting that the cord on this ancient phone was so short. He had to lean over me to speak. He was close enough for me to feel his breath on my cheek and give me a close up of his face as he quickly became absorbed in the conversation. He closed his eyes tightly against what was obviously more bad news.

He handed me the receiver and said, "Look, I have to go out for a while and help put this thing out of its misery. Will you behave yourself here?"

I nodded. My brain was still working on ways to save the case. As he was about to go out my apartment door, I called, "Nelson, wait. Can you get them to wait just one more day? I may be able to find information that will keep the case open."

His green eyes narrowed and that mellifluous voice developed harsh edges of suspicion. "What information?"

"I'm not sure, but if they can wait just until tomorrow . . . Look no matter how you try to hide it, real estate leaves a paper trail and I am really good at that kind of investigation."

He looked to the ceiling and shook his head with the impatience of a long-suffering parent. "No more lies, Diana. These guys deal in hard facts. If you have anything real, tell me now."

I don't have those facts yet, but let me at least try, let me do what I do best. Give me one day.

As he hesitated, I thought about Maude's little invitation. Internal debate paralyzed me. Every bit of my experience screamed against telling Nelson. Every hard lesson I had learned had taught me to keep the secrets of my cases closely guarded. Trust no one. Today Sam had warned me against misusing my true friends, but he hadn't told me what to do when you weren't sure who they were. Nelson wasn't a friend. He was The Group, and I was just his source. But now, I was asking him to trust me. As I debated, he turned to leave.

To stop him, I blurted out, "Maude's having a little tea party tonight at 7:30. She has commanded me to be there. I don't know who will attend or what's on the agenda, but it might be a chance to find out how they're planning to 'tie up the loose threads.'"

He had stopped when I started to speak, turned slowly to face me, fury in his eyes. "Still playing them close to the chest huh, Diana? Has it occurred to you that you might be one of the loose threads on the agenda?"

"Yes."

"When were you going to tell me? When you needed me to run in and take the bruises for you?"

"Nelson, please. I am telling you. I'm telling you because I want to help The Group on their case. Please, I want to see some real justice out of this thing. I want to get those guys. Please just hold off one day."

He pushed his left sleeve back and studied his watch as his little finger tapped rhythmically against his arm. Ticking off the seconds, he considered my request and then finally met my eyes. "I don't know if I can. I'll see."

THIRTY-THREE

As soon as Nelson was out of sight I went into my secret room to take another look at the grant deeds and trust deeds for the two pieces of property recorded in the names of the homeless. I had, of course, studied these documents before when I copied them in the Recorder's office. Now I was looking for something different, some unifying element, some criteria which might be used to find other properties. I examined every line. Finding nothing new, I felt a slight panic. Was I as good as I had bragged? Could I really find the "hard facts" that would tie up this case? What made me think I could do what an entire team of hotshot investigators had failed to do?

Unfortunately the property addresses and ownership lines were of no help without Gunter's green ledger. The seller was the same, Senator Simpson's company, but what chance was there that all the properties LA LA Land bought would be from the same source? A quick check of the database revealed more than two thousand entries for Simpson's company in L.A. County alone. Each one would have to be copied and investigated to see if ownership was suspicious. I'm good at this type of search because I don't just do computer searches like most PI's do. I pull all the documents and examine each one, searching for pieces that don't fit, finding clues other miss. On this case was no time for such tedious research.

The sales were both financed by Bankhaus Von Kleimur, but there was no way to search the database by lender.

If they used the same notary on each sale we could subpoena all the notary's records and depose him. Time consuming, but possible. I looked for the notary's signature and got a nasty shock. On both of the documents the name was Ralph Jenson--Maude's attorney, the one Robby had spoken to. Could it be a coincidence of two men with the same name? No. Here was the hard evidence I had been looking for and hoping I wouldn't find. Not only was Maude a board member to the bank, but she, or at least her attorney, was up to his notary stamp in the actual transactions. "Damn!"

I finished checking the documents and found nothing else that looked useful. We could try subpoenas on both Simpson and Jenson, but it could take months to get compliance and then would probably be useless.

I still felt certain there had to be a way. I just hadn't thought of it yet. I sat down at my computer, pulled up my Property Quick database, and printed out the records for these two properties. I compared the data to the facts available on the trusts and deeds. The data compiled by this service comes not from the Recorder's office, but from the tax assessor's office. It took only one look at these printouts to find what I needed. It was so easy that I laughed out loud.

When the county prepares your tax bill each year, they want to make sure that the tax bill gets to the person responsible for paying the taxes whether that person lives on the property or not. They therefore have two addresses on the records: the "site address," where the property exists, and the "mailing address," where the bill payer is. The mailing address for the tax bills on my homeless guys' properties was none other than One Avenue of the Stars, Suite 2700. That was Mono Hano Property Management. "Eureka!"

It was so obvious I kicked myself for not thinking of it earlier. I input the search criteria: Mailing Address: One Avenue of the Stars, Suite 2700, then opened a log to catch the data and turned on the printer as well. The printer began to hum and clatter and spit out pages and pages of data. I scanned the items as they darted rapidly up the blue screen of my laptop. When it finished I couldn't help a broad smile. I had all we needed.

As I looked over my list, I heard a knock at the apartment door. I gathered up the printout sheets, shut the secret room, and went to the door to let Nelson in.

He was dressed in black sweats and a loose-fitting windbreaker. As he unzipped the windbreaker I could see that it covered a shoulder holster and a large pistol.

Assuming his attire meant The Group had said yes, I handed him the list of properties. "Feast your eyes on this!"

I left him to study it while I went into the bedroom to change into black sweats, black tennies, and a waistband holster and belt.

He asked no questions until I came back into the living room. Feeling quite smug about my coup, I was expecting excited congratulations. Instead, he shook the papers at me, crumpling them angrily in his clenched hand, and with uncontrolled fury asked, "When and how?"

I dug my Walther 32 out of the suitcase and loaded a clip. As I put the gun in my holster and an extra clip into my fanny pack, I answered his questions. "While you were gone. On an ordinary computer, in an ordinary, legal, public records database. If you doubt me, check the printout date and time."

"How? Every property is under a different name."

"Right, but look at the mailing address. Every property has to provide an address for the tax collector. See who pays the taxes?" I topped my outfit with a navy blue windbreaker with large pockets.

He looked back down at the list. As he went through the stack of printouts he mumbled, "Mono Hano, the property management firm."

I stuffed a pair of brown kid gloves and a black ski mask into the pockets of my windbreaker. "Exactly. All I had to do was ask for all properties with Mono Hano's mailing address."

"Hell! We didn't need to go busting in there and blow the case."

I noticed that it was no longer me, but "we" who had blown the case. "I know," I said. "You exposed the investigation and Robby lost his life, all over a little green ledger that wasn't even needed. It wasn't until you told me about the destruction of evidence that I started trying to figure out some other way."

"At least you thought of it. The Group is supposed to have the best investigative minds in the country. None of us thought of this."

I had taken so much guff from Nelson the last day or so that I couldn't help gloat just a bit. "Yeah, well, you law and order types are usually focused on street action rather than paper chase. In fact a lot of police stations don't have or use the databases I use daily."

"Maybe The Group better recruit you."

"Well, for now, Hunter Investigations has recruited you. Unless, of course, this list makes a difference. Are you still with me?"

"Here's the problem. Robertson, the guy I report to, said that there is already so much political muscle lined up to squash this case that even if he had the green ledger, he wouldn't be able to continue the investigation. The client who hired us has backed off and is running for cover. We may not even get paid for a lot of what we have done. He gave me twenty-four hours to see what you and I could come up with. Frankly, I don't think even this list can get the case back on track. We would have to come up with something so powerful it could change the political landscape. Any ideas?"

"Maybe. If Woodward and Bernstein could do it, so can Hunter and Langly. Let's start with tonight's trip to Maude's and see what we can stir up in the next twenty-four hours."

THIRTY-FOUR

We took Nelson's rental car, less conspicuous than my T-Bird, and drove slowly north along the ocean, planning to eventually end up on L.A.'s west side at Maude's compound. We were in no hurry. At a little shop in San Pedro that sold all kinds of ocean charts and maps, we bought a topographical map that included Maude's Hill, and verified my hunch. There was a natural wash that ran parallel to the street and wound its way up the hill to Maude's.

After a dinner in Santa Monica, we drove to a spot downhill from Maude's where we could intersect the wash. Nelson parked the car. It was about 5:45 and with short November days, it was already getting dark. We needed no conversation at this point and began walking quietly up the wash.

I was alert and calm but hyper sensitive to every bird call or rustle in the bushes as I made an almost soundless assault on the compound at the top of the hill. As I picked my way carefully, I remembered all those cold winter hunting trips with my dad and thanked him for the lessons learned. I even forgave him the hours of misery I had suffered as I followed him in the predawn darkness, with my toes and fingers feeling nearly frozen.

I realized that I could not hear Nelson and looked over my shoulder to make sure he was there. Just a few steps behind me, he followed as silently as a hunting cat. I couldn't remember the last time I had shared that skill with anyone and wondered if Sam had taught him his woodsman's skills.

The climb to the top of the hill took about forty minutes and it was fully dark by the time we arrived. It was not hard, however, to see the landmark I was leading us to because its dark silhouette stood out against the ambient light of the city sky. Just to the left of the main gate was the grand old oak tree I had noticed the day I visited Maude. As a kid, trees had been my special friends. Many of them had housed secret places where I kept a store of candy or stashed my latest secret code book, or hid out from my Dad. I learned that if you were in a tree you were almost invisible. More than once I escaped detection by sitting quietly in a tree while someone walked below me calling and searching. I pretended this was because the trees held magic and deliberately hid and protected me. Even then, of course, I knew the truth. People simply don't look up.

Nelson and I studied the dark limbs of Maude's oak and gauged our best climbing route. Then, covering the white of our hands with gloves and our heads and faces with the ski masks, we started quietly and carefully up the tree.

I was disappointed to find that my tree climbing skills were not what they used to be and that the fearlessness of youth had given way to a healthy respect for the possibility of a fall. Nonetheless, I made it to a big fat limb that grew laterally over the top of the wall. Stretched out comfortably on this perch, I could see the roof of the house to the north and the guard shack and gate only thirty or forty feet away. Nelson joined me on the next limb.

Since I had been ordered to appear at 7:30, we timed our arrival for 6:30 so we could see what preparation was being made for my command attendance. The guard sat comfortably in a plastic lawn chair, smoking and talking to someone on his cell phone. I could only catch a word or two here and there but he seemed to be gossiping about other people at work.

There was no indication of anything unusual until about ten to seven when a number of people came from the direction of the house. The guard got to his feet and struck the appropriate pose for an alert security guard. When the parade got close enough to be recognized, he seemed to relax again. The group began piling into a car parked near the gate and someone yelled, "Open the gate, Dennis, the slaves have been freed."

"What is this? She fire everyone?"

"Nope, night off, with pay no less."

"Everyone in the house is off? Boy, the ol' girl must have a hot date tonight."

At the gate one passenger rolled down a window and said, "Here, she sent down a list of guests to be let in. We're all heading to Stoner's. Join us if she cuts you loose later."

Dennis opened the gate, then stood in the light at the corner of the guardhouse and read his instructions. I was certain I knew who some of the other guests would be, and I had very little time to wait to verify my suspicions.

At seven o'clock Maude's limo pulled up to the gate and was ushered in.

One of the guests exited the limo.

"Good evening, Dennis."

"Good evening, Mr. Jenson."

Dennis peeked inside the limo and took a quick head count. "I have approval here for, let's see, for Senator Simpson and Mr. Von Kleimur."

"Yes, they are with me."

"But, sir, if you pardon me, I have clearance for three people and you seem to have four plus the driver."

"That is because Maude is giving you the night off." A huge man got out of the car. "Ellery here will be on gate duty. Here is a little bonus for you and the rest of the staff to celebrate your night off."

As Ellery turned toward the light, my stomach turned over. He was the goon who had provided me with my black eye when I was at Von Kleimur's.

Dennis hesitated, fingering the cash and looking thoughtfully at Johnson. He took a second look into the car and then at Ellery, as if evaluating the guest who would be given unfettered access to his employer. He probably knew Jenson, Simpson and Von Kleimur, but not Ellery.

"Go on." said Jenson. "We saw the rest of the staff headed downhill as we came up. Go catch up with them. Maude is just having a quiet evening with three old friends and wants you to have a great night off."

Finally, Dennis said,. "I just have to give Mrs. McCallvoy one last message. Excuse me." He went to the guard shack and called the house. When he came out he was smiling broadly, "Thank you, Mr. Johnson," he said waving the cash. Then he climbed into his car and left.

I wasn't sure who had called this little tete-a-tete, and I had wondered if sending off Maude's guard was her idea or Jenson's. But Dennis was no one's fool. He had checked with Maude.

The limo with the three guests drove up the path to the house and Ellery took up his post in the chair by the gate.

The phone rang in the guardhouse, and I almost jumped off my limb. Ellery went to answer it, and I nodded to Nelson. This was as good a time as any to leave our perch.

I climbed down to the next limb and then out to the sagging end. From there I jumped to the ground but hit harder and louder than intended and froze in position. Nelson landed beside me. I looked around to the guardhouse to see if we had disturbed Ellery. No sign of him.

"I don't want any surprises tonight," I whispered.

Nelson nodded and crept off toward the guardhouse.

I ran to the road that led to the house and took cover in the chaparral on the far side. Crouching in the shadows of the shrubs, I ran until I was within visual range of the house, then waited there for Nelson.

He arrived a little breathless and waved a role of silver duct tape. Quietly, he informed me, "Well, Ellery ducked out for a little while."

I smiled and watched as he crammed the tape into his windbreaker pocket. He asked, "I make Simpson, Von Kleimur and Ellery, but who's the Jenson guy?"

"Ralph Jenson. He's Maude's corporate attorney, notary on Senator Simpson's property sale to the homeless, and the person Robby McCallvoy spoke to about Dorica's fraud a week or so before he was killed."

Nelson absorbed this while we appraised the current situation. This was the first time I had been close enough to see her home and I was surprised to find that the house was not built in some grand architectural style. It was designed like a very large, rustic hunting lodge. Not what I had expected of Maude.

A wooden veranda encircled the two story house and was filled with large comfortable-looking chairs and even a porch swing. Seated on the porch, near the door, was the chauffeur. He looked like another of Gunter's goons.

Most of the house was dark and the surrounding grounds even darker. The only light blazed from a large living room with a panoramic window that opened onto the night and displayed Maude and her guests like characters in a lighted shadow box.

The focal point of the room was a rock fireplace of gigantic proportions. A cheery fire burned brightly and yet seemed dwarfed by the size of the hearth. Maude, Simpson, Von Kleimur, and Jenson stood in front of the fire. No one had drinks or food and no one looked very happy. From our hiding place in the chaparral we watched the players perform a pantomime upon the lighted stage. Body language and facial expression told me that there was a lot of anger in this tableau, but no one appeared ready to pull a weapon or try to do my client in. The scene had more the air of a hostile board meeting and I suspected that was what it was. Here they all were, the bankers, the corporate barons, the bought and paid for government representatives; collectively the Corporatocracy whose clandestine activities ran the world.

"Well, let's do it," I said. "I'll join the board meeting."

"And I'll join the guy on the porch."

THIRTY-FIVE

Slipping around the side of the house, I found an unlocked window and quietly let myself inside. I peeled off the ski mask and gloves, stuffed them into my pockets and pulled a small flashlight from my fanny pack. The room I had entered was a bedroom that looked clean but had a musty smell, as if it wasn't frequently used.

I drew my Walther 32. Not something I do lightly. But this week I had been attacked, beaten, and had my life threatened twice. Considering that my invitation to Maude's could be a trap to make good on those threats, the Walther was a justifiable precaution.

I made my way around the semicircle of outer rooms until I was in a small bar next to the room with the fireplace. From there I could hear the senator's voice, but not quite make out his words.

I put the flashlight into the fanny pack and pushed open the door, No one even noticed me when I stepped into the room. I slammed the door behind me. Complete silence and startled expressions greeted my entrance. To my delight, I saw that Von Kleimur was wearing a neck brace and let out a yelp of pain as he turned his head to see me. I was delighted.

They all eyed the pistol as I said, "Maude, as ordered, I am here precisely at 7:30. Please stand perfectly still. Gentlemen, very slowly and carefully remove your jackets and place them across the back of the couch."

The only hint of Maude's reaction to my surprise entrance was a slight widening of her eyes. Her face locked down in the expressionless mask I had seen before during our debates at Rick's salon. It showed her control but also revealed her need for defense.

Jenson followed my instructions and put his coat over the couch. Von Kleimur and Simpson looked to the veranda where a man stood with his back to the room. Von Kleimur bellowed, "Max!"

As the man turned to face the room, he swivelled a porch chair around to reveal that Max was now gagged and neatly duct-taped to the chair. Nelson raised his nine millimeter and let himself in though the sliding glass door.

"Your jackets, gentlemen," I repeated. This time they complied.

Maude observed me coldly as I searched the coat pockets with my free hand. I netted a couple of large checkbook wallets, a folded wallet, two cell phones, and a pocket-size computer.

Her voice deadly, her tone threatening, Maude said, "I don't know what you think you're doing, Diana, but this is hardly . . ."

With a harshness matching hers I said, "Shut up, Maude."

Her mask slipped. Her eyes widened again and her mouth opened slightly. I doubted anyone ever addressed her in that tone or with such words.

"Gentlemen, move to the wall. Place your hands on the wall and step back two paces." Bereft of their trusty guard dog on the veranda, the men revealed their Beta status as their eyes turned toward Maude in silent request for leadership. No doubt about it, Maude was the Alpha dog in this pack.

I fired three shots into the floor, each one at the feet of one of the men. They obeyed my last command, rapidly turning to the wall. "Now spread your legs."

Once they were sufficiently off balance, Nelson frisked them but came up with nothing more deadly than a one-inch Swiss pocket knife. He had them sit down on the floor. As Nelson had the situation in hand, I put my Walther back into my holster and confronted the seated group: a rotund senator, a pompous banker, and a lanky lawyer, trying to maintain their dignity while looking like over-grown kindergartners waiting for story time.

"Aren't we missing someone? Where is the Daring Duo of Repo Real Estate?" They exchanged looks. "Don't tell me that Dorica and Gunter weren't invited to this little tea party?"

Maude knew me too well to even try, but Jenson leaped in. "I assure you, Ms. Hunter, that we were all shocked to learn of the fraud that was perpetrated by those two."

At his statement I laughed out loud. He sounded like Captain Renault in Casablanca and I quoted,: "I'm shocked, shocked to learn gambling is going on in here." My movie reference was totally lost on him and he hesitated a moment, confused by my laughter and quote.

He continued lamely, "In fact that is why this meeting was called. We intend to contact the police and the FBI and lend our assistance to their investigations. Ms. Grizel and Gunter will be arrested for fraud."

"Ah, get all your stories straight for a fraud case, huh?" I was still facing the men, but with my eyes I also watched Maude for reaction to the next question. "Who will be arrested for Robby's murder?"

A swift furtive look passed between Von Kleimur and Simpson while Jenson seemed genuinely surprised by my question.

Jensen answered, "Why that deranged veteran, of course. Didn't you read about him?"

"Oh, yeah. The crazy vet." I looked directly at Maude. "Is that who killed Robby, Maude?"

She did not answer but her eyes moved from me to the senator and Von Kleimur. Under her visual examination, both men immediately dropped their eyes.

Maude looked up from the men and met my eyes. Color left her face and she lost her stiff proud stance as her whole body went limp. She sat in the chair next to her.

Nelson's expression told me that he hadn't the vaguest idea where I was going with this and was not pleased to be in the dark. His eyes narrowed and mouth line hardened as he forced himself to keep quiet and continue backing me up with his nine millimeter Glock.

Not only did Maude and I both have a sixth sense for reading people, but we also had experience with one another. She understood exactly where I was going.

Having gotten an answer to my most important question, I turned my attention back to the men. "So, the murder problem is taken care of very cleanly. However, it must be quite a problem finding enough evidence to charge Dorica and Gunter, without incriminating yourselves."

The three men looked to Maude but found no guidance. The senator took over.

"I'm afraid you have some misconception there, Ms. Hunter. We are all innocent victims of this fraud and stand to lose a great deal of money."

"Right, and it was his innocence that made Von Kleimur call Gunter and his goons to San Francisco to beat me up."

Simpson continued, "Yes, in a sense it was. Gunter lied to us. He told us that you were involved in the robbery at LA LA Land that led to the tragic death of Robert McCallvoy. You must know that when we learned that you were in reality working for Maude, we immediately set out to correct the situation. Even in her grief, Maude went to the police and personally cleared your name. Naturally, Leonard feels terrible about what happened and wishes to make amends. Isn't that right, Leonard?"

Leonard Von Kleimur studied Simpson a moment as if trying to decide whether he wanted to agree or not. Eventually he said, "Yes, madame, you have my most sincere apologies and if you would be so good as to return my wallet, I would be happy to write you a check for, say, $25,000 for your pain and suffering."

I almost laughed but instead turned to Maude. "What do you say, Maude? Think I ought to buy that?"

She didn't even answer, but gave me a look of impatience and a slight shake of her head. Though I knew that negative sign was displeasure with what I was doing, rather than an answer to the question, I turned back to Von Kleimur. "Gee, no, Leonard, Maude doesn't seem to think that's enough. There were all the extra travel and expense. Then there was . . ."

"Fifty thousand."

I smiled. "That's a nice round figure. Keep in mind, however, I will probably have to do a great deal more work to assist you in compiling all the 'right' evidence regarding Gunter and Dorica."

"Very well, one hundred thousand. If your expenses should go higher than that, I might be forced to look into another murder." He looked pointedly at Nelson. "You see, one of Gunter's employees suffered a broken neck when someone broke into my home in San Francisco."

I looked at Maude. "Guess I better take it, huh, Maude?" I picked up Von Kleimur's wallet checkbook with attached pen and tossed it to him.

Maude did not control her expression as well as before. I could see surprise and confusion on her face, while the look on Nelson's face showed open astonishment.

"Nelson, while Von Kleimur writes me a check, please take the senator and Jenson out and tape them to chairs. Then come back for the banker. I want to have a private conversation with my client."

Nelson gave me a not-too-subtle look of annoyance but obediently removed the men one at a time.

Once alone with Maude, I said, "Okay, Maude. What was the real reason you hired me to watch Robby?"

Maude did not hesitate in her answer or insult my intelligence by pretending not to understand the implications of my question. "When Robby spoke to Jenson about fraud at LA LA Land, Jenson managed to read some of the information Robby had. One of the suspect properties was owned by an HMS subsidiary. I needed to find out if there was anything fraudulent in that transaction."

With the events of the past week and the tragedy they unleashed, her subtle lies triggered my pent up emotions. My fury exploded. "Bullshit, Maude! You could easily have looked into one lousy real estate deal and cleaned your own dirty laundry. Why did you put me on Robby?"

Echoing my anger, Maude dropped her mask of impassive control. She stood up from the chair, her face flushed a deep red and her expression contorted by emotion. She growled out a response that seemed to emanate from her gut and push its way past clenched teeth. "Because if Robby was involved it could never be as simple as one bad property. Robby made it his lifetime career to attack everything my family had spent three lifetimes building. At the center of his black heart was a hatred for me and for everything I stood for. You and the press all thought Robby was some sort of saint, out there living like a pauper and doing sainted works. The truth was that every ounce of his energy was spent in an attempt to destroy me. He organized ecological protests against my oil companies, boycotted my agricultural products, and brought charges of substandard maintenance against my residential properties. Most of the time the charges were patently untrue and unfair. The truth is he was just a willful, hurtful, ungrateful child. He picked his causes for one purpose and one purpose only. That was to stick another poison dagger into me, the woman who bore him. I was constantly having to make arrangements to protect my companies and my political friends from the self-righteous zeal of my own son."

In the heat of anger, I hurled words back at Maude for which I will always be sorry. "Well, Maude, I guess now you've finally made the ultimate 'arrangement' regarding Robby."

Maude turned so pale I was afraid she might pass out. Her rigid posture wilted as she sank back into the chair. In a barely controlled voice she said, "Diana, I have always credited you with a high level of ability, but until now I had greatly underestimated your capacity for cruelty."

To my astonishment, large tears formed in Maude's eyes and she said in a passion-choked voice, "Get out of my house."

With shock I realized what I had misunderstood about Maude. I looked away from her and into the dancing flames of the fire. Too late, I realized what I should have known. Maude's hatred of Robby's activities was not due to the political or financial peril to her corporate dominion, but to the personal pain of a mother rejected by her own son. I remembered the slight joy that crept into her voice when she told me she and Robby had a pleasant lunch together the day he talked with Jenson. She had seen hope in the fact that he had come to her with this investigation. She would never have harmed him, and had still hoped to some day win him back. That was the real reason she had hired me.

Aloud, but almost to myself, I said, "How sharper than a serpent's tooth it is, to have a thankless child!" I looked back at her and said, "I'm sorry, Maude."

She shut her eyes, and as the tears fell down her cheeks, her hand flew to her mouth as if she could stop her crying or hide it from public view. She turned away from me. I started to reach out to touch her but realized she wouldn't allow it.

I could think of nothing else to say or do, so I turned to leave, then hesitated and turned back. I knew Maude would want to know. "Maude, your son wasn't killed by a crazy vet. For what it's worth, I intend to see that the police get the real killer."

She turned and looked at me with red tear-filled eyes. In a weak, almost child like plea she asked, "Who?"

"It was one of Gunter's goons. Probably an ex FBI agent named Paul Kennedy. I would appreciate it if you kept this from your associates on the porch. I need a day or two more . . ."

She nodded silently.

THIRTY-SIX

I wasn't sure how much time Maude would allow us before she cut her friends loose, so we borrowed her golf cart and drove it down the hill to Nelson's car. Nelson didn't say a word all the way down. At the car, we both unloaded our weapons and tossed them in the trunk along with the gloves and ski masks. I could feel his silent anger as he unlocked the car doors.

As he put the car in gear and headed toward Bluff Beach he said, "So, is that it? Your idea of 'getting' those guys was ripping off the banker for a hundred grand?"

His question angered me, but with deliberate calm I said, "I know you don't know me very well. Maybe you can't make any better estimate of my character or my actions, but you do seem like a fairly observant investigator. I would have thought that you could at least have picked up on the subtext in that room."

He took a deep breath and a moment to think before he answered me in a slightly cooler tone. "I don't know what you mean by subtext, and I can't know what you were up to in there because you never told me."

"Nelson, I didn't keep anything from you. I didn't know what was going to happen until I got in there. I had to read their responses, then play the thing by ear."

"What the hell does that mean?"

I realized Nelson really didn't understand. He was like my ex-husband Martin, in that regard. People have different ways of perceiving. When Martin and I would go to a party, he saw the physical. He could give details of everyone's physical description and tell you what color and style of clothes everyone wore. With my poor visual memory, I couldn't even tell you the color of people's eyes and hair unless I deliberately committed it to verbal memory.

On the other hand, I could pick up on the unspoken communication between people. When we would leave the party I would tell Martin who was sleeping with whom, who was about to get a divorce, and which employees secretly hated each other. My skill at interpreting the hidden agendas was accurate. At first Martin didn't believe me. He would ask, "Who told you that?" I had to have an authority or it couldn't be true. When, in time, I would be proven correct, he hated it even more. He called it witchcraft. Nelson wasn't going to understand or trust this skill any more than Martin had. Instead of getting mad, I tried to explain.

"I've known Maude for a couple years, so maybe I could read her a little easier than you could. By subtext I mean sensing the emotions and action of others, reading in something that is only implied and not said. It's picking up on subtle signs that tell you who is doing what to whom and why."

"Okay," he answered, "I sensed four well-heeled crooks covering their collective asses. Since we had a gun on them they decided bribery was better than murder. And I see my new partner, the one pledged to righteously crusade for justice, accepting a check that looks very much like a bribe. Does that about cover it?"

"In a shallow, insensitive way, perhaps. Now let me tell you what I saw in there." I thought a minute about where to start.

"Maybe you need a little background first. Maude had allowed her attorney, Jenson, to invest some of her corporate capital in a deal with her political protege, Senator Simpson. The deal was financed and run through Bankhaus Von Kleimur. Until recently, all had gone well and been very profitable. When Robby came in to talk with Jenson about fraud, Jenson had recognized one property as owned by an HMS subsidiary. Jenson told Maude, and Maude hired me to learn what Robby was up to. Unfortunately, Jenson also told the senator.

"Somehow, probably through Simpson, Gunter found out that someone was snooping around LA LA Land. I doubt he had any idea it was Robby McCallvoy. Between this warning and our various encounters with them, they were on the alert when Robby and Ben broke into the office."

"Is that all conjecture and subtext or did Maude tell you all that?"

Exactly like Martin, I thought. He's got to ask who told me. Patiently I explained, "Some of it I learned during my investigation, some Maude told me and some I read in their reactions.

"Okay, for the sake of argument, we will assume that is fact. What did you think you were doing in there?"

"The reason I came here tonight was to learn what Maude's role was. I had to know why she commanded me to be here this evening and how much she knew about Robby's death. "

"What did you conclude?"

"You remember when Simpson was explaining that it had all been a big mistake, that Gunter had lied to them about me being in on the robbery at LA LA Land?"

He nodded and I continued.

"He also said that Maude had already given a statement to the police clearing my name. Maude's little pals wanted me to know that and to know the cover story so I didn't say anything else to the police. That is why I was invited. But, and this is what I really needed to know: until we walked in tonight, Maude still believed Ben had killed Robby. When I questioned that, it took only one hard look at Von Kleimur and Simpson for her to know that they had been lying to her."

"Did she tell you that?"

"No, that's part of what I saw in there. I could read her question in the look on her face. I could see Von Kleimur and Simpson were unable to look at her as her steel gray eyes bored into them. I could see her eyes widen slightly as the truth registered. I could see her chest move more rapidly as she breathed faster and more shallowly and fought to control her anger. I could see her collapse into the chair as she realized what had happened. That's part of the subtext you missed.

"Here's the rest. When we came in, Von Kleimur, Simpson, and Jenson were all appeasing Maude and making sure she would play the cover-up game. They had already decided that Gunter and Dorica could take the fall for the fraud and Ben for the murder. After listening to Maude's opinions for the last two years, I doubt she was overly distressed by the fraud she had unknowingly participated in. She was going to go along with them to protect her corporate empire. It was good policy. Things changed when she saw they had lied to her about Robby."

"So what do you think you learned? You figure now Maude is on our side?"

"Our side? Are you being sarcastic or naive?"

"Neither one. You just said that Maude only learned tonight who killed Robby. Don't you think she will want to get even with her pals?"

"Oh, she'll get even all right and it would be delicious to see. But her revenge will never see the light of day. She is a member of the Corporatocracy, the bankers, corporation heads and government leaders who wield the real power.

Maude's vengeance will be executed behind the curtain and according to Corporatocracy rules. As to our own search for justice, we are on our own.

THIRTY-SEVEN

I knew he believed me and thought I had answered all his questions, but he seemed to be waiting for something more. "So you see I couldn't tell you what I was going to do because I didn't know until I was in the middle of it."

He was silent a moment. When he began to speak, his voice had taken on a deep, personal tone and a firmness that left no doubt about the finality of his position. "I don't think that's your real reason, Diana. I think it's part of your control, your lack of trust of anyone. Sure, you may need to stay flexible when you're scamming the bad guys, but that doesn't mean you have to scam your partner at the same time. And I'm telling you right now, I won't play by those rules. If we're partners, we must be full and equal partners. Either you trust me, brief me completely on all your plans, or I'm out."

He was the third person this week who had leveled the same complaint at me. I needed some time to digest what he had said and consider the consequences of my response. The immediate result would be that I either retained Nelson's help on this case or went on alone. I could see, however, that much more than that was involved.

I thought about Jenny and how many times I had dragged her along blindly. She had just put up with it. I had sometimes even endangered her life, without revealing the details of my plans. I had been scamming my best friend. How had she put up with it and stayed my friend so long?

I watched Nelson as he drove. He was silent and kept his eyes on the road, waiting for my response.

Finally I said, "You're right, Nelson, and I am sorry. I'll be straight with you about this case, but remember, that goes both ways. You also withheld information."

His entire body seemed to relax as if he had been holding his breath while I thought this thing out. He pulled to the side of the road, turned toward me, and studied my face a moment. "That's a deal." Then he smiled and took my hand in his. "I think we might make a pretty good team. I just need to know we are a team."

I felt my entire body go rigid. He was still talking partner talk but the way he was holding my hand in both of his said much more. The panic inside me began to rise like bile. He was moving toward taking our relationship to a level of reality I hadn't dared visit in years. We had just met and our brief time together had been intense and exciting and I was attracted to him, but hardly ready to jump into a relationship. What would happen to me if I opened up to Nelson and let myself really care? Could I stand the pain if it didn't work?

I saw subtle changes in Nelson's expression and realized he had read my tension quite accurately. Maybe he read people better than I thought. He began to release my hand and I felt a new panic. In that moment I knew the risk of caring couldn't be worse than continuing this pretense of a life. I closed my hand on his and said, "Just slow down a bit. I need time to think."

He looked back into my face, searching my expression for intent, then leaned forward and kissed me. It was a gentle, friendly kiss. "We probably both do," he answered and put the car in gear. "So, partner, what about the last question. Were you just pretending to take a bribe? Are you going to tear up that check?"

"Yes and no. Yes, I was just pretending to take a bribe, and no, I am not going to tear up the check. You and I are going to assist Mr. Von Kleimur in making cash contributions to a good cause or two, all in his name mind you."

He didn't object but gave me a quizzical look.

"And those contributions are just the beginning. As I understand the problem, your case is folding, not due to lack of evidence but because your client, an agency of the U.S. government, is being told to back off. Someone is wielding a scary amount of power there. Someone is able to command a legal government agency to drop a legitimate criminal investigation because the bad guys are men too powerful to bust. Makes about as much sense as banks too big to fail. But I think if the truth of this fraud got out to the public, the government agency involved might find that 'change in the political landscape' you said you needed. I think I know a way to get the truth out. It may sound a bit crazy. It's a Diana Hunter special, the type of action I use when my client can find no legal remedy to his problem. It will use our friends at LA LA Land and may even be fun."

The rest of the way back to Bluff Beach I filled Nelson in on the details of my solution to this case. I told him everything. To my surprise, I found it actually felt good.

When I finished he was quiet a while, then he said, "First, we could never pull that off by ourselves. Once Gunter gets a whiff of what we're up to at LA LA Land, he'll turn his dogs loose and we'll end up dead. We'll need back up. And second, I could never participate in pulling a stunt like that on my own. I do have to answer to an organization. We're going to have to pitch it to the Group and see if it flies.

THIRTY-EIGHT

The Group was represented by three suited, short haired, law and order types. They were older than Nelson by twenty years. Throughout my presentation they maintained a stiff, unsmiling, deadly serious countenance. I explained in detail the way I felt we could expose the truth and why I thought this was necessary to get the case back on track, but they didn't look like they were buying it. When I finished there was silence while they traded looks.

Finally, Mr. Robertson looked at me and said, "Miss Hunter, I appreciate your passion and your desire of be of assistance, but you must understand this has been a two year investigation carried out internationally by a team of professional investigators. Playing a game of charades as you are suggesting is not the sort of technique we employ, nor can I see how such action would be useful."

We were meeting in a small hotel room. They had remained standing during my entire presentation and did not offer me a chair. The implication was that we would not be there long enough to bother getting comfortable. But I had done my homework. I knew who I was meeting and what sort of reception I was likely to get. "Really, Mr. Robertson? When you were with the FBI I believe you received commendations and bonus checks for just such operations when you ran undercover scams that resulted in the arrest and prosecution of many criminals."

Robertson gave a quick angry look at Nelson, assuming he must be my source. I pulled out a large file from my brief case, opened it and set it on the small writing desk. "Frankly I was pretty impressed with the cunning and ingenuity of some of these." I pulled out several printouts of newspaper articles and even one large magazine piece featuring Special Agent Robertson during his FBI days. I spread them out and began commenting on each, admiring his creativity and his success. With obvious embarrassment, he stacked up the files and cut short my commentary.

"Thank you, Miss Hunter, but you must understand that there was a lot more to these cases than just the sting operation which made a big splash in the papers. There were months and sometimes years of careful, tedious, investigation resulting in the compilation of the hard evidence it took to get convictions in those cases."

"Yes, like the two years your professional investigative group has spent on an international investigation into this financial cabal. As I understand it, and please correct me if I am wrong, lack of evidence is not your problem. You have the evidence you need, especially with the list of suspect properties my investigation has supplied. Your problem is a political clash with the Corporatocracy Rules.

"The what?"

"As I understand it, the client who asked you to conduct this investigation was some agency of the Federal government. Your assignment was to quietly find the evidence to support prosecution of very powerful people in the international financial world and thus stop activity both illegal and highly detrimental to our country. Once you had obtained the evidence you were to turn it over to the client agency and let them handle the prosecution and reap the glory. Right?

"Yes, . . . but . . ."

"But the power behind the scenes, the Corporatocracy that really pulls the puppet strings of our government got to your client agency and pulled the plug."

"I wouldn't put it that way."

"I think the way you put it to Nelson was that there was already so much political muscle lined up to squash this case that even if you had the green ledger, you wouldn't be able to continue the investigation. That the client who hired you was running for cover and that you might not even get paid for the work you had done. Right?"

"Yes, but frankly, I can't see how this stunt you propose could do anything positive for the case, and it would most likely endanger both you and Nelson."

"It will do what you said you need. Once my 'stunt' is out there in the press, it will 'change the political landscape' and put the spine back in your client agency."

He looked uncomfortable. Before he could reiterate his refusal I charged in. "You have to know what you are fighting here. The political muscle you refer to is powered by large international corporations, banks and the political leaders indebted to them. I call it Corporatocracy because it has garnered so much power that it is rapidly rendering our democracy powerless. It's modern Fascism, the union of corporate and state power, overwhelming legitimate representation of the people.

"It's not just this case. Look at what they can do. Drug companies and other lobbyist write legislation and have indebted legislators pass it regardless of public welfare. Regulatory agencies in every sector of our lives are stopped from legitimate investigation and regulation because it might be bad for business. Food and drug, environment, traffic and air safety, banking and securities . . .it's not what's good for the people that counts. It's what's good for the corporations. Judges at every court level receive substantial donations toward their elections if they have the *right* attitude toward corporate rights. Even the Supreme Court—hell, they may have driven the final nail in the coffin of our republic by allowing corporations to spend unlimited amounts of money on election campaigns. There won't be a judge, a senator or a representative they can't buy. International policy, including wars that kill our children and other peoples children is decided not by what is moral, legal, and democratic, but by what will give our corporations the most imperial control over the worlds resources.

'We may not be able to tackle all that but we can strike one small blow for real justice but letting the people know the truth in this one case. The only weapon we still have against this power is the press and media. Since those same corporate interests own most of the press and media, you can't just leak the story. You do that and the story will never be published. Someone up the corporate ladder will be a Corporatocracy board member and the story will be killed. For this story you must have action by real live flesh and blood people in front of a whole room of witnesses and plenty of press and media present. You have to have a story that happens on camera before anyone can shut it down."

There was complete silence in the room and once again the three exchanged looks, then all of them looked at Nelson. Mr Robertson turned to me and asked, "What makes you think the press will show up?"

"Are you kidding? Robby McCallvoy was murdered last week at LA LA Land. Not only has the press loved covering his bizarre activities, but he's the son of the corporate titan, Maude McCallvoy. She's another press favorite who has been known for years as the Black Widow. In addition to that drawing card I'll send out a few special invites to friends in the press with hints of a big story."

Nelson chimed in. "I think we could also alert a few of our contacts. The press and media will show."

Robinson tuned to Nelson."You really willing to pull this stunt, Nelson?

You think it can work?"

"Yes, sir. Diana and I both worked undercover at LA LA Land. We know the layout and we know the subjects involved."

"You realize The Group can't be openly associated with this operation?"

Nelson nodded. "I've been thinking about that. I believe if we quietly hire off-duty police for backup and call in any press and media people we know to cover the event, Diana and I can handle the rest."

Robertson sighed and looked again at his two associates for consultation. One gave a slight shrug and tilt of his head. The other said, "The investigation's dead. This can't do any worse."

Robertson turned to Nelson and me and said, "Ok, Nelson. Just make sure the 'real flesh and blood' we see isn't yours and Miss Hunter's."

THIRTY-NINE

On my fourth attempt to reach Jenny, her son Michael finally picked up the phone. "Hi, Diana. Mom just left."

"She just left? So she heard my last three messages?"

Silence.

"Did she leave on her bike?"

Pause. "Yeah. She's pretty pissed. Maybe you ought to give her a while to cool off."

"Why?"

Pause. "Well, the last time you called, you really scared her, and then you wouldn't tell her what was going on. Then she read about that murdered guy and she freaked."

"I see. Okay, thanks for the warning."

I put the bike on the car rack and drove to an entrance to the trail that was below where Jenny and I usually begin our ride. I waited on my bike, and when she rode up I pushed off and rode beside her. She frowned and said, "Go away, Diana."

I paced her for about a quarter mile, not knowing where to start. Finally I said, "I'm sorry, Jenny. I don't know if you can believe this, but I promise, I will never leave you in the dark again."

Her only answer was a snort of disbelief. I tried to think of what else I could say, how I could convince her I had learned something this week and understood what I had been doing to her. Every approach I thought of sounded hollow and untruthful even to me. For lack of anything better, I just started babbling. I started with the murder and then told her everything that had happened. I told her what was going on when I called her from the hotel and told her about San Francisco. I told her my last call was only to keep her safely away from LA LA Land and that if I had any reason to believe she or her family were known to Gunter or in any danger, I would have told her.

When I wound down, there was silence as I waited for her to respond. We rode for a full mile before she said a word. "All well and good, Diana, but there will always be the next time. I don't want to hang around for that."

We were quite a ways down the trail before I got up my courage to say what I knew I had to say. I opened up my soul and told Jenny what I had done to Sam and what I had done to Nelson and how deeply the lesson had cut.

"Jenny, I know, we both know and have talked about the fact that I have put up a wall against getting involved with another man since Martin. But, I thought that was all of the problem. This week I had three friends tell me I was playing them for suckers by keeping them in the dark. Honest to God, I didn't know I was doing that. I really believed it was all part of the game. But now, I have seen it and I promise I'll never do it again. I don't care if you want to stop working with me; in fact, I couldn't blame you at all for that, but please don't stop being my friend. Relationships and the effect of relationships, good or bad, are all our souls take from this life. I don't want to lose yours."

We reached the end of the trail in silence. She got off her bike and turned to me. "Let's put this to the test. Join me for breakfast and we'll talk."

At the end of the river sat a great little restaurant, almost on the sand of the beach. We locked our bikes and took a table at the edge of the patio where we could eat and watch the wind surfers, oil tankers, sailboats, and volleyball players.

Once we had ordered, she looked at me and said, "Okay, so tell me what you plan to do next." It wasn't a statement, it was a challenge. Her real question was, would I tell her the whole truth and nothing but the truth?

For the second time in twenty-four hours I provided a complete, blow-by-blow description of how I believed we could impact the political power grid around the bad guys and get a little justice done. To my surprise I found that Jenny not only began to talk like she was in, but also provided insight and analysis that helped improve points in my plan that were weak. On the ride home we finalized the plan, chose up tasks, and parted friends. I felt wonderful.

FORTY

My early morning ride with Jenny had thrown my schedule behind and I had very little time left before Nelson would show up to start our next part of my plan. Fortunately, Yeabot was not only very fast but could find records which were not on your standard public databases. I have never asked Sam how this was done, and he has never volunteered any information. With the guilty suspicion that it might not be exactly legal, I used Yeabot's special skills infrequently.

This morning, after only thirty-four minutes, I had tracked Walter Johnson to a church home for the indigent in downtown L.A. and had discovered that the Cannons were registered at a cheap motel out in the desert near Barstow. I had my end ready.

When Nelson got to my apartment he had the attorney, Michael Amilio, with him. We loaded everything we needed into a rental car, then the three of us headed for Barstow.

The attorney and I watched from the car as Nelson waited at the corner of the motel. The curtains on the motel window had been tightly pulled all morning and the door had remained closed. Only the slight swaying motion of the curtains as someone brushed past them had verified that the Cannons were still there. It was just before noon and we had almost reached the cut-off time for doing this the easy way.

When the door started to open, I held my breath, hoping it would be Ben coming out.

I spoke into the neck mic. "It's Ben. One hand is in his jacket. Looks like the pistol must be in his waistband. Shit! It's the whole family. Plan two."

I started the rental car and put it in gear, timing my arrival at the corner of the motel to coincide with Ben's rounding that corner on his way to his car.

As he turned the corner, Nelson grabbed him, immobilizing his arms. At the same moment, Mary Anne screamed and the kids jumped. I slammed on the brakes, put the car in park, and leaped out, leaving my car door open. My first move was to grab Ben's gun from his waistband. I tossed it into my car and slammed the door.

Mary Anne was so hysterical she didn't even recognize me. Ben yelled for her to take the kids and run, but instead, she was trying to get around Ben to scratch Nelson's face. I grabbed Mary Anne, saying, "Mary Anne, stop! It's me, Diana. We're here to help you, not hurt you."

She whirled on me, and for a second I thought I would be the target for those nails. Then she blinked and really looked at me.

"Ouch, Goddamn it. Call off the kid," said Nelson.

Their oldest boy was doing his best to kick Nelson's shins. Nelson was using Ben as a shield.

Mary Anne grabbed hold of the boy. "Benjamin. Stop! It's all right. They're friends."

Ben was almost frantic. "Mary Anne, they're not friends. We have no friends. They're here to either arrest me or kill us all. Take the kids and get out of here."

Battered by months of shock and disaster, Mary Anne had lost touch with reality. She was incapable of dismissing Ben's paranoid frenzy. She backed away, again looking terrified, but this time there was an almost childlike expression on her face, begging me to say it wasn't true.

I reached out for her hands, looked steadily into her face and said, "No, Mary Anne. We are here to help you. If Ben were thinking clearly he would realize that he and I are witnesses to Robby McCallvoy's murder. We are the only ones who can help the police arrest Gunter and Kennedy for that crime."

Emotionally fragmented, Mary Anne began to sob. I pulled her to me and held her for several moments and spoke to her quietly. I could hear Nelson talking softly and calmly to Ben.

When both were calmed, I said, "Ben, the man you knew as Mac was actually Robby McCallvoy."

"I read that," he interrupted angrily. "I also read that they think I killed him."

"Not anymore. Maude McCallvoy and I have already made our statements to the police. They know you didn't kill Robby and that you witnessed the murder. You're the only one who really saw it happen. They need you to testify. If you come back with us, you may still have to defend yourself on charges of assault with a deadly weapon and trespass. But the police and DA are already aware that you and Robby were material witnesses cooperating with an investigation of LA LA Land."

I expected him to demand an explanation of that cover story, but he was focused much more personally.

"I can't even take care of my family. How can I defend myself?"

From my windbreaker pocket I pulled out a small maroon bank book and a folded piece of legal-size paper. I handed Ben the savings account book and opened it to the first page, which showed a $25,000 balance in his and Mary Ann's name. He stared at it dumbly. Then I unfolded the paper which was headed RETAINER AGREEMENT and showed receipt of $25,000.

"There has been an anonymous donation to your defense fund of a total of $50,000. Half was put into a saving's account to keep you afloat until you get settled. A good criminal defense attorney has agreed to take your case and his fee will come out of the other half." I opened the back door to my car. "Ben, I'd like you to meet your attorney, Michael Amilio."

After dropping the Cannons and their attorney at a small rental apartment in LA we picked up a second attorney and headed across town to All Faiths Church Home. The attendant in charge registered neither surprise nor suspicion. She ushered us into the child-care room without as much as asking our names.

I spotted Walter in a corner by a window. He was seated on a kid-size yellow chair with his feet flat on the floor and his long thin legs bent at the knees. He looked like a contented grasshopper. One child sat in his lap. Two others cuddled in small yellow chairs on each side of him, like tiny bookends. He was deeply absorbed in reading aloud from *Horton Hatches an Egg* and didn't even notice our approach.

The little girl in his lap looked up at me with big round eyes and smiled. "Hello," she said, causing Walter to stop mid-sentence and look up at us.

He frowned a moment as he tried to place us. Then a cautious smile developed slowly on his face.

"Well, I'll be. If it ain't the lady who sees what she's seein' with the man who done lost all his old gray hair. You two cleaned up a bit since I saw you. Umhum."

From the look on Nelson's face, it was obvious that Walter's powers of observation and recollection had astounded him. I was not even a little bit surprised.

Walter looked at the man with us. He assessed him top to bottom and up again. Then somewhat suspiciously he asked, "What you two need with this lawyer fellow? You two get in trouble or you tryin' to get me in trouble?"

The looks on both Nelson's face and the attorney's face were so incredulous I had to laugh. I also had to admit that this Sherlockian feat of observation and deduction surprised even me.

"Remind me never to try to put one over on you, Walter. This attorney is for you, but not because you're in any trouble." I unfolded the grant deed to Walter's piece of real estate and handed it to him to read.

"You once told me that no one would let you do a real estate deal, but you were wrong. When Gunter put your name down in that little green ledger, he was using your name to hide and secretly hold some real estate. That property is worth more than five million dollars."

It was now Walter's turn to look incredulous. He looked at the paper and then looked suspiciously at me. His look dared me to convince him this could be true.

"We're not sure how it will all work out, but this lawyer believes he can help you get a substantial settlement from the litigation over this property. Walter, I would like you to meet your attorney, Steven Colman."

After Colman had a few words with his new client, he left saying he would catch a taxi back to his office. Nelson and I took Walter aside, detailed our plans because they included him. We warned him that it could be dangerous, but ask if he would be willing to help us. He looked at Nelson, then at me. He took so long in answering, I was afraid he was going to refuse. Then he gave us a knowing look that gradually grew into a smile, then an all-out belly laugh. When he finally brought the laugh under control he said, "Oh man! I wouldn't miss this for the world."

We gave him the new suit, hat and shoes we had bought for him and told him we would be back for him shortly.

———————————————————————————————

As we climbed back into our car Nelson tried to sound casual as he asked, "What plans do you have for the last $25,000?"

Nelson knew nothing about our last stop and I wanted him to understand. I wanted him to know that I hadn't held out anything to do with the case. This was just something personal I felt compelled to do. I began trying to explain.

"The night before we met at LA LA Land, I was wandering around downtown. I don't know what I thought I was doing. I just wanted to see the world that these people live in. I expected to see drunks and drug deals, and I did. But I got a lot more than I bargained for. I saw a woman, younger than me, with two very small children. They were huddled in a doorway under a thin hospital blanket. The mother had some kind of club under the blanket. That was the only defense she had for herself and her children."

I was quiet for a minute as I tried to put my feelings into words. He understood and didn't interrupt.

"You know, there are panhandlers everywhere you go anymore. The number of homeless just keeps growing. I don't know why and I don't know what to do or believe about it. When somebody bums from me I feel guilty if I don't give them something and I feel like a sap if I do. I hear stories about people who make a very good living bumming. Some say it's just another kind of con or that anything you give them just goes to booze or drugs. I don't know if that's true or how often it's true. I know I do see an awful lot of seemingly able-bodied men and women trying to bum quarters. I don't know why.

"But that woman with her children. She hit me where I live. When Martin first left me, I came close to being on the street myself. I thought, if enough bad things happened to a person all at once, it could happen to anyone. Maybe. I don't know."

"You can't save the world, Diana."

"I know. I'm not going to try. I just have to do something about this one thing."

He nodded.

I found her on the same doorstep where I had tripped over her before. This time, however, I knew what to say to her. From the back seat, I picked up a cloth bag with a thermos and cups, and while Nelson waited in the car I sat on the steps far enough away that I was not threatening. I talked quietly. When the two babies poked their heads out from under the blanket, I poured two cups of lukewarm coco out of a thermos, handing them to the mother and letting her check them out before giving them to the kids. Then I poured her one. That was the turning point. She began to talk to me and in few minutes the three of them were loaded into the back seat of the car and settled in with the thermos of chocolate and a picnic basket of chicken sandwiches.

As we pulled to a quiet stop at the church shelter where we had found Walter, Nelson leaned over and said quietly, "You sure this is the best idea? They might not have room."

"Oh, I think they will. This is where Von Kleimur made his last $25,000 donation."

He smiled. "I see. Then, I guess that's the last of our arrangements."

We left the mother and her children in the care of the church and picked up Walter who was now all slicked up in a new suit. The three of us headed for LA LA Land.

Nelson looked over at me. "Are you ready for the final act?"

What we had planned sounded good on paper, but a million things could go wrong. I took a deep breath and answered, "Ready as I'll ever be."

FORTY-ONE

Nelson and I had already had a full day, but the main event was yet to come. As we waited across the street from LA LA Land, I went over the details in my mind, hoping nothing crucial had been overlooked.

He looked at his watch. "Well, it's almost show time." He laid his hand on my shoulder. "Look, we don't know what sort of reaction they are going to have to this, but we know it could be violent. Are you sure you don't want to just give the press a handout and let it go at that?"

I shook my head. "No. If we are going to succeed in sicking the press onto powerhouses like Simpson and Von Kleimur, they will need a truly compelling story. The kind that produces pictures and video."

He looked into my face for a very long moment, showing me an expression I hadn't seen before and couldn't read. My stomach clenched and I felt an unexpected thrill at his touch and his nearness. Then he wrapped both arms around me, drew me closer, and kissed me.

As he prepared for his reconnaissance of the theater, Nelson put on a tummy pad to widen his girth, a plaid jacket, a long brown wig, sideburns and beard. I smiled but refrained from laughing.

When he returned from the theater, he allowed himself a little smile and said, "Your reporter friend and Robertson both made good on their promises. Representatives from every newspaper and television station in town are set up just in front of the orchestra pit. It's a zoo in there. Dorica and Gunter must wonder what the hell is happening."

"They'll put it down to Robby's murder, which in fact did help get the coverage for tonight. Did you spot Jenny?"

"Yeah, Jenny's all set with her boxes of press releases. They are thick suckers with all those properties attached"

"How about my mic? Did you get the pick-up hooked into the musicians' amplifier?"

He nodded. "Yeah, all set. If Gunter cuts the stage sound, your mic will keep blasting."

"There's one other little thing I noticed while I've been waiting for you. There are police, not Gunter's private security, but regular L.A.P.D. in uniform at all entrances. Robertson must have come through with the promised backup.

"You mind?"

"Heck, no! I'm grateful."

"It's time," he said. We headed toward the rear stage entrance. On the way, I signaled to Walter who was waiting patiently in my rental car. He climbed out, straightened his new suit, and ambled across the street to meet us. He brought me the large purse that I had entrusted to his care.

"You still feel sure about doing this, Walter?"

"Now, girl, don't even think about leaving me out of this at this point."

"Okay. Just stick with us, keep very quiet, and get off the stage and down to Jenny as soon as your part is played."

He nodded.

As I had noticed before, the crew had the door open to allow cool air into the hot, crowded backstage area. We walked in and joined the milling crowd of guest speakers. Most of them where pigging out on the hors d'oeuvres and champagne as they waited their turn to give testimonial to Dorica's wonderful real estate secrets.

The stage crew was busy creating the magic on stage and took no notice of Nelson, Walter and me. I pulled back the curtain at the left side of the stage just enough to peek out and survey the audience. The place was standing room only and the crowd seemed even more exuberant than usual. The fellow with the one-man-band was providing emphasis to every punch line as Dorica's comic warmed up the crowd with cutting jokes spiked with class-strife and mortgage melt-down tragedy. The crowd was eating it up, writhing with anger at being victimized. How would they respond, I wondered, when I told them the truth about who was victimizing them?

I tuned back to Nelson and Walter and we made our way to the old circular staircase that led to the basement under the stage. As we descended the stairs, the noise of the show diminished but could still be heard over the sound system of the theater. As the comedian wound up his act the crowd roared. His last joke had evidently hit home and the response sounded more like fury than humor. It was the cry of the Roman Coliseum to bring out the lions. Would my news make them want to throw Dorica to the lions, or me.

Gunter took the stage before the roar of the crowd died down and began pounding home his message of anger and bile, delivering mind-poisoning hatred of "them" as a proven method of harnessing the masses. His "them" included the poor, the immigrants, the rich, the bankers, the socialists and the corporations. Logic didn't matter. He used any catch phrase, any sound bite he had picked up from professional hate mongers on radio and TV, anything that grabbed the baser human emotions. It amazed me how easily a mob can be manipulated by hate. They could be lead to loath the very thing that is in their own self-interest and embrace the very thing that does them the most harm.

The basement beneath the stage was a damp, musty rat's nest of old sets, furniture, boxes, and miscellaneous junk. Light glowed in the far corner of the room but was swallowed up by the aged collection, as if the dingy props and paraphernalia still grasped greedily for the lime light.

We moved silently through the shadows and peered over the piles of boxes at Dorica who sat at a dressing table and prepared her makeup in the light of a vanity mirror cerca 1950. When we reached the elevator, I signaled Walter to wait for us there.

Nelson and I moved to a large oak wardrobe that stood just behind Dorica. She was in the process of putting on a long glittering earring and was looking intently into the mirror. It had one of those three-piece hinged mirrors to provide the viewer with profiles as well as a frontal view.

At Nelson's signal we stepped around the wardrobe and stood at the back of Dorica's chair, giving her multiple reflections of us. She jumped and turned toward Nelson. Then her expression shifted from startled to recognition to rage. She looked toward the stairs and opened her mouth to shout for help.

Before she could yell, Nelson grabbed her arms, pinning her to her chair, and I slipped a gag into her open mouth. Those cold eyes showed no fear, only fury. Then Nelson lifted her from the chair and stood her on her feet while I unzipped her dress and slipped it down. I was a little shocked to see she wore no underclothes of any kind. I considered covering her, but thinking about my photo taken at LA LA Land, I decided that leaving her this way was no more than tit for tat. Out of the corner of my eye I spotted Walter peeking around the edge of the elevator, a broad grin on his face.

While Nelson plunked her naked bod back in the chair, I dug into my large purse for a coil of slender, strong rope, then dropped the purse onto the vanity. She wriggled and fought and made muffled yells for help but with the noise on stage and in the audience there was no way she would be heard.

As I slipped out of my clothes and climbed into her dress, Nelson began to tie her and her vanity chair to a large, load-bearing cement column. When he completed his task, I was still trying vainly to finish getting into Dorica's dress. I turned my back to Nelson. "Can you help me zip this?"

He examined the problem and pulled the zipper to just above my waistline. "That's about as far as it's going to go. You have a good four-inch gap topside. Just don't turn your back on the audience."

I looked in the mirror and took off the scarf I had been wearing. Richard had prepared me a black wig, a perfect imitation of the Victorian coif that was Dorica's trademark.

"Okay. From the audience it will work. But if Gunter catches my side profile from the wings, it's going to be up to you to keep him at bay until Walter and I finish our act."

"Don't worry. Gunter leaves the stage after his act and goes to the lobby to line up his army of cashiers who march in to take everyone's money. He never has his goons around backstage either. It's too crowded with shills swigging down Dorica's wine and snacks. Just keep it very short, like we rehearsed and then get off the stage and down to the press. Let's do it."

As Nelson went back upstairs, I pulled a wireless mic from my purse and joined Walter. We stepped into the elevator and waited for our cue to rise to the stage. The elevator was an ancient little box with no door. It had a single lever that raised it one short floor, through the trap door to the stage, and lowered it again to the basement. After the elevator in my building, operating this one would be a snap.

Gunter had completed his bit and Walter and I could hear the testimonials as true believers and shills alike told stories of financial salvation and success. Then, as the testimonials ended, the little man with the marvelous electronic orchestra began building the musical introduction for Dorica. I shoved the lever upward and the little box began its climb to the stage.

FORTY-TWO

We arrived at stage level a moment or two before the crescendo but close enough. Just before the spotlight hit us, I shoved the elevator lever into its hold position.

Dressed in Dorica's white bejeweled dress and coiffed in her dramatic Victorian hairstyle, I raised my arms Heavenward in her standard pose of welcome. The audience had been worked to a fever pitch with a half hour of "hate them" and a half hour of love our savior Dorica. The applause and cheers roared out.

Walter stood in back of me in the open elevator, blinking in the bright lights and waiting for his cue.

I could see very little beyond the footlights and only a couple feet into the wings. I knew that Nelson was watching for any move by Gunter, but I had no idea how much time he might be able to buy me. I also had no idea which way the stimulated crowd might respond to the unexpected message I brought them. My stomach was in knots as I waited for the applause to end.

As soon as the applause began to wane I turned on my mic and tried to quiet the audience.

"Ladies and gentlemen, please, thank you, ladies and gentlemen, please, we have an important guest tonight. Thank you." The applause died down, ending in a couple shrill whistles. I could see Jenny, just beyond the footlights, handing out the press releases. I called Walter to my side and glanced nervously toward the wings.

"You may have noticed that we are honored to have an exceptionally large group from the press and media."

That brought another round of applause. I waited nervously for a moment, then spoke louder trying to talk over them. "I would like you . . . please folks, time is short. I would like you all to meet a man who has just learned that he has gone from being homeless to being the vested owner of a 5.7 million dollar office building. Ladies and gentlemen, Mr. John Morgan."

This brought a burst of applause that I couldn't quiet. Beaming ear to ear, Walter took a deep, sweeping bow which prolonged the applause. Video lights blazed and cameras flashed. Almost blinded, I grabbed Walter out of his third deep bow and pushed him to the steps. If this thing blew, I wanted him down into the waiting arms of the press and out of harm's way.

As Walter descended the stairs, Jenny grabbed him and ushered him to Doris Whitmore, one of my friends from the *Times*. Once again, I quieted my audience and rushed to tell the main points of my story.

"Ladies and gentlemen of the press. You have each just been handed a thick press release. In that you will find details on Mr. Morgan's property as well as fifty-five other properties. You will want to look very carefully at each of these transactions because each case is a total fraud."

There was a momentary pause, then confused mutters from the audience. "Yes, I said fraud. On every one of those properties is in the name of a homeless person, a homeless person who took temporary shelter here at LA LA Land , a homeless person who knows nothing about any real estate in his name. And . . ." The audience mumble grew. "And they were never supposed to learn about it. This is a fraud! The names of the homeless are on these papers just as strawmen, to hold the properties for wealthy crooks who don't want to pay their share of taxes."

The audience began to yell questions. Confusion was turning to anger. I ripped the wig off my head and tossed it down on the stage. "Dorica June Grizel is as phony as that wig and you folks have every right to be angry. You are the ones struggling against job loss, credit crunch, and home loss. You are the ones who really believe in the American dream and believe that if you are willing to work hard and try new things you can survive the financial disaster the banking and security firms have plunged the entire world into. You are the ones struggling, hanging on by your fingernails, trying to succeed while Dorica preys on everyone, the helpless taxpayer supports this shelter, the hopeful suckers search for and find her properties, and the homeless become her strawmen so she can make her rich friends richer."

At that point I saw Gunter, running down the isle toward the stage stairs.

"LA LA Land is the bottom rung of an international financial cabal operated by and for the super rich creating hidden money, hidden investment, hidden profits, with no taxes, and you are all unknowing pawns. "

Gunter leaped up the stairs to the stage. As he bounded onto the stage, I fully expected him to rush me. I yelled, "Nelson, Gunter's on stage!"

Instead of making for me, however, Gunter headed for the wings and started the curtain closing, then he turned to follow the closing curtain. In seconds he would be on me.

Before he got two feet, however, Nelson emerged from backstage, wrapped a powerful arm around Gunter's neck, and dragged him back to the wings.

Nelson had at least bought me a few more seconds. Peering out at the now confused audience and speaking as rapidly as I could, I continued giving the press some vital details. "On each trust deed you will find the lender is the German bank, Bankhaus Von Kleimur. On many transactions you'll see the signature of Senator Bernard Simpson. . ."

The curtain was within four feet of closing when suddenly Paul Kennedy vaulted over the brass rail surrounding the orchestra pit and landed heavily on the first keyboard. He almost lost his balance as the notes he stepped on blared out a discordant blast over the sound system.

I hadn't seen this guy since he attacked me outside of my apartment and I knew the police were after him for Robby's murder. How could he be here?

He held his arms out trying to maintain his balance. In his right hand was a large caliber pistol. Stepping first on an amplifier and then on a second keyboard, he leaped onto the stage.

Forgetting that I was talking into the mic, I said, "Oh, Hell! I thought he would be in jail!"

As the curtain closed, the last thing the press and the audience saw was the silhouette of a man landing on the stage, arms raised for balance, his right hand brandishing a weapon.

As Kennedy landed I shouted, "Nelson!"

After that, everything seemed to happen at once. Distracted by my yell, Nelson loosened his hold on Gunter. Kennedy took firing position and aimed at me. I backed away from him until I came up against the back wall of the elevator. Into my mic I yelled, "Police, we have a shooter on stage. We need police. Shooter on stage." At this pronouncement, the audience erupted into screams and pandemonium.

Holding Gunter with one hand and drawing his gun with the other, Nelson yelled, "Kennedy, you bastard!"

At Nelson's yell, Kennedy pivoted away from me, toward Nelson. Suddenly, Ellery, another of Gunter's goons appeared from behind Nelson and jumped into the fray.

As Nelson turned to defend himself against the new attacker, Gunter got free and was yelling, "Cut the mics." In his own futile attempt to silence me, Gunter yanked down on a power switch at the wings, plunging the stage into darkness.

I heard the blast and saw the flash of Kennedy's pistol. Someone in the wings yelled. I cried "Nelson!" I turned toward the wings and as I did, I saw a second flash of Kennedy's gun and heard the whine of the bullet as it zinged past my head. I backed into the elevator again, yanked downward on the shift lever, and ducked to the floor of the little box. As the box descended into the basement, a second and third shot thudded into the elevator wall above me.

As soon as I was down, I jumped out of the elevator and stumbled my way across the cluttered basement toward the stairs. With my eyes adjusted to the darkness of the stage, I could see well in the low-lit basement. Dorica's eyes followed me.

I could still hear the screams and clamor of the audience and, above all, Gunter yelling, "Get the girl, get the girl."

I was almost to the bottom of the circular stairway when I heard heavy feet hitting the top steps. I ran back among the boxes and looked frantically around for another way out. I would never make it up in the elevator before Kennedy would have another shot at me. Down here, with better light, his aim would be more accurate.

I ran for the only hiding place I could find and climbed into the old oak wardrobe. To my horror, I found that it was not as solid as it looked. As I stepped to the back, I heard the supporting wood crunch and felt the wardrobe almost tip over. There was no time to pick a new hiding spot. I quickly shifted my weight to the front and pulled the doors closed. The lock that had once secured the doors had been pried off leaving a small hole in the wood. Through this peephole I looked directly into the vanity mirror.

I could no longer hear Kennedy's footsteps but he soon came into view, reflected in the left wing of the mirror. He moved though the basement in a crouched position, weapon held ready. In the right mirror I could see Dorica tied to her chair. In the center loomed the huge wardrobe.

When Dorica spotted Kennedy, she began her muffled yelling. Kennedy fell into shooting stance and aimed at the sound. Dorica's voice ascended a full octave and her yells came shorter and faster. Kennedy pulled up on the pistol and held the shot.

He stood straight and stared open-mouthed at Dorica's naked body tied in the chair. It would almost have been comical if I hadn't been terrified. She attempted to form words out of her muffled sounds and nodded her head toward my hiding place.

He cocked his head to one side like a confused hound. Finally the light dawned and he crouched again into his hunting position, turning in the direction of Dorica's head motion. I held my breath, too panicked to think of any way out.

To my amazement, Kennedy did not open the doors to my hiding place but turned to walk behind it toward the elevator. At this momentary reprieve my brain clicked through the possible options for escape. I estimated the amount of time I would have to reach the steps and climb up out of view, and judged that a slim chance.

Dorica now was stamping her feet, shaking her head wildly, and straining her voice in a frantic attempt to correct Kennedy's course. Just before he disappeared from view behind the wardrobe, I saw him turn a confused look toward Dorica. As he paused there trying to read her, I saw my only chance.

With all my might, I heaved my body against the back of the wardrobe and prayed the heavy old thing was really as unbalanced as it had seemed. The rotten wood on the back supports gave a loud splintering crash and with a suddenness that was almost too fast for me, the wardrobe tilted and began to fall heavily backward. I turned and groped for the wardrobe doors, fighting my way out through opening. Landing off balance on the basement floor, I half ran and half stumbled across the room to the stairs. I wasn't sure what condition Kennedy was in and I had no desire to stop and check it out. I vaulted the steps two at a time.

As I rounded the top step I saw the stage lights were back on. Nelson was trying to pull away from one police officer. Two others were in the process of cuffing Gunter.

"Nelson," I yelled as I ran toward him.

"Diana, thank God, thank God," he answered as he pulled away from the officer and threw his arms around me.

"Is this the lady you were worried about?"

I turned my head to see the police lieutenant who had been trying to hold

Nelson back.

"This is my lady," said Nelson, as he smiled down at me and pulled me to him.

I laid my head on his chest and felt something wet on my face. I drew back sharply and looked at the dark red stain on his clothes. Fear and pain wrenched me. "Nelson, you're hurt!"

"No, no, love. That's *his* blood." He pointed to Ellery lying on the stage floor. "Kennedy got him instead."

"Kennedy! Oh my God, I forgot about Kennedy. Lieutenant, the shooter is down in the basement."

The police lieutenant drew his gun and called to one of the other officers. I touched his sleeve to detain him. "I don't know what shape he's in. I hit him with a wardrobe."

"You hit him with a what? Is he out?"

"I don't know. Also there's someone else down there. Dorica Grizel. She's sort of, uh, tied up, though."

We watched a moment as the officers made their way cautiously toward the basement. The officer with Gunter was opening the stage curtain for the paramedics and additional police officers who were arriving. Most of the crowd had left. The press and a few of the curious waited at the steps, held back from the stage by a lone police officer. As the paramedics and officers were admitted, Jenny and Doris Whitmore wormed their way past the officer to me.

Jenny hugged me a moment and then stepped back and gave me her "mother" look. She touched her fingers to the red goo on my cheek, examining me carefully for injury, then closed her eyes and shook her head in disgust. "If you don't stop this craziness you are going to succeed in getting yourself killed. Is that what you're trying for?"

The officers returned half carrying and half dragging Paul Kennedy, and dumped him beside Gunter and Ellery.

Doris whipped out her ever ready camera and popped off three quick pictures of the three suspects in custody.

The lieutenant turned to a young officer and I heard him say, "The shape that other one's in, we better call for a couple police women to arrest her."

"Hell of a show you put on here, Diana," said Doris as she opened her note pad. "For you, I called in all my competitors on this story. You definitely owe me some kind of exclusive. You want to tell me what all happened back here after the curtain closed?"

I looked at Doris. I looked at the basement steps. I smiled wickedly and looked at Nelson. He shrugged.

"Come with me, Doris. I'll give you a photo that I guarantee no one else will have."

FORTY-THREE

We had left the louvers of the door and windows open so we could fall asleep to the muted crash of the breakers on the rocks below. All night their exotic music underscored the romance of our Baja cabana and our delightful sense of discovery of one another.

I didn't worry anymore. The defenses weren't worth it. I had decided that I would simply take joyous pleasure in our being together at this moment. I would let tomorrow take care of itself.

At first light, I awoke chilled by a cold damp wind that carried the misty fragrance of the sea through the open louvers. I pulled up the blanket and snuggled over, warming myself in Nelson's arms.

We had arrived late at night and exhausted ourselves in pent-up love making. Then, eager to fill each other in on the history of our lives before LA LA Land, we talked until the wee hours in the morning. Though we had little sleep, we were both awake early and lay placidly entwined. We talked idly about things which were of very little consequence but enjoyable to share. We were interrupted by a knock on the door.

Nelson pulled on a robe and answered it. Ernesto had brought him a telegram.

I looked sharply at Nelson as he opened it. "Hell, the outside world arrives. Who did you tell we were here?"

He heard the slight accusation that crept into my voice. Apologetically he said, "I had to check in, Diana, especially after the shooting."

After he opened and read it he said, "I'm sorry. I'm going to have to make some calls. It might take a little while."

"Sure," I said. "I need some breakfast, anyway." I saw the look on his face. Unlike Maude's subtext, he had no trouble reading me. I had to admit that in this instance, it wasn't hard. My voice had been sharp.

Escaping into the bathroom I dressed in jeans and a sweatshirt. When I came out, Nelson was engrossed in his phone calls and hardly noticed me slip out the door. I headed to the main lodge to get some breakfast and get my mind off Nelson. I sat alone on the glassed-in patio trying not to think. The sky was a solid lumpy gray mat and the wind was up. The killer storm that had swept into southern Mexico was headed northeast, but Baja was still in for its own share of rain and wind as the edges of this storm blew toward Arizona and New Mexico. From the safety of my high perch at the edge of the bluff, I could watch as the swells grew taller and the white caps increased.

I downed the last swallow of coffee and found myself chewing grounds. Washing them down with water, I nibbled slowly at the last bites of mango and papaya. At last, reluctantly, I headed for my room.

I had come down to Ernesto's Hacienda de la Playa with Nelson to have that R and R he had promised me. For one night I had been happier than I had been in years. One lousy night. Of course, I had known that eventually The Group would call him back and he would disappear on a plane to wherever. I didn't expect it to last forever. But one lousy night.

I tried to be philosophical about it but found my mood was too depressed to manage that. I shifted to thinking about work but since the only case looming on the horizon seemed to involve a crazy person who believed in Martians, that didn't help either. Maybe I could just stay here at Ernesto's and earn my keep making beds. No, that wouldn't do. Financial reality would put an end to this pleasant exile.

As I walked along the cliff, the sea-scented gusts of wind were growing stronger and colder. The wind blew through my hair, whispering mystic threats of danger in the coming storm. I savored the feeling as I faced into the wind. Some perverse and primal part of my being responded to that siren lure with a vague but joyous excitement. I laughed aloud at myself. For me the threat of danger was both the thrill and the promise that made me get up in the morning.

I reached the door to my cabana and paused. Nelson. That was my real problem. I had tried so hard for so many years to keep my emotional distance so that I would never be this needy and vulnerable to pain. In one short week, I had learned to care all over again. Now, there was nothing to do about it but hurt. I turned the handle and walked in.

He was showered, shaved, and dressed, and smelled deliciously of aftershave. His small duffel bag lay stuffed with the few things he had brought. He was exuberant. How dare he be so happy as he prepared to leave me.

"Hey, where you been? How's your Spanish?"

I wanted to be angry but he was infectiously happy. I laughed. "Pretty good. Much of my misspent youth was in mining camps in South and Central America. Why? You need help on a long-distance call or something?"

"No, on a long-distance case. Guatemala to be precise."

"Oh, they're sending you to Guatemala?" I asked enviously.

"Wrong. They are sending 'us' to Guatemala."

I stared blankly at him. He took my face in his hands and kissed me.

"They are pretty impressed with your solution to the LA LA Land thing. The shit is already hitting the fan in papers around the nation. With the muck the press is raising, they might even get a second shot at a criminal charge or two. I have orders to do everything in my power to recruit you to The Group." He wrapped his arms around me and pulled me close. "I told them I would do so only if you were assigned as my partner."

My mouth dropped open and I inhaled sharply in surprise. My emotions surged ahead of my mind.

He put a finger to my lips and said, "Don't answer yet. You haven't heard the sales pitch. Now it may not be as exciting as your own business and the pay is probably a lot less, but you know you'll have a paycheck every month. You know you'll have the backup of a lot of good people. And most importantly, you know that the work you do is, well, it's clean and worthwhile. You can feel good about yourself at the end of the day."

I smiled at him. "You mean Truth, Justice, and the American Way?"

"Now don't try to act like a cynic. You're a believer, I know you are. I've seen you work. Besides, I haven't given you the best argument yet."

He then laid a kiss on me that left me utterly limp in his arms. When he spoke again, the huskiness of his voice showed that his whammy had worked on him as well. "And if that's not enough to convince you, I'll have you talk to Sam. He says no one else could put up with either one of us and we had better save two other people from a lifetime of misery by sticking together. What do you say?"

There it was. Him and me and The Group, happily ever after. Just what I had been wishing for. Sort of. Or was it? It's surprising what can happen to your wishes when they are granted. I had wanted so badly to continue with this wonderful relationship we had started, both professional and personal, but somehow, the way he put it, the price was too high. What I had really wanted was for this romantic night to last. I hadn't really been ready to surrender my business, my lifestyle, and my independence. Having a steady paycheck and good people to back you up also meant having total dependence on people who could control your every move. Not that I didn't want Nelson, I would just have to negotiate the terms. I wasn't quite ready for complete surrender.

I smiled up at him and said, "Guatemala, huh? I would love to work with you . . ."

He waited. He could hear the "but" or "however" in my voice and his expression changed from joyous to guarded.

I gave him a kiss. "But, not at the cost of my own business. By coincidence, Hunter Investigations has a case in Costa Rica. How would you feel about teaming up on both cases?"

His relief showed plainly on his face and he smiled. "One of your high-paying clients?"

Crossing my fingers behind his back and said, "Sure. Will The Group approve of you working for Hunter Investigations?"

"Sure," he answered.

As we kissed, I happened to look at the mirror on the bathroom door. His fingers were also crossed. Very interesting. So much for the honesty we had promised each other. I remembered that night, those promises, and both the fear and delight that moment had brought. At that time, I had really meant those promises and I suspected he had also. But our natures and our experience made it hard to change our spots.

The relief that swept over me is hard to fathom. Instead of further depressing me that realization actually released me from the fear. Somehow it put everything back in perspective and brought me back to reality. I was no longer the young innocent. I would never be as vulnerable again as I was with Martin. I had moved on and grown up. I knew one night here is all there would ever be and that was alright. To paraphrase Bogie's line in Casablanca: "We'll always have Baja."

Joan Francis is a licensed private investigator and owner of Francis Pacific Investigations. She has also worked as a librarian and a newspaper reporter and is author of previous Diana Hunter thrillers, *Old Poison* and *Silent Coup*. She spent her childhood in small mining towns and camps in the western United States and in South America with her two sisters, mother, and mining engineer father. Moving from place to place as her father opened up new mine sites, she attended fifteen schools before graduating with a B.A. in history from the University of Washington in Seattle. Married with three grown children, she and her husband now live in a secluded valley of the Tehachapi Mountains.

Other books by Joan Francis

For more information go to

www.joanfrancis.net

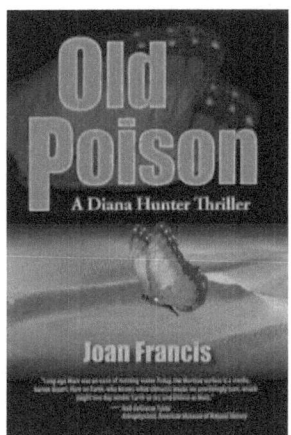

PI Diana Hunter is confronted by corporate greed with deadly intent when she investigates a cover-up regarding an alternative fuel that could have disastrous effects on global warming and climate change.

Private Investigator Diana Hunter inherits not only her Uncle Bennett's hidden wealth but also his life-long quixotic cause, fighting fascist minded foes who covertly work for the destruction of our democracy.